Hickory Flat Public Library
2740 East Cherokee Drive
Canton, Georgia 30115

The Darkest Part of the Forest

BY HOLLY BLACK

LITTLE, BROWN AND COMPANY
NEW YORK BOSTON

Quote by Kenneth Patchen, from BUT EVEN SO, © 1968 by Kenneth Patchen. Reprinted by permission of New Directions Publishing Corp.

Little, Brown and Company

Hachette Book Group
1290 Avenue of the Americas, New York, NY 10104
Visit us at lb-teens.com

Little, Brown and Company is a division of Hachette Book Group, Inc.
The Little, Brown name and logo are trademarks of Hachette Book Group, Inc.

The publisher is not responsible for websites (or their content) that are not owned by the publisher.

First Edition: January 2015

Library of Congress Cataloging-in-Publication Data

Black, Holly.
    The darkest part of the forest / by Holly Black.—First edition.
        pages cm
    Summary: In the town of Fairfold, where humans and fae exist side by side, a boy with horns on his head and ears as pointed as knives awakes after generations of sleep in a glass coffin in the woods, causing Hazel to be swept up in new love, shift her loyalties, feel the fresh sting of betrayal, and to make a secret sacrifice to the faerie king.
    ISBN 978-0-316-21307-3 (hardcover)—ISBN 978-0-316-21305-9 (ebook)—
ISBN 978-0-316-36492-8 (library edition ebook)   [1. Fairies—Fiction.
2. Magic—Fiction. 3. Love—Fiction.]   I. Title.
    PZ7.B52878Dar 2015
    [Fic]—dc23

                                                                              2014002549

10 9 8 7 6 5 4 3 2 1

RRD-C

Printed in the United States of America

For Sarah Rees Brennan,
a great friend and an inspiration

Come now, my child, if we were planning to harm you,
do you think we'd be lurking here beside the path
in the very darkest part of the forest?

—*Kenneth Patchen*

CHAPTER 1

Down a path worn into the woods, past a stream and a hollowed-out log full of pill bugs and termites, was a glass coffin. It rested right on the ground, and in it slept a boy with horns on his head and ears as pointed as knives.

As far as Hazel Evans knew, from what her parents said to her and from what their parents said to them, he'd always been there. And no matter what anyone did, he never, ever woke up.

He didn't wake up during the long summers, when Hazel and her brother, Ben, stretched out on the full length of the coffin, staring down through the crystalline panes, fogging them up with their breath, and scheming glorious schemes. He didn't wake up when tourists came to gape or debunkers came to swear he wasn't real. He didn't wake up on autumn weekends, when girls danced right on top of him, gyrating to the tinny sounds coming from nearby iPod speakers, didn't notice when Leonie Wallace lifted her beer high over her head, as if she were saluting the whole haunted forest. He didn't so much as stir when Ben's best friend, Jack Gordon, wrote IN CASE OF EMERGENCY, BREAK GLASS in Sharpie along one side—or when Lloyd Lindblad took a sledgehammer and actually tried. No matter how many parties had been held around the horned boy—generations of parties, so that the grass sparkled with decades of broken bottles in green and amber, so that the bushes shone with crushed aluminum cans in silver and gold and rust—and no matter what happened at those parties, nothing could wake the boy inside the glass coffin.

When they were little, Ben and Hazel made him flower crowns and told him stories about how they would rescue him. Back then, they were going to save everyone who needed saving in Fairfold. Once Hazel got older, though, she mostly visited the coffin only at night, in crowds, but she still felt something tighten in her chest when she looked down at the boy's strange and beautiful face.

She hadn't saved him, and she hadn't saved Fairfold, either.

"Hey, Hazel," Leonie called, dancing to one side to make room in case Hazel wanted to join her atop the horned boy's casket. Doris Alvaro was already up there, still in her cheerleader outfit from the game their school lost earlier that night, shining chestnut ponytail whipping through the air. They both looked flushed with alcohol and good cheer.

Waving a hello to Leonie, Hazel didn't get up on the coffin, although she was tempted. Instead she threaded her way through the crowd of teenagers.

Fairfold High was a small-enough school that although there were cliques (even if a few were made up of basically a single person, like how Megan Rojas was the entire Goth community), everyone had to party together if they wanted to have enough people around to party at all. But just because everyone partied together, it didn't mean they were all friends. Until a month ago, Hazel had been part of a girl posse, striding through school in heavy eyeliner and dangling, shining earrings as sharp as their smiles. Sworn in sticky, bright blood sucked from thumbs to be friends forever. She'd drifted away from them after Molly Lipscomb asked her to kiss and then jilt Molly's ex, but was furious with her once she had.

It turned out that Hazel's other friends were really just Molly's friends. Even though they'd been part of the plan, they pretended they weren't. They pretended something had happened that Hazel ought to be sorry about. They wanted Hazel to admit that she'd done it to hurt Molly.

Hazel kissed boys for all kinds of reasons—because they were cute, because she was a little drunk, because she was bored, because they let her, because it was fun, because they looked lonely, because it blotted out her fears for a while, because she wasn't sure how many kisses she had left. But she'd kissed only one boy who really belonged to someone else, and under no circumstances would she ever do it again.

At least she still had her brother to hang out with, even if he was currently on a date in the city with some guy he'd met online. And she had Ben's best friend, Jack, even if he made her nervous. And she had Leonie.

That was plenty of friends. Too many, really, considering that she was likely to disappear one of these days, leaving them all behind.

Thinking that way was how she'd wound up not asking anyone for a ride to the party that night, even though it meant walking the whole way, through the shallow edge of the woods, past farms and old tobacco barns, and then into the forest.

It was one of those early fall nights when wood smoke was in the air, along with the sweet richness of kicked-up leaf mold, and everything felt possible. She was wearing a new green sweater, her favorite brown boots, and a pair of cheap green enamel hoops. Her loose red curls still had a hint of summer gold, and when she'd looked in the mirror to smear on a little bit of tinted ChapStick before she walked out the door, she actually thought she looked pretty good.

Liz was in charge of the playlist, broadcasting from her phone through the speakers in her vintage Fiat, choosing dance music so loud it made the trees shiver. Martin Silver was chatting up Lourdes and Namiya at the same time, clearly hoping for a best-friend sandwich that was never, ever, *ever* going to happen. Molly was laughing in a half circle of girls. Stephen, in his paint-spattered shirt, was sitting on his truck with the headlights on, drinking Franklin's dad's moonshine from a flask, too busy nursing some private sorrow to care whether the stuff would make him go blind. Jack was sitting over with his brother (well, *kind of* his brother), Carter, the quarter-back, on a log near the glass coffin. They were laughing, which made Hazel want to go over there and laugh with them, except that she also wanted to get up and dance, and she also wanted to run back home.

"Hazel," someone said, and she turned to see Robbie Delmonico. The smile froze on her face.

"I haven't seen you around. You look nice." He seemed resentful about it.

"Thanks." Robbie *had* to know she'd been avoiding him, which made her feel like an awful person, but ever since they'd made out at a party, he'd followed her around as though he was heartbroken, and that was even worse. She hadn't dumped him or anything like that; he'd never even asked her out. He just stared at her miserably and asked weird, leading questions, such as "What are you doing after school?" And when she told him, "Nothing, just hanging out," he never suggested anything else, never even proposed he might like to come over.

It was because of kissing boys like Robbie Delmonico that people believed Hazel would kiss *anyone*.

It really had seemed like a good idea at the time.

"Thanks," she said again, slightly more loudly, nodding. She began to turn away.

"Your sweater's new, right?" And he gave her that sad smile that seemed to say that he knew he was nice for noticing and that he knew nice guys finished last.

The funny thing was that he hadn't seemed particularly interested in her before she lunged at him. It was as though, by putting her lips to his—and, okay, allowing a certain amount of handsiness—she'd transformed herself into some kind of cruel goddess of love.

"It is new," she told him, nodding again. Around him, she felt as coldhearted as he clearly thought she was. "Well, I guess I'll see you around."

"Yeah," he said, letting the word linger.

And then, at the critical moment, the moment when she meant to just walk away, guilt overtook her and she said the one thing she knew she shouldn't say, the thing for which she would kick herself over and over again throughout the night. "Maybe we'll run into each other later."

Hope lit his eyes, and, too late, she realized how he'd taken it—as a promise. But by then all she could do was hightail it over to Jack and Carter.

Jack—the crush of Hazel's younger, sillier years—looked surprised when she stumbled up, which was odd, because he was almost never caught off guard. As his mother once said about him, Jack could hear the thunder before the lightning bothered to strike.

"Hazel, Hazel, blue of eye. Kissed the boys and made them cry," Carter said, because Carter could be a jerk.

Carter and Jack looked almost exactly alike, as if they were twins. Same dark, curly hair. Same amber eyes. Same deep brown skin and lush mouths and wide cheekbones that were the envy of every girl in town. They weren't twins, though. Jack was a changeling—*Carter's* changeling, left behind when Carter got stolen away by the faeries.

Fairfold was a strange place. Dead in the center of the Carling forest, the haunted forest, full of what Hazel's grandfather called Greenies and what her mother called They Themselves or the Folk of the Air. In these woods, it wasn't odd to see a black hare swimming in the creek—although rabbits don't usually much care for swimming—or to spot a deer that became a sprinting girl in the blink of an eye. Every autumn, a portion of the harvest apples was left out for the cruel and capricious Alderking. Flower garlands were threaded for him every spring. Townsfolk knew to fear the monster coiled in the heart of the forest, who lured tourists with a cry that sounded like a woman weeping. Its fingers were sticks, its hair moss. It fed on sorrow and sowed corruption. You could lure it out with a singsong chant, the kind girls dare one another to say at birthday sleepovers. Plus there was a hawthorn tree in a ring of stones where you could bargain for your heart's desire by tying a strip of your clothing to the branches under a full moon and waiting for one of the Folk to come. The year before, Jenny Eichmann had gone out there and wished herself into Princeton, promising to pay anything the faeries wanted. She'd gotten in, too, but her mother had a stroke and died the same day the letter came.

Which was why, between the wishes and the horned boy and the odd sightings, even though Fairfold was so tiny that the kids in kindergarten went to school in an adjacent building to the seniors, and that you had to go three towns over to buy a new washing machine or stroll through a mall, the town still got plenty of tourists. Other places had the biggest ball of twine or a very large wheel of cheese or a chair big enough for a giant. They had scenic waterfalls or shimmering caves full of jagged stalactites or bats that slept beneath a bridge. Fairfold had the boy in the glass coffin. Fairfold had the Folk.

And to the Folk, tourists were fair game.

Maybe that's what they had thought Carter's parents were. Carter's dad was from out of town, but Carter's mom was no tourist. It took a single night for her to realize that her baby had been stolen. And she'd known just what to do. She sent her husband out of the house for the day and invited over a bunch of neighbor ladies. They'd baked bread and chopped wood and filled an old earthenware bowl with salt. Then, when everything was done, Carter's mom heated a poker in the fireplace.

First it turned red, but she did nothing. It was only once the metal glowed white that she pressed the very tip of the poker against the changeling's shoulder.

It shrieked with pain, its voice spiraling so high that both kitchen windows shattered.

There'd been a smell like when you toss fresh grass onto a fire, and the baby's skin turned bright, bubbling red. The burn left a scar, too. Hazel had seen it when she and Jack and Ben and Carter went swimming last summer—stretched out by growing, but still there.

Burning a changeling summons its mother. She arrived on the threshold moments later, a swaddled bundle in her arms. According to the stories, she was thin and tall, her hair the brown of autumn leaves, her skin the color of bark, with eyes that changed from moment to moment, molten silver to owl gold to dull and gray as stone. There was no mistaking her for human.

"You don't take our children," said Carter's mother—or at least that was how the story Hazel heard went, and she'd heard the story a lot. "You don't spirit us away or make us sick. That's how things have worked around here for generations, and that's how things are going to keep on working."

The faerie woman seemed to shrink back a little. As if in answer, she silently held out the child she'd brought, wrapped up in blankets, sleeping as peacefully as if he were in his own bed. "Take him," she said.

Carter's mother crushed him to her, drinking in the rightness of his sour-milk smell. She said that was the one thing the Folk of the Air couldn't fake. The other baby just hadn't smelled like Carter.

Then the faerie woman had reached out her arms for her own wailing child, but the neighbor woman holding him stepped back. Carter's mother blocked the way.

"You can't have him," said Carter's mother, passing her own baby to her sister and picking up iron filings and red berries and salt, protection against the faerie woman's magic. "If you were willing to trade him away, even for an hour, then you don't deserve him. I'll keep them both to raise as my own and let that be our judgment on you for breaking oath with us."

At that, the elf woman spoke in a voice like wind and rain and brittle leaves snapping underfoot. "You do not have the lessoning of us. You have no power, no claim. Give me my child and I will place a blessing on your house, but if you keep him, you will come to regret it."

"Damn the consequences and damn you, too," said Carter's mom, according to everyone who has ever told this story. "Get the hell out."

And so, even though some of the neighbor ladies grumbled about Carter's mother borrowing trouble, that was how Jack came to live with Carter's family and to become Carter's brother and Ben's best friend. That was how they all got so used to Jack that no one was surprised anymore by how his ears tapered to small points or how his eyes shone silver sometimes, or the way he could predict the weather better than any weatherman on the news.

"So do you think Ben's having a better time than we are?" Jack asked her, forcing her thoughts away from his past and his scar and his handsome face.

If Hazel took kissing boys too lightly, then Ben never took it lightly enough. He wanted to be in love, was all too willing to give away his still-beating heart. Ben had always been like that, even when it cost him more than she wanted to think about.

However, even he didn't have much luck online.

"I think Ben's date will be boring." Hazel took the beer can from Jack's hand and swigged. It tasted sour. "Most of them are boring, even the liars. Especially the liars. I don't know why he bothers."

Carter shrugged. "Sex?"

"He likes stories," Jack said, with a conspiratorial grin in her direction.

Hazel licked the foam off her upper lip, some of her previous good cheer returning. "Yeah, I guess."

Carter stood, eyeing Megan Rojas, who'd just arrived with freshly purpled hair, carrying a bottle of cinnamon schnapps, the pointed heels of her spiderweb-stitched boots sinking into the soft earth. "I'm going to get another beer. You want something?"

"Hazel stole mine," Jack said, nodding toward her. The thick silver hoops in his ears glinted in the moonlight. "So grab another round for us both?"

"Try not to break any hearts while I'm gone," Carter told Hazel, as if he was joking, but his tone wasn't entirely friendly.

Hazel sat down on the part of the log that Carter had vacated, looking at the girls dancing and the other kids drinking. She felt outside of it all, purposeless and adrift. Once, she'd had a quest, one she'd been willing to give up everything for, but it turned out that some quests couldn't be won just by giving things up.

"Don't listen to him," Jack told her as soon as his brother was safely on the other side of the casket and out of hearing range. "You didn't do anything wrong with Rob. Anyone who offers up their heart on a silver platter deserves what they get."

Hazel thought of Ben and wondered if that was true.

"I just keep making the same mistake," she said. "I go to a party and I kiss some guy who I would never think of kissing at school. Guys I don't even really like. It's as though out here, in the woods, they're going to reveal some secret side of themselves. But they're always just the same."

"It's just kissing." He grinned at her; his mouth twisted up on one side, and something twisted inside her in response. His smiles and Carter's smiles were nothing alike. "It's fun. You're not hurting anybody. It's not like you're *stabbing* boys just to make something happen around here."

That surprised a laugh out of her. "Maybe you should tell that to Carter."

She didn't explain that she wasn't so much wanting something to happen as not wanting to be the only one with a secret self to reveal.

Jack draped an arm over her shoulder, pretend-flirting. It was friendly, funny. "He's my brother, so I can tell you definitively that he's an idiot. You must amuse yourself however you can among the dull folk of Fairfold."

She shook her head, smiling, and then turned toward him. He stopped speaking, and she realized how close their faces had become.

Close enough that she could feel the warmth of his breath against her cheek. Close enough to watch the dark fringe of his eyelashes turn gold in the reflected light and to see the soft bow of his mouth.

Hazel's heart started pounding, her ten-year-old self's crush coming back with a vengeance. It made her feel just as vulnerable and silly as she'd felt back then. She hated that feeling. She was the one who broke hearts now, not the other way around.

Anyone who offers up their heart on a silver platter deserves what they get.

There was only one way to get over a boy. Only one way that ever worked.

Jack's gaze was slightly unfocused, his lips slightly apart. It seemed exactly right to close the distance between them, to shut her eyes and press her mouth to his. Warm and gentle, he pressed back for a single shared exchange of breath.

Then he pulled away, blinking. "Hazel, I didn't mean for you—"

"No," she said, leaping up, her cheeks hot. He was her friend, her brother's *best* friend. He mattered. It would never be okay to kiss him, even if he wanted her to, which he clearly did not, and which made everything much worse. "Of course not. Sorry. Sorry! I told you I shouldn't go around kissing people, and here I am doing it again."

She backed away.

"Wait," he started, reaching to catch her arm, but she didn't want to stay around while he tried to find the right words to let her down easy.

Hazel fled, passing Carter with her head down, so she didn't have to see his knowing told-you-so look. She felt stupid and, worse, like she deserved to be rejected. Like it served her right. It was the kind of karmic justice that didn't usually happen in real life, or at least didn't usually happen so fast.

Hazel headed straight for Franklin. "Can I have some of that?" she asked him, pointing to the metal flask.

He looked at her blearily through bloodshot eyes but held the flask out. "You won't like it."

She didn't. The moonshine burned all the way down her throat.

But she slugged back two more swallows, hoping that she could forget everything that had happened since she'd arrived at the party. Hoping that Jack would never tell Ben what she'd done. Hoping Jack would pretend it hadn't happened. She just wished she could undo everything, unravel time like yarn from a sweater.

Across the clearing, illuminated by Stephen's headlights, Tom Mullins, linebacker and general rageaholic, leaped up onto the glass coffin suddenly enough to make the girls hop off. He looked completely wasted, face flushed and hair sticking up with sweat.

"Hey," he shouted, jumping up and down, stomping like he was trying to crack the glass. "Hey, wakey, wakey, eggs and bakey. Come on, you ancient fuck, get up!"

"Quit it," said Martin, waving for Tom to get down. "Remember what happened to Lloyd?"

Lloyd was the kind of bad kid who liked to start fires and carried a knife to school. When teachers were taking attendance, they were hard-pressed to remember whether he wasn't there because he was cutting class or because he was suspended. One night last spring Lloyd took a sledgehammer to the glass coffin. It didn't shatter, but the next time Lloyd set a fire, he got burned. He was still in a hospital in Philadelphia, where they had to graft skin from his ass onto his face.

Some people said the horned boy had done that to Lloyd, because he didn't like it when people messed with his coffin. Others said that whoever had cursed the horned boy had cursed the glass, too. So if anyone tried to break it, that person would bring bad luck on themselves. Though Tom Mullins knew all that, he didn't seem to care.

Hazel knew just how he felt.

"Get up!" he yelled, kicking and stomping and jumping. "Hey, lazybones, time to waaaaaaake up!"

Carter grabbed his arm. "Tom, come on. We're going to do shots. You don't want to miss this."

Tom looked unsure.

"Come *on*," Carter repeated. "Unless you're too drunk already."

"Yeah," said Martin, trying to sound convincing. "Maybe you can't hold your booze, Tom."

That did it. Tom scrambled down, lumbering away from the coffin, protesting that he could drink more than the both of them combined.

"So," Franklin said to Hazel. "Just another dull night in Fairfold, where everyone's a lunatic or an elf."

She took one more drink from the silver flask. She was starting to get used to the feeling that her esophagus was on fire. "Pretty much."

He grinned, red-rimmed eyes dancing. "Want to make out?"

From the look of him, he was as miserable as Hazel was. Franklin, who'd barely spoken for the first three years of grammar school and who everyone was sure ate roadkill for dinner sometimes. Franklin, who wouldn't thank her if she asked him what was bothering him, since she'd wager he had almost as much to forget as she did.

Hazel felt a little bit light-headed and a lot reckless. "Okay."

As they walked away from the truck and into the woods, she glanced back at the party in the grove. Jack was watching her with an unreadable expression on his face. She turned away. Passing under an oak tree, Franklin's hand in hers, Hazel thought she saw the branches shift above her, like fingers, but when she looked again, all she saw were shadows.

CHAPTER 2

The summer when Ben was a baby and Hazel was still in their mother's belly, their mother went out to a clearing in the woods to paint en plein air. She spread out her blanket over the grass and sat Ben, slathered in SPF-50 and gumming a chunk of zwieback, on it while she daubed her canvas with cadmium orange and alizarin crimson. She painted for the better part of an hour before she noticed a woman watching from the cool shadows of the nearby trees.

The woman, Mom said when she told the story, had her brown hair pulled back in a kerchief and carried a basket of young green apples.

"You're a true artist," the woman told her, crouching down and smiling delightedly. That was when Mom noticed her loose dress was hand-loomed and very fine. For a moment Mom thought she was one of those ladies who got into homesteading and canned stuff from her garden, kept chickens, and sewed her own clothes. But then she saw that the woman's ears rose to slim, delicate points and realized she was one of the Folk of the Air, tricksy and dangerous.

As is the tragedy of so many artists, Mom was more fascinated than afraid.

Mom had grown up in Fairfold, had heard endless stories about the Folk. Had known about the nest of redcaps who dipped their hats in fresh human blood and who were rumored to live near an old cave on the far side of town. She'd heard about a snake-woman sometimes spotted in the cool of the evening near the edges of the woods. She knew of the monster made of dry branches, tree bark, dirt, and moss, who turned the blood of those she touched to sap.

She remembered the song they sang while they skipped rope as girls:

> *There's a monster in our wood*
> *She'll get you if you're not good*
> *Drag you under leaves and sticks*
> *Punish you for all your tricks*
> *A nest of hair and gnawed bone*
> *You are never, ever coming—*

They'd shouted it with great glee, never saying the last word. If they had, the monster might have been summoned—that was what it was supposed to do, after all. But as long as they never finished the song, the magic wouldn't work.

But not all the stories were terrible. The generosity of the Folk was as great as their cruelty. There was a little girl in Ben's playgroup whose doll was stolen by a nixie. A week later that same girl woke in her crib with ropes of gorgeous freshwater pearls wound around her neck. That was why Fairfold was special, because it was so close to magic. Dangerous magic, yes, but magic all the same.

Food tasted better in Fairfold, people said, infused as it was with enchantment. Dreams were more vivid. Artists were more inspired and their work more beautiful. People fell more deeply in love, music was more pleasing to the ear, and ideas came more frequently than in other places.

"Let me draw you," Mom said, pulling her sketchbook from her bag, along with some charcoals. She thought she drew better in Fairfold, too.

The woman demurred. "Draw my beautiful apples instead. They are already given over to rot, while I will remain as I am for all the long years of my life."

The words sent a shiver down Mom's spine.

The woman saw her face and laughed. "Oh yes, I have seen the acorn before the tree. I have seen the egg before the hen. And I will see them all again."

Mom took a deep breath and tried again to persuade her. "If you allow me to draw you, I'll give you the picture once it's done."

The elf woman considered this for a long moment. "I may have it?"

Mom nodded, the woman assented, and Mom got to work. All the while that Mom sketched, they spoke of their lives. The woman said she had once belonged to an easterly court but had followed one of the gentry into exile. She told Mom of her newfound love of the deepness of the forest, but also of her longing for her old life. In turn, Mom told her of her fears about her first child, who'd grown fussy and bored, whimpering on his blanket and in need of a new diaper. Would Ben grow up to be someone completely unlike her, someone who would be uninterested in the arts, someone dull and conventional? Mom's parents had been disappointed in her again and again because she wasn't like them. What if she felt that same way about Ben?

When Mom was done with the drawing, the elf woman drew in her breath at the loveliness of it. She knelt down on the blanket beside the baby and brought her thumb to his temple. Immediately, he began to howl.

Mom grabbed for the woman. "What have you done?" she cried. On her son's brow, a red stain was spreading in the shape of a fingertip.

"For the gift of your drawing, I owe you a boon." The woman rose, towering above Mom, taller than seemed possible, while Mom wrapped her arms around a squalling Ben. "I can't change his nature, but I can give him the gift of our music. He will play music so sweet that no one will be able to think of anything else when they hear it, music that contains the magic of faerie. It will weigh on him and it will change him and it will make him an artist, no matter what else he desires. Every child needs a tragedy to become truly interesting. That is my gift to you—he will be compelled to art, love it or no."

With that, the elf woman took her drawing and left my mother huddled on her blanket, weeping, arms around Ben. She wasn't sure if her son had been cursed or blessed.

The answer turned out to be both.

But Hazel, floating in the tideless sea of amniotic fluid, was neither. Her tragedy, if she had one, was to be as normal and average as any child ever born.

✦ CHAPTER 3 ✦

Hazel got home from the party late that night to find Ben eating cereal at the kitchen table, dragging his spoon through the milk to scoop up the last pieces of granola. It was a little after midnight, but their parents were still awake and still working. Light blazed from the windows of their shared art studio out back. Sometimes, when they were inspired or on deadline, one of them even wound up sleeping out there.

Hazel didn't mind. She was proud of the ways they were different from other people's parents; they'd raised her to be. "Normal people," they'd say with a shudder. "Normal people think they're happy, but that's because they're too dumb to know any different. Better to be miserable and interesting, right, kiddo?" Then they'd laugh. Sometimes, though, when Hazel walked around their studio, breathing in the familiar smells of turpentine and varnish and fresh paint, she wondered what it would be like to have happy, normal, dumb parents, and then she felt guilty for wondering.

Ben looked up at her with cornflower-blue eyes and black brows, like her own. His red hair was messier than usual, the loose curls disheveled. There was a leaf stuck in it.

Hazel moved to pluck it out, grinning. She was drunk enough to feel blurry around the edges, and her mouth was a bit abraded from the way Franklin had mashed his lips against hers, all details she wanted to be distracted from. She didn't want to remember any of the night, not Jack nor how much of an idiot she'd been, not any of it. She pictured a huge trunk slamming down on those memories, a padlock coiling around the trunk, and then the trunk falling to the bottom of the sea. "So how was your date?" she asked him.

He gave a long sigh, then pushed his bowl away, across the worn tablecloth. "Basically awful."

Hazel put her head down on the table, looking over at him. He seemed insubstantial from that angle, as though if she squinted, she might be able to see right through him. "Was he into something weird? Rubber suits? Clown costumes? Rubber clown costumes?"

"He was not." Ben didn't laugh. His smile had gone a bit strained.

Hazel frowned. "Are you okay? Did something—"

"No, not like that." Ben spoke quickly, shaking off her concern. "We went back to his apartment and his ex was there. As in, his ex still *lived* there."

She smothered a gasp, because that did sound awful. "Seriously? He didn't mention that beforehand?"

"He said he had an ex—full stop. Everyone has an ex! Even me! I mean, you have, what, millions?" He grinned, so she'd know he was kidding.

Hazel wasn't in the mood for that particular joke. "Can't have an ex if you never go on a date," she said.

"Anyway, we go in the door, and this guy is sitting in front of the television looking crushed. Like, clearly, he's not okay with my being there, and, clearly, he wasn't prepared for it, either. My date, meanwhile, is talking about how his ex is cool and he'll even sleep on the couch so we can hang out in the bedroom. Which is how I realize there's only one bedroom in the apartment. Right then I decide that I have to get out of there. But what am I supposed to do? I feel like I can't say anything, because that would be rude. Mutually constructed reality, the social contract, *something*. I just can't."

Hazel snorted, but he ignored her.

"So I say I have to go to the bathroom, and I hide in there, trying to get my nerve up. Then, taking a breath, I walk out and just keep going until I'm through the apartment door and down the stairs. When I hit the sidewalk, I book it."

She laughed, picturing him enacting this less-than-subtle plan. "Because running away isn't rude at all."

Ben shook his head solemnly. "Less awkward."

That made her laugh harder. "Have you checked your e-mail? I mean, he's going to write and ask where you went. Won't that be awkward?"

"Are you kidding? I am never going to check my e-mail again," Ben said, with feeling.

"Good," said Hazel. "Boys on the Internet lie."

"All boys lie," Ben said. "And all girls lie, too. I lie. You lie. Don't pretend you don't."

Hazel didn't say anything, because he was right. She'd lied. She'd lied a lot, especially to Ben.

"So how about you? How was our prince tonight?" he asked.

Over the years, Hazel and Ben had made up a lot of stories about the horned boy. They'd both drawn endless pictures of his beautiful face and curving horns with Dad's markers, Mom's charcoals, and, before that, their own crayons. If Hazel closed her eyes, she could conjure the image of him—his midnight-blue doublet stitched with dark gold thread picking out phoenixes, griffins, and dragons; pale hands folded over each other, each adorned with glittering rings; nails unusually long and subtly pointed; boots of ivory leather that came to his calves; and a face so beautiful, with features so perfectly shaped, that looking at him for too long made you feel as though everything else you saw was unbearably shabby.

He must be a prince. That was what Ben had decided when they first saw him. A prince, like the ones in fairy tales, with curses that could be broken by their true loves. And back then, Hazel was sure she would be the one to wake him.

"Our prince was the same," Hazel said, not wanting to talk about the night, but not wanting to be obvious about it, either. "Everyone was the same. Every*thing* was the same."

She knew it wasn't Ben's fault that she got frustrated by her life. Her bargains were made. There was no point in regretting them, and even less point in resenting him.

After a while, their dad staggered in from the studio to make a cup of tea and shooed them off to bed. Dad was on deadline, trying to finish up the illustrations he was supposed to drive to the city with on Monday. He was likely to stay up all night, which meant he'd notice if they stayed up, too.

Mom was probably keeping him company. Mom and Dad had started dating in art school in Philadelphia, bound by a love of kids' books that led to Ben and Hazel both being named, humiliatingly, after famous rabbits. Soon after graduation, Mom and Dad moved back to Fairfold, broke, pregnant, and willing to get married if that meant Dad's family would let them live rent-free in his great-aunt's farmhouse. Dad converted the barn behind it into a studio and used his half to paint illustrations for picture books, while Mom used hers to paint landscapes of the Carling forest that she sold in town, mostly to tourists.

In the spring and summer, Fairfold was clogged with tourists. You could spot them eating pancakes with real maple syrup over at the Railway Diner, picking up T-shirts and paperweights with clover suspended in resin at Curious Curios, getting their fortunes told at Mystical Moon Tarot, taking selfies sitting on the prince's glass casket, picking up sandwich boxes from Annie's Luncheonette for impromptu picnics out near Wight Lake, or strolling hand in hand through the streets, acting as though Fairfold was the quaintest and kookiest place they'd ever been.

Every year, some of those tourists disappeared.

Some got dragged down into Wight Lake by water hags, bodies cracking the dense mat of algae, scattering the duckweed. Some would be run down at twilight by horses with ringing bells tied to their manes and members of the Shining Folk on their backs. Some would be found strung upside down in trees, bled out and chewed upon. Some would be found sitting on park benches, their faces frozen in a grimace so terrible that it seemed as though they must have died of fright. And some would simply be gone.

Not many. One or two each season. But enough that someone should have noticed outside Fairfold. Enough that there should have been warnings, travel advisories, something. Enough that tourists should have stopped coming. They didn't.

A generation ago, the Folk had been more circumspect. More inclined toward pranks. A stray wind might grab an idle tourist, sweep her up into the air, and deposit her miles away. A few tourists might stagger back to their hotel after a late night, only to realize six months had passed. Occasionally one would wake up with his or her hair in knots. Things they'd been sure were in their pockets went missing; strange new things were discovered. Butter was eaten right off a dish, licked up by invisible tongues. Money turned into leaves. Laces wouldn't untie, and shadows looked a bit ragged, as though they had slipped away for some fun.

Back then it was very rare for someone to die because of the Folk.

Tourists, the locals would say, a sneer in their voices. And they still did. Because everyone believed—everyone had to believe—tourists did stupid things that got them killed. And if someone from Fairfold very occasionally went missing, too, well, they must have been acting like a tourist. They should have known better. The people of Fairfold came to think of the Folk as inevitable, a natural hazard, like hailstorms or getting swept out to sea by a riptide.

It was a strange kind of double consciousness.

They had to be respectful of the Folk, but not scared. Tourists were scared.

They had to stay clear of the Folk and carry protections. Tourists weren't scared enough.

When Hazel and Ben lived briefly in Philadelphia, no one believed their stories. Those two years had been bizarre. They had to learn to hide their strangeness. But coming back had been difficult, too, because by then they knew how weird Fairfold was compared with places outside it. And because, by the time they'd returned, Ben had decided to give up his magic—and his music—entirely.

Which meant he could never, ever know the price Hazel had paid for them to go in the first place. After all, she wasn't a tourist. She should have known better. But sometimes, on nights like the one she'd just had, she wished she could tell *someone*. She wished she didn't always have to be so alone.

That night, after she and Ben went up to bed, after she stripped off her clothes and got into her pajamas, after she brushed her teeth and checked to make sure the scattered bits of salted oatmeal were still under her pillow where they might keep her safe from faerie tricks, then Hazel had nothing left to distract her from remembering the dizzying moment when her mouth had met Jack's. Only, as she slid off into dreams, it wasn't Jack she was kissing anymore, but the horned boy. His eyes were open. And when she pulled him closer, he didn't push her away.

⁓

Hazel woke up feeling out of sorts, restless, and melancholy. She put it down to drinking the night before and swigged back some aspirin with the last dregs of a carton of orange juice. Her mom had left a note to pick up bread and milk clothespinned to a ten-dollar bill in the giant pottery catchall bowl that sat in the center of the kitchen table.

With a groan, Hazel went back upstairs to put on leggings and a baggy black shirt. She shoved the green hoops back into her ears.

Music was on in Ben's room. Even though he didn't play anymore, Ben always had a continuous sound track in the background, even as he slept. If he was up, though, she hoped she could persuade him to run Mom's errand, so that she could go back to bed.

Hazel knocked on Ben's door.

"Enter at your own risk," he called. Hazel opened it to find him holding a cell phone up to his ear as he hopped his way into a pair of mustard-colored skinny jeans.

"Hey," she said. "Can you—"

He waved her over, speaking into the phone. "Yeah, she's up. She's right in front of me. Sure, we'll meet you in fifteen minutes."

Hazel groaned. "What are you agreeing to?"

He tossed an easy grin in her direction and said good-bye to the person on the other end of his cell. The person she was pretty sure was Jack.

Ben and Jack had been friends for years, through Ben coming out and his obsessive relationship with the only other out boy at school, which ended in a huge public fight at the homecoming bonfire. Through Jack's bleak depression after being dumped by Amanda Watkins, who'd told him that she was dating him only because she really wanted to date Carter and dating him was like dating Carter's shadow. Through both of them liking different music and different books and hanging out with different people at lunch.

Surely, a little thing like her kissing Jack wouldn't even ripple the waters. But that didn't make her eager for the moment Ben found out what she'd done. And she wasn't looking forward to Jack's watching her warily all afternoon as though she might lunge at him or something.

But, despite herself, she was looking forward to seeing him again. She couldn't quite believe they'd kissed, even just for a moment. The memory filled her with an embarrassing jolt of happiness. It felt like an act of real daring, the first she'd committed in a long time. It was a horrible mistake, of course. She could have wrecked things—she hoped she hadn't wrecked things. She could never do it again. At least she couldn't think of a way it would be possible to do it again.

Hazel wasn't sure when her crush on Jack had started. It had been a slow thing, an exaggerated awareness of him, a thrill at his attention, accompanied by a constant stream of nervous chatter when he was around. But she remembered when her crush had become acute. She'd walked over to remind Ben he was supposed to be home for a music lesson with one of Dad's deadbeat friends and found a whole group of boys in the Gordon kitchen, making sandwiches and goofing around. Jack had made her one with chicken salad and carefully sliced tomato. When he was turned away to get her some pretzels, she had snatched his partially chewed gum from where it was stuck to a plate and shoved it into her mouth. It had tasted of strawberry and his spit and had given her the same pure shock of agonized happiness that kissing him had.

That gum was still stuck to her bed frame, a talisman she couldn't quite give up.

"We're going to Lucky's," Ben offered, as though maybe he should inform her of the place she hadn't agreed to go. "We'll get some coffee. Listen to records. See if any new stuff came in. Come on, Mr. Schröder probably misses you. Besides, as you are so fond of pointing out, what else is there to do in this town on a Sunday?"

Hazel sighed. She should tell him no, but instead she seemed to be running toward trouble, leaving no stone unturned, no boy unkissed, no crush abandoned, and no bad idea unembraced.

"I guess I could use some coffee," she said as her brother picked up a red blazer, apparently matching his outfit to a sunrise.

——

Lucky's was in a big, old restored warehouse on the duller end of Main Street, beside the bank, the dentist's office, and a shop that sold clocks. The place smelled like the dust of old books, mothballs, and French roast. Mismatched shelves filled the walls and defined the aisles down the center. Some of the bookshelves were carved oak, others were nailed together from pallets, and all had been picked up for cheap at garage sales by old Mr. and Mrs. Schröder, who ran the place. Two overstuffed chairs and a record player sat beside big windows that overlooked a wide stream. Customers could play any of the old vinyl albums in stock. Two big thermal dispensers held organic, fair-trade coffee. Mugs sat on a painted table with a chipped jar beside them marked: HONOR SYSTEM. FIFTY CENTS A CUP.

And on the other side of the room were racks and racks of second-hand clothes, shoes, purses, and other accessories. Hazel had worked there over the summer, and a big part of her job had been going through what seemed like hundreds of garbage bags in the back, sorting what could go on the shelves from stuff that was ripped or stained or had an unpleasant smell. She'd found a lot of good stuff, hunting through those bags. Lucky's was more expensive than Goodwill—which was where her parents liked for her to shop, claiming that buying things new was for the *bourgeois*—but it was nicer, too, and she got a discount.

Jack, whose family definitely qualified as bourgeois to Hazel's parents, and who bought his clothes new from the mall, came to Lucky's for stacks of biographies of the obscurely famous, which he read with the frequency other people smoked cigarettes.

Ben came for the old records, which he loved, even though they skipped and hissed and degraded over time, because he said the grooves mirrored the sound's original waveform. He claimed they gave a truer, richer sound. Hazel believed that what he truly loved was the ritual, though—taking the vinyl out of the sleeve, placing it on the turntable, bringing down the needle in just the right place, and then balling his hands into fists so he wouldn't tap out the notes against his thigh.

Well, he might not love that last part, but he did it. Every time.

The day was bright and chilly, the wind slapping their cheeks on the walk over, turning them rosy. As Hazel and Ben entered the shop, a dozen crows rose from a fir tree, cawing as they flew up into the sky.

Mr. Schröder looked up from where he was napping when the bell over the door jingled. He winked at Hazel, and she gave him a wink in return. He grinned as he slumped back into his armchair.

On the other end of the room, Jack was putting a Nick Drake album on the turntable. His sonorous voice filled the shop, whispering about golden crowns and silence. Hazel tried to study Jack without his noticing, gauging his mood. He was his usual slightly rumpled self, wearing jeans, two-tone oxfords, and a wrinkled green shirt that seemed to bring out the silver shine of his eyes. When he saw Hazel and Ben, he smiled—but was Hazel imagining that his smile looked a little forced and didn't quite reach his eyes? Either way, it didn't matter, because his gaze slid over her and went to her brother. "So what's all this about ditching your date like Bruce Wayne after spotting the bat signal?"

Ben laughed. "That's not what happened!"

What had she been thinking, kissing him? Just because she'd had a crush on him when they were kids? Just because she'd wanted to?

"Yeah," she forced herself to say. "Batman would never ditch."

Ben was happy to tell the story of his disastrous date again. They scrounged up change for honor-system coffee as Ben's new version became more exaggerated and dramatic. The roommate was even more wildly in love with Ben's date and even more furious at Ben. Ben was even more comically incompetent at sneaking out. By the end, Hazel had no idea how much of it was true anymore, and she didn't care. It reminded her of how compellingly Ben could tell a story and how many of her most beloved tales about the horned boy had been ones he'd made up.

"So what about you guys?" Ben asked finally. "Hazel says nothing even remotely interesting happened last night."

Jack's laugh stopped. "Oh," he said after a pause that was just a couple of seconds too long. There was an odd light in his amber eyes. "She didn't tell you?"

Hazel froze.

Her brother was watching them curiously, brow furrowed. "Well? What?"

"Tom Mullins got wasted, climbed up on the glass coffin, and tried to smash it. He's cursed for sure, poor bastard." Jack's smile was tilted, rueful. He ran his fingers over his tight brown curls, rumpling them.

Hazel let out her breath a little dizzily.

Ben shook his head. "What makes people do that? Bad stuff happens whenever somebody messes around with the coffin. Tommy doesn't care about the prince, so what's the temptation?" He looked honestly frustrated, but then Ben and Tom Mullins used to be friends, before Ben moved away and Tom became a drunk.

"Maybe he was tired of the same old parties and the same old people," Jack said, perching on a table arranged with stacks of books, belts, and scarves and looking at Hazel. "Maybe he wanted something to *happen*."

She winced.

"Okay, enough with the weirdness," Ben said, leaning forward in his chair, cradling his cup. His red curls looked gold in the light filtering through the dirty windowpanes. "What's wrong with you guys? You keep staring at each other like creepers."

"What? No," said Jack softly. "Nothing's wrong."

Hazel shook her head, going to refill her coffee cup. "Huh," she said, eager for a subject change. "Is that a sequined tube top I spy with my little eye?"

It was, and nearby was a big, gauzy prom dress in bright mermaid aqua that she danced around the room in. And beside that was a herringbone suit that looked as if it could have been worn on one of the early seasons of *Mad Men*. Jack put on a Bad Brains vinyl, Ben tried on the suit, some tourists came in to buy postcards, and everything started to feel like a regular Sunday afternoon.

But then Ben put his hands into the pockets of the jacket he was peacocking around the store in, daring them to say it was a little tight on him, and Hazel picked up his red blazer, folding it over her arm. Something fell out of one of the pockets. It bounced once on the ground and then rolled against Jack's shoe. A walnut with a thin bow of grass tied around it.

"Look at that," said Jack, frowning down at her discovery. "What do you think it is?"

"Was it in my coat?" Ben asked.

Hazel nodded.

"Well, let's open it." Jack slid off the table, a bowler hat sitting cockeyed on his head. He had a relaxed, loose-limbed way of moving that made Hazel think the exact sort of thoughts that had got her into trouble in the first place.

The grass unfurled easily, and the two halves of the walnut came apart. Inside was a small scrap of paper, rolled up like a scroll.

"Let me see," Hazel said, reaching for it. Unfurling the thin piece of parchment, a shiver went up her spine as she read the spidery lettering, *Seven years to pay your debts. Much too late for regrets.*

They were all silent for a long moment, and Hazel concentrated on not dropping the paper.

"That doesn't make sense," said Jack.

"It's probably some old thing a tourist bought in town." Ben's voice was a little unsteady. "Bullshit fake magic fortune walnut."

There was a shop near the end of Main Street called the Cunning Woman that sold souvenirs to faerie seekers. Incense, bags of salt mixed with red berries for protection, maps to "sacred" faerie sites around town, crystals, hand-painted tarot cards, and iridescent window dazzlers. Cryptic faerie notes in nuts was the sort of thing they might carry.

"What kind of fortune is that?" Jack asked.

"Yeah," Hazel added, trying to sound as if her heart weren't thundering, trying to behave as though she didn't know for whom the note had been meant, pretending everything was still normal.

"Yeah." Ben put the shell and the note back in his pocket with a little laugh. "Creepy, though."

After that, Hazel could only pretend to be having fun. She watched Ben and Jack, memorizing them. Memorizing the people and the place, the smell of old books and the sounds of normal stuff.

Ben bought a polka-dot bow tie, and then they walked over to the general store, where Hazel picked up the carton of milk and loaf of bread. Jack was heading back to his parents' for dinner because they had a tradition of playing family board games on Sundays, and no matter how dorky Jack or Carter felt that was, neither was allowed to skip out on it. Hazel and Ben went home, too. Outside their front door, Hazel squatted to pour a little milk into the ceramic bowl Mom kept next to the stone walk. Everyone in Fairfold left food out for the faeries, to show them respect, to gain their favor.

But the milk glubbed out in thick chunks. It had already gone sour.

↣ CHAPTER 4 ↢

That night, Hazel tossed and turned, kicking the sheets, willing herself not to worry about promises made and debts coming due. She imagined them away, bound up in a hundred barnacle-encrusted safes, a thousand buried chests, chains tight around every one.

In the morning, her limbs felt heavy. When she rolled over to hit the snooze on her phone alarm, her fingertips stung. Her palms looked red and abraded. There was a splinter of glass the length of a pin nestled under the swell of her thumb, and a few smaller shining splinters scattered across her fingers. Her heart began to race.

She kicked off the covers, frowning, only to find that her feet were caked in mud. Chunks of it dropped off her toes as she got up. Dirt spatter clung to her leg all the way to her knee. The hem of her nightgown was stiff and filthy. When she pulled back the sheet, her bedclothes looked like a nest, with grass and sticks everywhere. She tried to think back to the night before, but there were only vague dreams. The more she concentrated on them, the more they receded.

What had happened? What had she done, and why couldn't she remember any of it?

Hazel forced herself into the shower, turning the tap to as hot as she could stand it. Under the water, she was able to work glass splinters out of her hand, tiny beads of blood swirling away down the drain. She was able to wash away the mud and to stop trembling. But she was still no closer to having any answers.

What had she done?

Her muscles hurt, as though she'd strained them, but that and the dirt and the shards of glass didn't add up to anything. She was breathing too fast, no matter how much she tried to tell herself to be calm, no matter how much she tried to tell herself that she'd known this was coming, that the hardest part was waiting, and that she ought to be glad that she could finally get it over with.

Five years ago, when Hazel was nearly eleven years old, she'd made a bargain with the Folk.

She had crept down to the hawthorn tree on a full-moon night, just before dawn. The sky was still mostly dark, still dusted with stars. Strips of cloth fluttered from the branches above her, the ghosts of wishes. She'd left her sword at home, out of respect, and hoped that even though she'd hunted some of the Folk—the bad ones— they would still bargain with her fairly. She was very young.

Keeping what she wanted in mind, Hazel crossed the ring of

white stones and waited, sitting on the dew-wet grass under the haw-thorn, her heart beating mouse-fast. She didn't have to wait long. A few minutes later a creature loped from the woods, a creature she had no name for. It had a pale body and crept on all fours, with claws as long as one of her fingers. It was pink around the eyes and around its too-wide mouth, which was filled with jagged, sharklike teeth.

"Tie your ribbon to the tree," hissed the creature, a long pink tongue visible when it spoke. "Tell me your wish. I bargain on behalf of the Alderking, and he will give you all that you desire."

Hazel had a strip of cloth she'd cut from the inside of her favorite dress. It fluttered in her hand when she took it from her pocket. "I want my brother to go to music school in Philadelphia. Everything paid for, so that he can go. In return, I'll stop hunting while he's away."

The creature laughed. "You're bold; I like that. But, no, I'm afraid that is no sufficient price for what you want. Promise me ten years of your life."

"Ten years?" Hazel echoed, stunned. She'd thought she was pre-pared to bargain, but she hadn't guessed what they'd ask for. She needed Ben to be better at music. She needed them to be a team again. When she went hunting without him, she felt lost. She had to make this bargain.

"You're so very young—*stuffed* with years yet to come. Won't you give us a few?" asked the creature. It padded closer, so that she could see its eyes were as black as pools of ink. "You'll hardly miss them."

"Don't you all live forever?" Hazel asked. "What do you need anybody's years for?"

"Not anyone's years." It sat, its claws kneading the dirt in a way that made the creature appear both bored and menacing. "Yours."

"Seven," said Hazel, remembering that Folk were fond of certain numbers. "I'll give you seven years."

The creature's smile went even wider. "Our bargain is made. Tie your cloth to the tree and go home with our blessing."

Lifting her hands, fabric fluttering between her fingers, Hazel hesitated. It had happened so quickly. The creature had agreed without any counteroffers or negotiation. With cold, creeping dread, she became more and more sure she'd made a mistake.

But what was it? She understood that she'd die seven years sooner than she would have, but at ten, that was so vastly far in the future it seemed closer to *never* than *now*.

It was only on the walk home through the dark that she realized she had never *specified* that those years be taken from the end of her life. She'd *assumed*. Which meant they could carry her off any time they wanted, and, given how differently time was said to run there, seven years in Faerie might be the rest of her life in the mortal world.

She was no different from anyone who'd ever gone to wish at the tree. The Folk had gotten the better of her.

Ever since that night, she'd been trying to forget that she was living on borrowed time, trying to distract herself. She went to all the parties and kissed all the boys, shoring up fun against despair, against the suffocating terror that loomed over her.

Nothing was ever quite distracting or fun enough, though.

Standing in that shower, Hazel thought again of the walnut and the message inside: *Seven years to pay your debts. Much too late for regrets.*

She understood the warning, even if she didn't understand why the Folk were being so considerate as to give her one. Nor did she understand why, if now was the time that she was to be taken, she was still in her bedroom. Had she been taken last night and returned? Is that why she woke up muddy? But then why did they return her? Were they going to take her again? Had seven years passed in a single mortal night? No one, certainly not her, would get that lucky.

Padding to her closet, towel clutched around her, she tried to think of what she could do.

But the note was right. It was much too late for regrets.

Picking out a navy dress dotted with tiny pink-and-green ptero-dactyls and matching green wellies with a clear umbrella, Hazel hoped that the cheerful outfit would help her stay cheerful, too. But as she sat on the bed to pull on the boots, she noticed there was a mess by the window. Mud, streaking the lintel, smeared on the glass pane—and something written in mud on the wall beside it: AINSEL.

Hazel went closer and squinted at the word. It could be the name of someone who was helping her, but it seemed just as likely to be the name of someone she should fear, particularly scrawled as it was, horror-movie style, across the pale blue paint of her wall.

It was incredibly creepy to think of some creature following her back to her room, one of the Folk crouched on her bedroom floor, painting the letters with a bony finger or sharp claw.

For a moment she considered going downstairs and telling her brother everything—the bargain, the note, waking up with the mud on her feet, her fear that she was going to be taken without ever getting to say good-bye. Once, he'd been the person she trusted most in the world, her other half, her co-conspirator. They'd hoped to right all the wrongs of the town. Maybe they could be close like that again, if only there were no more secrets between them.

But if she told him everything, then he might think what was happening was his fault.

She was supposed to take care of herself—that was part of what she'd promised him. She didn't want him to know how badly she'd failed. After Philadelphia, she didn't want to make things worse again.

Taking a deep breath, steeling herself to not say anything, she went downstairs to the kitchen. Ben was already there, packing his backpack with stuff for lunch. Mom had left a plate of homemade kale-granola-raisin bars sitting on the table. Hazel grabbed two while Ben poured coffee into mason jars.

On the way to school, Ben and Hazel barely spoke, eating their breakfast and letting the scratchy speakers of his Volkswagen Beetle fill the car with the nearest college station's morning punk playlist. Ben yawned and seemed too sleepy to talk; Hazel watched him and congratulated herself on acting normal.

By the time they got to Fairfold High, she'd managed to mostly convince herself that she wasn't about to be stolen away by the Folk at any moment. And if they were messing with her, like a particularly cruel cat with a mouse, then getting upset wasn't going to help anything. It was with that resolve that she stepped through the entrance of the school. Jack and Carter were walking down the hallway, mirror images of each other at that distance, except one of Carter's arms was slung over the shoulders of a smug-looking Amanda Watkins. Apparently, Amanda had finally gotten Carter. No more shadows; somehow she'd managed to score the real thing.

Hazel's first thought was that Carter was a hypocrite for hassling her about breaking hearts when he was going to help Amanda break his brother's.

Her second thought was that maybe Carter didn't know that Amanda had called Jack his shadow. Hazel glanced at the careful blankness of Jack's face as he walked beside them and was willing to bet he'd never told his brother.

It made her furious to think of Jack pining away for Amanda while Amanda was *right there*, fluttering her eyelashes at Carter. It made her want to channel her feelings of helplessness about her own situation into punching Amanda in the stomach. It made her want to kiss Jack again—kiss him so hard that the power of that kiss drove Amanda right out of his head, kiss him so wildly that all the other guys, even Carter, would be impressed by Jack's powers of attraction.

But when she imagined crossing the hall and actually doing it, she thought of the odd, pained expression Jack had worn when he pulled back from their kiss at the party. She didn't want him ever looking at her like that again.

"What's going on up there?" Ben asked, drawing her attention toward a knot of church youth-group kids gathered in front of the auditorium doors, a crowd forming around them.

"He just *wasn't there* anymore," Charlize Potts was saying, her arms folded over the giant slouchy Hollister sweatshirt she wore with pink jeggings, white-blond hair spilling down her back.

"We were out in the woods this morning before school, trying to pick up a little, you know, so the tourists don't trip over all the bottles you losers leave out there. Pastor Kevin doesn't want the town to be embarrassed. The coffin was empty. Smashed. Somebody finally broke into it, I guess."

Hazel froze. All her other thoughts washed away.

"He can't just be gone!" someone said.

"Someone must have stolen the body."

"It's got to be a prank."

"What happened Saturday night?"

"Tom's in the hospital with two broken legs. He fell down some steps, so he couldn't have gone back out there."

Hazel's heart sped. They couldn't be talking about what she thought they were talking about. They couldn't be. She took a slow step closer, feeling as though she were moving through something far more solid than air. Ben's long legs took him past her into the crowd.

A few moments later he glanced back at Hazel, eyes shining. She didn't need to hear him say it, but he did, grabbing her shoulder and whispering in her ear as if he were confiding a secret, even though everyone was talking about it.

"He's awake," he said, breath ruffling her hair, his voice low and intense. "The horned boy—the prince—is free. He's loose and he could be anywhere. We have to find him before anyone else does."

"I don't know," Hazel said. "We don't really do that anymore."

"It'll be like old times," Ben said, a grin pulling at his mouth. His eyes hadn't been that bright in years. "The lone gunfighter coming out of retirement for one last battle, trusty sidekick at the ready. And do you know why?"

"Because he's our prince," Hazel said, and felt the truth of it. They were supposed to be the ones to save him. *She* was supposed to be the one to save him. And maybe she and Ben would have one last adventure along the way.

"Because he's our prince," Ben echoed, the way another person might have responded to a familiar prayer with "amen."

❧ CHAPTER 5 ❧

Once upon a time, a little girl found a corpse in the woods.

Her parents had raised the girl and her brother with the same benign neglect with which they'd taken care of the three cats and dachshund named Whiskey that already roamed around the little house. They'd have their long-haired, alt-rock friends over, drink wine, jam on their guitars, and talk about art late into the night, letting the girl and boy run around without diapers. They'd paint for hours, stopping only to fix bottles and wash the occasional load of laundry, which even clean managed to smell faintly of turpentine. The kids ate food off everyone's plates, played elaborate games in the mud outside by the garden, and took baths only when someone snatched them up and dumped them in a basin.

When the little girl looked back on it, her childhood seemed like a glorious blur of chasing her brother and her dog through the woods wearing hand-me-down clothes and daisy-chain crowns. Of running all the way to where the horned boy slept, singing songs and making up stories about him all afternoon, and coming home only at night, exhausted, wild animals returning to a den.

They saw themselves as children of the forest, creeping around pools and hiding in the hollows of dead trees. They glimpsed the Folk sometimes, movements out of the corners of their eyes or laughter that seemed to come from every direction and nowhere at once. And they knew to wear the charms, to keep a bit of grave dirt in their pockets, and to be both cautious of and polite to strangers who might not be human. But knowing the Folk were dangerous was one thing, and finding the remains of Adam Hicks was another.

—

That particular day, Hazel had been dressed up like a knight, a blue dishrag tied around her neck for a cloak and a scarf for a sash around her waist. Her red hair whipped behind her as she ran, shining with gold in the lazy, late-afternoon sun.

Ben had been sword fighting with her all day. He had a plastic He-Man sword that their mother had brought home from the secondhand store, along with a book on King Arthur's knights with stories about Sir Pellinore, who'd supposedly been one of the Folk himself before he joined Arthur's court, the story of Sir Gawain breaking a curse on a loathly lady, and a list of the virtues knights had—strength, valor, loyalty, courtesy, compassion, and devotion.

Hazel had received a baby doll that, if you filled it with water, you could squeeze and make it pee, even though she'd wanted a sword like her brother's. Ben, delighted to have the better present, chased her around, knocking sticks out of her hands with the plastic blade. Finally, frustrated, Hazel went into their dad's toolshed and found a rusty old machete in the back. Then she smacked Ben's plastic sword so hard that it cracked. He stomped back to the house for glue while she danced around in nine-year-old triumph.

She spent a while whacking at a patch of dried-out ferns while pretending they were the terrible monster of legend, the one that lurked in the heart of the forest. She intoned a few lines of the rhyme under her breath, feeling quite daring.

After a while, she got bored and went looking for blackberries, sheathing her machete in her sash and skipping through the tall weeds. Whiskey followed her at first, but then wandered off. A few moments later he started barking.

Adam Hicks was lying in the mud of the bank beside Wight Lake, his lips bluish. Hollow pits where his eyes should have been stared up at the sky, maggots squirming inside, pale as seed pearls. The bottom half of his body was submerged in the water. That was the part that had been eaten. White bone peeked out from flesh that hung in tatters and ribbons, waving in the water like ripped strips of cloth. There was a smell in the air, like when she'd accidentally left raw hamburger overnight on the counter.

Whiskey was running back and forth, sniffing the body, howling as if he thought he could wake Adam up.

"Come away from there," Hazel tried to call, but her voice came out like a whisper. She knew that not enough time had passed for her brother to be on his way back yet. She knew that it was just her and the dog alone out there.

She began to tremble all over.

Adam's parents had moved to Fairfold a year before, making him not quite a tourist, but not local, either. Dangerously indeterminate, tempting to the Folk. They are twilight creatures, beings of dawn and dusk, of standing between one thing and another, of *not quite* and *almost*, of borderlands and shadows.

Looking out at the green water, trying not to stare at the red ruin of Adam's eyes, Hazel thought of all the knights in the book she'd read that morning. She remembered that she was supposed to be one of them and tried not to throw up.

Whiskey's barking got more intense and more frenzied.

Hazel was trying to shoo him back when a damp claw closed around her ankle. She screamed, fumbling for her machete, stomping on the grasping, toad-pale hand with her free foot. The hag rose up out of the muddy water, her face sunken like a skull with cloudy eyes and long green hair that spread out, floating on the surface of the lake. The touch of her hands burned like cold fire.

Hazel managed to swing the blade as the hag yanked on her leg. Hazel went down on her back, hard. Flies blew up from Adam's body in a black cloud. As Hazel felt herself dragged toward the water, she noticed with dim and terrible satisfaction that the hag was bleeding from a slash in her cheek. Hazel must have struck her.

"Little girl," the hag said. "Barely a mouthful. Stringy from running. Relax, little mouthful."

Closing her eyes, Hazel swung the machete wildly. The hag made a hissing sound like a cat and grabbed for the blade. It sliced into the hag's fingers when she caught it, but she held on, wrenching it from Hazel's grasp and tossing it into the middle of the lake. It landed with a splash that made Hazel's stomach turn.

Whiskey bit the hag's arm and growled.

"No!" Hazel shouted. "No! Go away, Whiskey!"

The dog held on, whipping his head back and forth. The hag lifted her long green arm high into the air. Whiskey rose, too, his hind legs off the ground, his teeth still embedded deep in her flesh, as though pressed against bone. Then the hag's arm came down, slamming him against the ground as if he weighed nothing, as if he were nothing. The dog went still, lying on the bank like a broken toy.

"Nononono," Hazel moaned. She reached out a hand toward Whiskey, but he was just far enough to her right to be out of reach. Her fingers clawed at the mud, digging runnels into it.

Strains of distant music floated toward her. Ben's reed pipes. He had slung them around his neck on a dirty string a week ago, calling himself a bard, and hadn't removed them since. *Too late. Too late.*

Hazel tried to crawl toward Whiskey's body, kicking against the cold grip of the hag. Despite her efforts, her feet hit the lake. Water splashed high into the air as she struggled.

"Ben," she shouted, her voice cracking with panic. "Ben!"

The piping went on, closer now, beautiful enough to make the trees bend low to hear him better, and utterly useless. Tears sprang to Hazel's eyes, fear and frustration combining into panic. Why didn't he stop playing and help? Couldn't he hear her? Her legs slid into the water, slime coating her skin. Hazel sucked in a breath, preparing to hold it as long as she could. She wondered how much it hurt to drown. She wondered if she had any fight left.

Then suddenly the hag's fingers went slack. Hazel scrambled up the bank, not bothering to notice why she got away until she was over a log and leaning against an elm tree, her breaths coming hard. Ben stood near the water, looking pale and scared, playing the pipe as though he was playing for his life.

No, Hazel realized. He'd been playing for *her* life. The water hag gazed at him, rapt. Her fish eyes didn't blink. Her mouth moved only slightly, as though she was singing along with the notes he played. Hazel knew the Folk loved music, especially music as fine as Ben's, but she'd had no idea it could do this to one of them.

She saw Ben notice Whiskey's body, saw her brother take a staggering half step forward, saw his eyes close, but he never stopped playing.

Hazel's gaze went to the bank where she'd fallen, the gouges her scrambling had made in the mud, Adam's rotting body and her dog's limp one beside it, the buzzing of flies in the air above them, and something else, something that shone in the sunlight like a hilt. A knife? Had Adam brought a weapon with him?

Slowly, Hazel crept back down the bank, back toward the water hag.

Ben looked over at her, eyes wide, shaking his head in warning.

Hazel ignored him, making her way to the knife in the mud, feeling numb and angry. She gripped the hilt and pulled. The mud made a sucking sound as the blade slid free. It was metal, blackened as though it had been in a fire, and gold underneath. It was much longer than she'd expected—longer even than her mother's biggest kitchen knife, with a groove down the middle. It was a *sword*. A real sword, the kind a grown-up knight would carry.

Hazel's mind was racing, but she kept going, concentrating on repeating over and over: *I am a knight. I am a knight. I am a knight.* A better knight could have saved Whiskey, but at least she could avenge his death. Wading into the silty water, she hefted the heavy sword like a baseball bat and brought it down, bashing the edge against the monster's head. Her skull split like a rotten melon.

The creature slumped over in the water, dead.

"Wow," Ben said, walking closer, dropping the pipes so that they hung around his neck again, tilting his head to one side and bending down to inspect the red mess of bone and lichen-covered teeth, to stare at the clumps of hair floating in the water. He pushed at it with his toe. "I didn't think you'd really kill it."

Hazel didn't know how to reply. She wasn't sure whether he thought what she did was bad or whether he was just surprised it had worked.

"Where did you get that?" he asked, pointing to the sword.

"I found it," Hazel told him, sniffing brokenly. Tears kept flooding her eyes, no matter how many times she tried to blink them back.

Ben reached out like he wanted to take the blade from her. Maybe he was thinking of his broken He-Man sword and how the one in her hand would make a good replacement. Hazel took a half step back.

He made a face, acting like he hadn't wanted it anyway. "With your sword and my playing, we could do something. Stop bad things. Like in stories."

Despite the dog's death, despite her tears, despite everything, she smiled and wiped the blood spatter off her nose with the sleeve of her shirt. "You think so?"

Children can have a cruel, absolute sense of justice. Children can kill monsters and feel quite proud of themselves. Even a girl who carries spiders outside instead of stepping on them, a girl who once fed a tiny fox kit with an eyedropper every two hours until wildlife rescue could come and pick it up—that same girl can kill and be ready to do it again. She can take her dead dog home and bury him and cry over his cooling and stiffening body, making promises as she digs a deep hole in the backyard. She can look at her brother and believe that together they're a knight and a bard who battle evil, who might someday find and fight even the monster at the heart of the forest. A little girl can find a dead boy and lose her dog and believe that she could make sure no one else was lost.

Hazel believed she'd found the sword for a reason.

By the time she was ten, Hazel and Ben had discovered two more monsters—two more faeries with tourist blood on their hands, two more creatures hungry to entrap them. Ben lulled them with his music, while Hazel crept up and struck them down with her sword— by then, honed and polished, gleaming with mineral oil, and painted over black to hide all the bright gold.

Sometimes they heard solitary Folk following them home from school, rustling at the edges of the woods. Hazel waited, but they never bothered her. Faerie morality isn't human morality. They punish the unmannerly and foolhardy, the braggarts and cheats, not the brave, not tricksters and heroes. Those, they claim for their own. And so, if the Alderking noticed the children, he chose to bide his time, waiting to see what they might yet become.

Which left Hazel and Ben to go on hunting monsters and dreaming about saving a sleeping prince, until the day Ben's playing faltered. They'd been tromping through the woods when a black-furred and flame-eyed barghest barreled toward them from the shadows. Hazel held her ground, drawing her sword from the scabbard she'd made, her eyes wide and teeth gritted. Ben began to play his pipes, but, for the first time, the notes sputtered out uncertainly. Surprised, Hazel turned toward him. It was just a moment, just a small shift in her body, just a glance toward her brother, but enough that the barghest was on her. Its tusk dug into her arm and she only slashed its side shallowly before it was past her. Panting, bleeding, she tried to keep her balance, tried to heft the sword up and be ready to strike again.

As it swung back around, she expected Ben to begin his song, but he appeared frozen. Something was very wrong. The barghest's hot breath steamed toward her, stinking of old blood. Its long tail swept the ground.

"Ben—" she called, voice shaking.

"I can't—" Ben said, nearly choked with panic. "Run! Run! I can't—"

And they did run, the barghest just behind them, weaving between trees like a leopard. They ran and ran until they managed to wedge themselves in the hollow of an oak tree, where they hid, hearts thumping, breaths held, listening for the sweep of a tail or the pad of a heavy step. They stayed hidden there until the late-afternoon sun was low in the sky. Only then did they dare creep home, balancing the odds the creature was waiting for them against the worse worry of being discovered by it in the woods after dark.

"We've got to stop—at least until we're older," Ben said, later that night, sitting on the steps behind their house, watching Mom grill burgers in cutoff shorts and an old, hole-pocked CBGB shirt. "It's harder than I thought it would be. What if something else goes wrong? What if you got hurt? It would be my fault."

You started this, she wanted to say. *You made me believe we could do this. You can't take it away.* But instead she said, "I'm not the one who messed up."

He shook his head. "Well, okay, that's worse. Because I could mess up again and doom us both. Probably I will. Maybe if I managed to get into that school, if I could learn to have more control over the music, maybe then..."

"Don't worry about me," she told him, bare toes digging in the dirt, chewing on a strand of her own red hair. "I'm the knight. It's my job to take care of myself. But I don't want to stop."

He let out a breath. His fingers tapped anxiously against his thigh. "We'll take a break, then. Just for a little while. Just until I'm better at music. I need to get *better*."

Hazel nodded. If that's what he needed so she could stay a knight, so they could continue their quest, so everyone could be saved, so they could be like characters from a story, then she vowed she'd find a way to get it for him.

And she had.

CHAPTER 6

During those heady, endless afternoons when Hazel and Ben had roamed the countryside, playing at quests and hunting real danger alike, Ben spun tales about how they were going to wake the prince. Ben told Hazel she might wake him by kissing the glass of his casket. It wasn't an original idea. If someone dusted that case, they'd probably find thousands upon thousands of lip prints, generations of mouths pressed softly to where the horned boy slept. But they hadn't known that then. In the stories, she would kiss the prince awake, and he would tell her that he could be freed only if his true love completed three quests—quests that usually included things like spotting the right kind of bird, picking all the blackberries on the bushes and then eating them, or jumping across the creek seven times without getting wet.

She'd never finish any of the quests Ben made up. She'd always leave a last berry on its branch or splash her foot on purpose, although she'd never have admitted that to her brother. She knew the quests weren't real magic. But every time she got close to completion, her nerve failed.

Sometimes Ben told stories about how he would free the prince, with three magic words—words he'd never say out loud in front of Hazel. And in those stories, the prince was always villainous. Ben had to stop him before he destroyed Fairfold—and Ben did, through the power of love. Because, despite his cruel heart, when the prince saw how much Ben loved him, he spared the town and everyone in it.

Back then, it hadn't seemed weird to Hazel to have the same imaginary boyfriend as her brother.

They were in love with him because he was a prince and a faerie and magical and you were supposed to love princes and faeries and magic people. They loved him the way they'd loved Beast the first time he swept Belle around the dance floor in her yellow dress. They loved him as they loved the Eleventh Doctor with his bow tie and his flippy hair and the Tenth Doctor with his mad laugh. They loved him as they loved lead singers of bands and actors in movies, loved him in such a way that their shared love brought them closer together.

It wasn't like he was real. It wasn't like he could love them back. It wasn't like he'd ever have to choose.

Except now he'd woken. That changed everything.

All of that hung between Ben and Hazel as they walked back out through the doors of the school and toward his car.

And a tiny voice nagged at her, a voice that whispered it could be no coincidence she'd woken with mud on her feet the very morning after something had woken the prince. She held that secret hope to her chest, being very careful to let herself think about it for only a moment or two, the way one might look at something so precious as to be overwhelming.

"Wait!" a voice called from behind them.

Hazel turned. Jack was running down the steps. Rain spattered his T-shirt, turning the fabric spotty and dark. He'd left his jacket inside.

They went around the corner of the building together, ducking under an awning, so that teachers couldn't see them, but it was dry enough to talk. They knew the spot because it was where all the janitors gathered to smoke, and if you didn't report them, they'd overlook whatever shady thing you were engaged in. She wouldn't have guessed that a good boy like Jack knew about the spot, but, clearly, she would have been wrong.

"We're going to find him," Ben said, grinning. He made it sound as though they were about to begin a game, but a very good game.

"Don't," Jack sighed, and looked out toward the football field. He seemed to be considering his next words carefully. "Whatever you think he is—he won't be what you're imagining." Then he visibly steeled himself to grit out the next bit. "You can't trust him. He's not human."

Silence stretched between them for a long moment. Ben raised his eyebrows.

Jack grimaced. "Yes, I *know*, okay. It's *ironic*, my telling you that, since I'm not human, either."

"So come with us," Hazel said, offering up her umbrella. "Share your invaluable inhuman insights."

Jack shook his head, smiling a little. "Mom would skin me alive if I missed my science quiz. You know how she is. Can't this wait until after school?"

Besides mandatory family games on Sundays, his mother was the kind of parent who packed lunches in stacked bento boxes, who knew exactly how her kids were doing in every subject, who monitored television time to make sure homework got done. As far as she was concerned, Carter and Jack were headed for Ivy League colleges, ideally close enough to Fairfold that she could drive up and do their laundry on weekends. Nothing was supposed to get in the way of that.

If Jack cut school, he'd be grounded for as long as she could make it stick.

"This is the single greatest thing that has ever happened around here," Ben said, rolling his eyes. "Who cares about a test? There will be a million more quizzes in your life."

Jack tipped his head forward, highlighting the sharpness of his cheekbones and the silver in his eyes. And his voice, when he spoke, took on an unfamiliar, lilting cant. "There are many things I am forbidden from telling you, for I am bound by both promises and strictures. Three times I will warn you, and that's all I am permitted, so heed me. Something even more dangerous than your prince walks in his shadow. Do not seek him out."

"Jack?" Hazel said, stepping back from him, unnerved. Although she'd almost been killed by creatures like the water hag and the barghest, there was something about the elegant, riddling faeries that terrified her more. Right then, Jack sounded like one of them—and not at all like himself. "What do you mean, *permitted*? Why are you talking that way?"

"The Alderking hunts for the horned boy. The Alderking hunts for whosoever broke the curse. And he is not alone. If you help the boy, you risk much wrath. No prince is worth that price."

Hazel thought of her hands, of the splinters, of the strangeness of her missing night and her dirt-covered legs.

"Wait, you're saying that the Folk in the woods are trying to kill him?" Ben asked. "So you've known secrets about him this whole time and never bothered to tell us?"

"I'm telling you what I may," Jack said. "Your prince may be in danger, but he's also dangerous. Let it be."

"But why? What did the prince do?" Hazel asked.

Jack shook his head. "That was your third warning, and I may say no more."

Hazel turned to her brother. "Maybe—"

Ben seemed frustrated, but not astonished. This strange new Jack did not seem so strange or new to him. "I appreciate what you're saying and all, Jack—we'll be as careful as we can—but I want to try to find him. I want to help."

"I expected nothing less." Jack smiled and was himself again, at least on the surface. But that familiar grin sent a cold chill up Hazel's spine. She'd always thought of Jack as a good boy, from an upstanding family, with good manners, one who made the occasional snarky remark and loved obscure biographies, but who was probably going to wind up a lawyer like his mom or a doctor like his father. She'd thought of his being a changeling as giving him an inner core of weirdness, sure, but in a town full of weirdness, it hadn't seemed *that* strange. But as she stood in the rain, staring up at him, it suddenly seemed a whole lot stranger. "Fine," Jack continued. "Try not to get killed by some handsome, paranoid elf who thinks he's stuck in a ballad. I'll try not to flunk out of physics."

"How could you—why did you say all that?" Hazel asked him. "How could you possibly know any of it?"

"How do you think?" he asked her softly. With that, he turned and started back to the front entrance through the rain, bell ringing in the distance. Hazel watched the muscles move under his wet shirt.

Leaving her to puzzle over his words and try to figure out—

Oh. To try to figure out how he could know things that *only his forest kin could possibly have told him.* She watched Jack's retreat into the school, wondering how she could have known him so long and not guessed. She'd thought he was happy in his human life. She'd thought he had only a human life.

"Come on," Ben said to her, heading for the car. "Before someone catches us cutting class."

Hazel slid into the passenger seat, folding her umbrella and chucking it into the back. Jack had unsettled her, but more than the danger he'd warned them about, she feared the possibility that they wouldn't find any trace of the horned boy at all. That he would become one of those mysteries that never got solved, the kind that became a story people in Fairfold told one another and no one really believed. *Remember when there was a beautiful, inhuman boy asleep in a glass coffin?* they would say to one another and nod, remembering. *Whatever became of him?* Stories like that were will-o'-the-wisps, glowing in the deepest, darkest parts of forests, leading travelers farther and farther from safety, out toward an ever-moving mark.

Hazel had seen a surfeit of faerie awfulness, but she was still lured by stories of the beauty and wonder of the Folk. She'd hunted them and feared them, but, like the rest of Fairfold, she loved them, too.

"Has Jack ever talked to you that way before?" Hazel asked as Ben pulled out of the lot, wipers sending waves of water across the windshield. The sky was a glorious bright gray, so uniform that she couldn't even see where one cloud ended and another began.

Ben glanced over at her. "Not exactly."

"It was freaky." She wasn't sure what else to say. She was still puzzling through what had happened. He'd let his mask slip, apparently on purpose, and she felt stupid that she'd only just realized he'd been wearing a mask at all. "So he talks to them?"

Ben shrugged. "His other family, you mean? Yeah."

Hazel didn't want to admit how thrown she felt. If Jack was keeping secrets, they were his secrets to keep—and, she guessed, it was Ben's job to keep Jack's secrets, too. "Okay, if we're supposed to find the prince against Jack's good advice, where are we going to look?"

Ben shook his head, then grinned. "I have absolutely no idea. Where do you look for somebody who doesn't even seem like he could be real?"

Hazel considered that, biting her lip. "Town would be strange. All the cars and the lights."

"If he goes back to his own people, he's dead, apparently." Ben sighed and hunched over the wheel, maybe going through the same thoughts she'd had before, the same fear this would amount to nothing, that it was playing a child's game they ought to have outgrown. Or maybe he was thinking about the ways magic had betrayed him before and was likely to do so again.

She was tempted once more to confess how she'd woken with mud on her feet and glass splinters in her hands, but now it seemed almost like bragging. And to explain why it wasn't, she'd have to say too much.

In general, her family wasn't very good at talking about important stuff. And of all of them, she was the least good at it. When she tried, it felt like all the chains on all her imagined safes and trunks started rattling. If she started to speak, she wasn't sure she'd be able to stop.

"His own people are the ones who cursed him. He knows not to go back to Faerie," Hazel said, watching the seesaw of the wipers. The familiar thrill woke in her: the hunt, the planning, the discovery of a faerie lair, and the tracking of a monster. Hazel thought she'd given up her dreams of knighthood years ago, but maybe she hadn't given them up quite as completely as she'd supposed.

Ben shrugged. "Okay. But then where?"

She closed her eyes and tried to imagine herself in the place of the horned boy, rousing from long dreams, not remembering where she was at first. He'd panic, slapping his hands against the inside of the glass case. Relief would flood him as he realized jagged pieces of it were missing, the glass smashed. Blinking into the leafy dark and with whatever memories he had from before the curse pounding in his head. But after that...

"I'd want food," she said. "I'd be super hungry, not eating for *decades*. Even if I didn't need it, I'd want it."

"He's not like us."

"Jack's like us," Hazel said, hoping it was true. "And he's like Jack."

Ben blew out a long breath. "Yeah, okay. But you're not going to go through the McDonald's drive-through. You don't have any cash. So what do you eat?"

"I'd forage for chestnuts." Hazel had bought a book identifying edible plants years ago during the library's get-rid-of-everything-ancient-or-tattered-or-oddly-sticky sale for twenty-five cents. With it, she and Ben had managed not to poison each other while gathering up a whole lot of dandelion leaves and wild onions and other edible plants. "But he'd have to roast them. Bird eggs would be good eating, although they'd be hard to come by this late in the year."

Ben nodded, clearly deep in thought. He steered the car toward the part of the wood where the horned boy had slept. "Or he could look for a hazelnut tree. You know, your namesake nut."

Hazel snorted, but there was a place she'd gathered hazelnuts before the worms could eat them. She remembered leaving them on a rock to dry in the sun. "I have an idea."

They parked by Wight Lake and walked from there. A hazelnut tree grew not far from the remains of an old stone building, now overgrown with vines. It was about a quarter mile into the woods, two miles from the glass coffin, and such a perfect place to hole up that her skin shivered with the possibility that she might be right.

The rain was still coming down hard, although the canopy of leaves stemmed the worst of it. Hazel was glad of her wellies while stomping through the mud and slick moss. She and Ben climbed over fallen and desiccated trunks of trees, past brambles and branches that snagged on their clothes. Past buckthorn and privet; past trout lily, closed up tight, and clumps of moonseed, its wide green leaves collecting water; past carrion flower, with Sputnik-shaped blooms bowed by the wind; past wisteria and bee balm; past jewelweed and milkweed and tufted knotweed; past dame's rocket and creeping jenny and maidenhair ferns in profusion. She used her umbrella as much to knock vines out of her way as to keep dry.

Then the stone building came into view, covered with ivy. Its roof had caved in years ago, and although rusted-out hinges held a strip of weather-beaten wood along one edge of the frame, the rest of the door was gone. Ben ran ahead of Hazel, and as he did, she slowed her step.

Her hand went to her side automatically.

Ben looked back at her, frowning. "What are you doing?"

Hazel shrugged. She'd been reaching for something—her belt? her pocket?—but there was nothing there.

"Going for your sidearm?" Ben asked, laughed, and kept on going.

Hazel had no more known what it was, exactly, that made her pause than she'd known what she'd been reaching for. But she thought about Jack telling them to be careful, about that curdled milk slopping into the bowl, about the note in the pocket of Ben's jacket, and about the memory of hunting faeries. With all that in her head, she closed her umbrella carefully.

Ben ducked through the doorway and then darted back out a minute later, a wondrous smile on his face. "You were right. I think you were right!"

Hazel followed her brother into the house. She'd been in the old stone building before with Ben, many years ago, when they'd been pretending to be witches and wizards just out of Hogwarts, cooking up cauldrons of weeds with a pail and some water. Rain drizzled through the remains of the roof. A weather-beaten table, gray and termite-eaten, was pressed against one of the stone walls.

On top of it were the skins of three persimmons, ripped open and scraped clean, the heady, spicy smell of them heavy in the air. A handful of bruised herbs rested nearby, of which Hazel recognized only mint. Tiny black elderberries and several chanterelles were scattered over the wood, like beads dropped from a necklace.

And beside all that was a knife, one with a handle of bone and a twisting blade of some golden metal. It reminded her of the sword she'd found when she was a kid.

"Shit," Hazel said, reaching toward it, stopping before her fingers touched the knife. She looked at Ben. He was grinning in a crazy, awed way.

"He was really here," she said.

"Well, he's got to come back for that, right?" Ben said. "If we wait, we'll catch him when he does."

Hazel nodded, feeling giddy. She found an area by the remains of the hearth and perched there while Ben leaned against a wall. After a few minutes the cold stone had numbed her butt. She watched water drizzling into a growing puddle near the empty hole of a window and tried to calm her nerves.

"You know how they say that once you eat faerie food, nothing else will satisfy you?" Ben asked suddenly.

"Sure," Hazel said, thinking of the pile of berries on the table.

"I wonder if Fairfold is like that. I wonder if I'd ever be happy somewhere else. Or if you would. I wonder if we're ruined for other places."

Her heart skipped a beat. He never talked about college, hadn't gotten any brochures in the mail. Hazel had no idea where he was headed after he graduated next year. "If you go away and don't like it, you can always come back," she said. "Mom and Dad did."

He made a face. "I'd really rather not turn into our parents. I keep hoping I'll meet someone with an awesome life so I can just slip into it."

Hazel remembered how a trick of the light had made it seem like she could see through him the night he came back from his last date. She wondered if that was more true than she'd imagined.

"The city's a lot like the deep, dark fairy-tale woods of Fairfold, right?" Ben went on. "In the movies, the city's where all the stories happen. It's the place people go to be transformed. Where people go to start over. I figure I can be anyone there. Maybe even someone normal."

Hazel thought of what her parents said about normal. And she thought about the fact that he was telling her this while out in the middle of the forest, looking for a lost elf prince. If normal was what he was trying for, he was going to have to try a lot harder.

Outside, the wind whipped against the trees. Hazel heard faint strains of music.

"Do you hear that?" she asked him.

Ben peered out in the direction she was looking. "Full moon tomorrow night."

Growing up in Fairfold, everyone knew to stay out of the forest on full-moon nights—and, to be on the safe side, on the nights surrounding them. That was when the Alderking had his revel, and every nixie, pixie, and sprite, every hobgoblin, water hag, phooka, and tree spirit would come from near and far to dance their circle dances and feast until dawn.

Unless the Alderking was too busy hunting the horned boy to have his party. Maybe those weren't the sounds of revelers, but the sounds of hunters.

They sat there for two hours in the cold drizzle, waiting. Eventually, the music faded away.

Ben yawned, then ran his fingers through rain-soaked ginger hair. His freckles stood out against his cold, pale skin. "I don't think he's coming back. So what do we do now?"

"We could leave him something," Hazel said after a moment's considering. "We could get him food and—I don't know—some clothes. Show him we're worth trusting."

Ben snorted. "I guess. I mean, I don't know if I'd prefer sweats to an embroidered doublet, no matter how long I'd been in it. But anything we could do to make him less freaked out would be good. To show we're friendly weirdos, not dangerous ones."

"You think he's freaked out?" Hazel pushed herself up and started to walk toward the doorway. She looked back at her brother, still leaning against the rough stone wall, moss clinging to it like shadows.

"I would be," he said.

Hazel raised an eyebrow at him. "I thought he wasn't like us."

Ben shook his head, then grinned at her. "Let's just go get the stuff."

Hazel ripped a piece of lined paper out of her book bag and wrote out a note with a ballpoint pen:

Hi, we're Hazel and Ben. We'll be back soon with some food for you and other stuff. It's yours if you want it. We're not asking for anything in return. We're just glad you're finally awake.

They were quiet on the way back, Hazel making a mental list of what they could pack: three cheddar-and-mustard sandwiches with relish, wrapped in tinfoil; a can of Coke; a big mason jar of coffee, with lots of milk and sugar in it; and two kale-granola-raisin bars. She thought there might be an old sleeping bag in the back of the attic; if it wasn't too musty and moth-eaten, he could use that, too. Ben could give up some clothes, and Dad had a pair of old army boots he wouldn't miss.

It all seemed like a poor offering for a lost prince of Faerie, but what else could they do?

Ben pulled the Volkswagen into their driveway. It was just after three thirty and Jack sat on the front stoop. He raised a hand in salute. The rain had stopped, but the lawn was still covered in shimmering beads of water.

Ben rolled down the window. "What are you doing here?" he called. "What happened to being forbidden from helping?"

"Not helping, just warning," Jack said, eyes flashing silver, bright against his dark skin and darker hair. "I might come over on a normal day, so I've decided to pretend this day is normal."

Hazel got out of the car.

"So did you find anything?" Jack asked, clearly expecting them to say they hadn't.

Ben shrugged. "Maybe."

"I just wanted you to understand," Jack said, glancing in her direction to make it clear he was speaking to both of them. "His waking was no accident. And whatever happens next will be no accident, either."

"Whatever," Ben said, walking toward the house. "We get it, okay? Gloom and also doom." The screen door banged behind him.

"What's with him?" Jack asked.

"He's in love," Hazel said, forcing a smile, because she was surprised at Ben's indifference to the warnings, too.

"You all are," said Jack softly, as though speaking to himself. "The whole town's in love."

Hazel sighed. "Come on in. Help me make sandwiches. I'll make you one, too."

He did. He sliced cheddar and she spread mustard, while Ben went through his clothes to find some stuff he thought might fit the horned boy. He brought down a gray hoodie, a pair of jeans, and two pairs of black boxers. He held up each for inspection. Hazel found the sleeping bag and boots in the attic and shook out any spiders on the lawn. They brewed fresh coffee and packed some in a large mason jar mixed with cream and sugar for the horned boy and in smaller jars for themselves. Ben found a basket to put all that in, along with the kale-granola-raisin breakfast bars, the soda, a pack of matches that Jack helpfully wrapped in plastic, and a bag of pretzels.

When the three of them got to the stone cabin, the golden knife was no longer lying on the table. The horned boy had come and gone again.

And he'd taken their note with him.

✦ CHAPTER 7 ✦

Gifted, they'd called Ben, since the elf woman touched his brow and a port-wine stain bloomed on his temple and he'd come home able to hear their music and make it, too. *Gifted*, they said, when he composed songs on a child-size ukulele that no adult could replicate. *Gifted*, when he played a tune on a xylophone that made their babysitter weep. *Gifted*, his sister called him, when he charmed faeries in the woods and saved her life. (And doomed it, too, maybe.)

But what he could do scared him. He couldn't control it.

Parents like theirs were kind of lazy and forgetful about things like paying bills on time or buying groceries or license renewals, but not about art. They might not make a dinner that was more than corn flakes and hard-boiled eggs or remember to sign field trip consent forms or bother about bedtimes, but they knew what to do with a musical prodigy. They called friends, and by the time Ben was twelve and Hazel was eleven, they had a referral to some crazy school where Ben could "fulfill his potential." At the audition, his playing of the piano made the entire admissions committee sit rapt and completely ensorcelled for a half hour. It was terrifying, he'd told Hazel later, like playing to a room full of the dead. Once he was done, they began to move again and told him how amazing his playing had been. He'd felt sick inside.

And he felt even sicker when Mom and Dad told him they couldn't afford to send him there. He wanted to go more than he'd ever wanted anything, because as strange as his audition had been, he knew learning about music was the only chance he had at controlling his power.

When the scholarship came in months later, long after he was sure they'd forgotten about him, he felt as though he'd won the lottery. They all went out for ice cream to celebrate, and he ate half of Hazel's along with his own.

He wasn't just glad he was going to a fantastic school to learn music. He was glad they were moving away. He was scared that Hazel was going to get hurt—really hurt, the kind of hurt people didn't come back from—and it would be because of him. He still remembered how invulnerable he'd felt when he realized that his music had immobilized the water hag, how amazed he'd been by the sight of his sister with the sword. He'd felt like they were born to be heroes. But actually hunting faeries was terrifying. And while he could make excuses to stop for a while, it was just a matter of time before she got fed up with him and went out on her own.

———

Dad rented out the house in Fairfold, and they got a cheap apartment in Philadelphia, where only a fraction of their stuff fit. Hazel didn't like it—didn't like anything about it. She didn't like that you could hear the neighbors through the walls. She didn't like the way she felt tired all the time there, even though her mother told her that was just adolescence and it happened to everyone. She didn't like the noises of the city or the smell of exhaust and rotting garbage outside the windows. She didn't like her public school, where her new friends made fun of her when she talked about faeries. She didn't like that she wasn't allowed to roam around by herself. And, most of all, she didn't like not being a knight anymore.

When she'd made the bargain, she'd thought only Ben would go away, not that she'd have to go with him. Not that the whole family would go.

"Think about all the takeout we can get," their mother had said, clearly remembering her favorite restaurants from when she was in art school. "We can have bowls of pho one night and tacos the next and injera with doro wat after that."

Hazel had made a face. "I don't want to eat any of those things. I don't even know what they are."

"Then think about your brother," their father had told her, not particularly sternly, ruffling Hazel's hair fondly as if he thought she was being adorably childish. "Wouldn't you want him to support you if you were following your dream?"

"My dream is to go back home," Hazel had said, crossing her arms over her chest.

"You just haven't found the thing that you're good at yet," her mother said, smiling. And that was that.

Hazel knew what she was good at; she just didn't know how to explain it. *That's not true*, she wanted to say. *I'm good at killing monsters.* But her mother didn't need to know that, and it would be foolish to say it. Mom might be horrified or scared. Mom might start paying attention to where she went and what she did. Besides, it was a delicious secret. She liked thinking of it almost as much as she'd liked the weight of her blade in her hand.

And if there was another part of her that wished her parents were the kind who might protect her from needing to kill monsters all on her own, at eleven she already knew that was unrealistic. It wasn't as if her parents didn't love her; it was just that they forgot things a lot and sometimes those things were important.

Which meant for two years, Ben learned to play different instruments (including wineglasses and a tuba) at the fancy school, while Hazel learned a new skill—how to be an unrepentant flirt.

Hazel wasn't the best in her classes, nor was she the worst. She might have been good at a sport, but she never bothered to try out for one. Instead, after school, she signed up for self-defense classes at the Y and practiced techniques she learned from YouTube videos of sword fighting. But, at twelve, Hazel discovered something she was weirdly better at than other people—making boys squirm.

She'd look at boys and smile if they caught her looking.

She'd twirl her red curls around her finger and bite her lip.

She'd prop up her boobs with her arm, the desk, or one of the new underwire bras she persuaded Mom to buy for her—all of them silky and brightly colored.

She'd tell people she was doing badly in all her classes—once or twice because it was true and then chronically when it wasn't.

Flirting didn't mean anything to her. There was no plan, no goal. It was just a little rush, just a way to be seen in a place where it would be easy to drown in invisibility. She never meant to hurt anyone. She had no idea that was even possible. She was twelve and bored and really didn't know what she was doing.

While she was flirting, Ben was falling in love for the first time, with a boy named Kerem Aslan. They met every day after school to whisper together over their homework and sneak kisses when they thought no one else was looking. Sometimes Ben would play snippets of a song he was working on, a thing he'd never done with anyone but Hazel before. She still remembered the way she'd seen Ben trace the boy's name along his arm in water. *Aslan*, like the lion from Narnia. Kerem looked a little bit like a lion, too, with golden-brown eyes and shaggy black hair.

Hazel and Ben went from having everything in common to having nearly nothing. They went to different schools, had different friends, different stories, different everything. Hazel was miserable, and Ben had never been happier.

But then Kerem's family found out about the relationship and his parents called to have a horrible awkward talk with Dad and Dad hung up on them. And Ben cried at the kitchen table, head buried in his folded arms, no matter how many times Dad hugged him and told him it was going to be okay.

"It's not," he whispered, insisting he would never feel any less miserable than he did in that moment. He insisted his heart was broken forever.

At lunch the next day Ben texted Hazel to say that Kerem had been avoiding him and talking shit to their mutual friends. After her classes were over, Hazel decided to walk to his school instead of going straight home. She knew his last period was a long individual study on the flute. After that, they could go get gelato at the place that poured a shot of espresso over it and maybe Ben would cheer up.

No one stopped her from going in; she slipped past the security guard and headed down the hall to the bench next to the music room. Perched there, she was surprised to see Kerem Aslan of the lion eyes and lion name walking down the hall toward her.

"Hey, little sister," he said. "You look pretty today."

Hazel smiled. It was automatic, half a reaction to a compliment and half the familiarity of smiling at him. She'd smiled at him a thousand times before.

"You know I always liked you. Whenever I came over to the

apartment, I'd ask if you wanted to come hang out with us, but Ben said that you were busy. He said you had a boyfriend." Kerem sounded as if he was flirting, but there was something in his face too close to fear for the words to be convincing.

"That's not true," Hazel said. She'd seen him and Ben, heads bent together as they whispered and laughed, oblivious to the rest of the world.

"So you *don't* have a boyfriend?" Kerem asked. She could tell from his tone that he was misunderstanding her on purpose, but it still flustered her.

"No, I mean—" she began.

And then, with a sideways glance down the hall, he leaned in and kissed her.

It was her first kiss, outside of grandmas and elderly aunts, outside of parents and brothers, despite all the flirting she'd done. His mouth was soft and warm, and while she didn't kiss him back, she didn't exactly squirm away.

It wasn't nice, her hesitation. It lasted only a moment, but it ruined everything.

"Stop it," she said, shoving him. Some other musical-prodigy kids looked over. A teacher came out of her classroom and asked if everything was okay. Hazel's voice must have been louder than she'd thought.

But everything wasn't okay, because Ben was staring at them. Then there was only the sight of her brother's backpack, the heels of his black Chucks, and the slam of the music room door.

"You did that on purpose," Hazel accused. "You wanted him to see."

"I told you I liked you," Kerem said, raising his eyebrows, but he didn't sound all that triumphant.

Her hands wouldn't stop shaking as she waited for Ben outside his classroom, listening to the strains of music that escaped the soundproofing. She wanted to tell her brother what really happened, explain that she hadn't wanted to be kissed. But she didn't get the chance, because a few minutes later his music instructor collapsed from a myocardial infarction that nearly killed her. The paramedics came, with Ben and Hazel's parents arriving soon after. Ben wouldn't talk to anyone, not then, not on the way home.

He'd played music when he was upset, when he was probably angry, and his instructor's heart had stopped. Hazel knew he must be blaming himself. Hazel knew he must be blaming the magic, and she knew he must be blaming her.

By the time she went up to Ben's room to try to apologize, he was sitting on the floor, door open, cradling his left hand.

"Ben?" she said. He looked up with haunted, red-rimmed eyes.

"I don't want to play anymore," he told her, voice weak, and she realized what he must have done to get his hand like that. He'd slammed it in the door. More than once, probably. The skin wasn't just red; it was *purple*, and his fingers were on the wrong angle.

"Mom!" Hazel screamed. "Mom!"

"It has to stop," he said. "I've got to stop. Somebody has to stop me."

They took a taxi to the hospital, where the ER doctors confirmed that he'd broken bones, lots of them. His instructors confirmed that he wouldn't be able to play anymore, at least not for a long while. He'd have to wait until the bones set and do exercises to give them greater mobility. He'd have to be very careful and diligent.

Even though Ben never said a thing to their parents about what he'd done or why he'd done it, even though Hazel never told, they got the message and moved the family back to Fairfold not long after, back to their sprawling mess of a house and their old life.

Ben was neither careful nor diligent with his hand.

He listened to music, lots of it. He gorged on music. But after they got back, he wouldn't even hum along. He didn't play again, which meant the next time a tourist went missing in Fairfold, Hazel hunted alone.

It was different without him, and it was hard going back into the forest after all the time away. The strap for her sword—the one that had allowed her to carry it on her back—no longer fit right. She had to adjust it for her hip, although she wasn't used to having it there, and the slap of the scabbard against her thigh was a constant distraction. She felt silly, almost a teenager, returning to a child's game. Even the woods had become unfamiliar. The paths weren't in the same places, and she kept finding herself putting a foot wrong when she tried to race through them the way she used to.

But she was taller and stronger and determined to handle things on her own—determined to show her brother that she didn't need him, determined to show herself she still could be a knight. She knew the trick to hunting the Folk was to keep your wits about you, to remember they were tricksy, to remember that the grass under your feet might move sideways, that you might be led in a circle. Hazel had turned her socks inside out before she set off, and her pockets were full of oatmeal, just as her grandmother had shown her and Ben when they were little kids. She was ready. She had to go back out there. She had to find the monsters. She had to fight the monsters, all of them, until she got to the monster at the heart of the forest and ended the corruption forever so that everyone could be safe always.

Sometimes, if she thought too much about that, her heart would race and panic would set in. Her quest was impossible, and she didn't know how much time she had left.

Panic was what she had to guard against, because it was easy to panic whenever she remembered she'd pledged seven years of her life to the faeries. And after panic came despair—and once despair set in, it was harder and harder to shake it off again. The trick was not to let herself think about it too much. Anything that stopped her from thinking would do. Anything that kept her from pressing her hand against her chest to feel the thudding of her own heart and know that each beat was another moment lost.

It took her three long days to find the missing girl, a tall and skinny teenager named Natalie. When Hazel did find her, the girl was still alive but unconscious, hanging from the branches of a thorn tree. A thin drizzle of her blood dripped from one of her arms into a wooden bowl. Two short faerie men with long reddened noses and pale eyes busied themselves adjusting the ropes, making the girl spin, making the blood drip faster.

Hazel had never found a tourist alive before.

She knew what the creatures with the girl were from stories, although she'd never seen one. They were redcaps, terrifying monsters who delighted in butchery and dyed their garments in blood.

For a moment Hazel looked at them and wondered what the hell she was doing. She'd gotten used to living in the city. She'd gotten used to a world without monsters. She'd gotten soft and scared. The pommel of the black-painted sword wobbled in her sweaty hands.

I am a knight. I am a knight. I am a knight. She repeated the words, lips moving soundlessly over them, but she wasn't sure that she entirely knew what they meant anymore. What she did know was that if she didn't get herself together, a girl was going to die.

Hazel burst from the brush, slashing downward. The first redcap cried out and then slumped over, entirely silent. Her stomach lurched, but she whirled on the second, ready to counter his attack, ready to slice him in half. She might have won, too. She was strong and fast, holding a glorious golden sword, and she'd taken the two redcaps by surprise. But there was a third she hadn't seen, and he knocked her to the ground with a single sharp blow.

They cut Natalie's throat. She had such little blood left anyway, they said, and the new one was much fresher. A rope went around Hazel's ankles, and they were preparing to haul her up like the other girl. She felt dizzy and sick and more scared than she'd ever felt in her life. She wanted to call for Ben, but there was no Ben to call for. She had only herself, and she'd failed. She hadn't saved anyone.

She hung upside down from the tree for hours, blood rushing to her head, before the redcaps departed for more firewood. Steeling herself, she swung over to where Natalie hung. The horror of the dead flesh under her hands was awful, but she climbed the girl's body until she could pull herself up onto a branch and undo the rope at her ankles. Tears wetted her cheeks, although she didn't remember crying.

She found her sword, stacked with an assortment of other stolen things, and headed for home, shaking so hard she was afraid she was going to shake apart.

That night, she'd discovered that thirteen-year-old ferocity was no match for ancient monsters, not alone. She had to admit that her knighthood was lost, along with Ben's music. When she finally made it home, she stood outside Ben's door for a long time, palm pressed against the painted wood. But she didn't knock.

Hazel had told him that she was sorry, that she had never meant for Kerem to kiss her, had never wanted it, had told him a thousand times. But in her heart of hearts she knew that wasn't entirely true. She'd flirted with Kerem at the apartment, because he was a cute guy and Ben had everything. She hadn't wanted the kiss when it happened, but she had thought about it before. And she'd let it happen, when maybe if she hadn't, Ben wouldn't have lost his music. Maybe he wouldn't have given up their quest, either. Maybe Natalie would still be alive.

She'd told Ben that the kiss meant nothing. And she wanted it to mean nothing.

She wanted to *prove* it meant nothing.

But no matter how many other boys she kissed, she couldn't bring Ben's music back.

CHAPTER 8

The night the prince went missing from his coffin, Mom made spaghetti with jarred sauce for dinner, along with shake cheese from the green can, and frozen peas. It was a typical deadline dinner, so familiar that Hazel craved it when she was sick the way other kids craved chicken soup. Dad was already gone and was going to stay in New York through the week for meetings. Mom tried to get them to talk about their day, but Ben and Hazel just stared at their food and answered stiltedly, too distracted by everything that had happened to make much of an effort at conversation. According to their mother, the mayor had already reached out to a local sculptor—a friend of hers—to inquire whether it might be possible to create a fake version of the prince, so his absence wouldn't affect tourism. The official story was that vandals had stolen him.

"When I was a girl, we all adored him," Mom said. "I remember there was this one—oh, you know her, Leonie's mom—anyway, she went out to that casket every Saturday with a roll of paper towels and a bottle of Windex to keep the glass shiny. That's how obsessed she was."

Ben rolled his eyes.

Mom looked pleased with the reminiscence. "And Diana Collins—Diana Rojas now—tried to wake him up by reenacting that Whitesnake video, rolling around on his casket like it was the hood of a Trans Am, wearing only a string bikini and baby oil. Ah, the eighties, right?" Absently, she rose and crossed the room to pull out an old, beat-up sketchbook from the bottom-most bookshelf. "You want to see something?"

"Sure," Hazel said, a little confused. The image of Megan's mother and baby oil was stuck in her head.

Mom flipped through the pages, only slightly yellowed by time. There, rendered in No. 2 pencil, in BIC pen, in colored markers, was the prince, asleep. The drawings were okay, not great, and it took Hazel a moment to realize what she was looking at.

"You drew these," she said, her voice coming out slightly accusatory.

Mom laughed. "Oh, I sure did. I used to go out to the woods after school, pretending that I was going to sketch trees and whatnot, but I always wound up drawing him. I did a big painting of him, too, in oils. It was one of the pieces that got me into college."

"What happened to it?" Hazel asked.

Mom shrugged. "Someone bought it off me for a couple of bucks when I was living in Philly. Hung it up in a coffeehouse for a while, but I don't know where it is now. Maybe I'll paint another, since he's gone. I'd hate to forget him."

Hazel thought of the knife stuck in the wood of the old table and wondered how gone he truly was.

After dinner, Mom opened her laptop in front of the television and watched some cooking show while Hazel and Ben stayed in the kitchen, eating grapefruit marmalade on toast for dessert.

"So what now?" she asked her brother.

"We better find the prince before Jack's warnings start coming true." Then, with a frown, Ben nodded at her hands. "You fall or something?"

She looked down at them, no longer red, healed to scabbed lines. *Something happened last night.* The words sat on her tongue, but she couldn't bring herself to speak them out loud.

After she'd nearly gotten killed by the redcaps all those years ago, after he'd seen the bruises and heard the story, he'd begged her never to hunt alone again. *We'll figure something out*, he'd promised her, although they never did.

If he knew she'd made a bargain with the faeries, he'd be really upset. He'd feel bad. And it wasn't like there was anything he could do about it now. "I must have got scraped out in the woods," she said. "Sticker bush or something. Ah well, totally worth it."

"Yeah," he said faintly, getting up and putting his plate in the sink. "So you think he's out there, somewhere, bedded down in our old sleeping bag? Eating our stale pretzels?"

"And drinking the drip coffee of our modern age? It's a nice thought. I hope so," Hazel said. "Even if he's the villainous prince from your stories."

Ben snorted. "You remember that?"

She turned her head, trying to summon up a smile. "Sure. I remember all of it."

He laughed. "God, I haven't thought about our telling each other all that stuff. It's so crazy, the idea that we get him—that he woke up in our generation."

"There's got to be a reason," Hazel said. "Something's got to be happening out in the forest. Jack's right about that."

"Maybe it's just time. Maybe his curse is up and he smashed the coffin himself." Ben shook his head, his mouth lifting at one corner. "If our prince was smart and wanted to be safe from the Alderking, he'd come straight to the center of town. Go door-to-door. He'd be invited to more dinners than a preacher on a Sunday."

"He'd be invited to more *beds* than a preacher on a Sunday," Hazel put in, to make Ben laugh, because Pastor Kevin was much lusted over by the youth-group kids for belonging to some semi-famous Christian rock band. The horned boy was a way bigger local celebrity, though. If he showed up in the middle of Main Street, the Fairfold Women's Auxiliary would probably hold a very sexy bake sale in his honor. Ben was right: If the prince didn't mind hiding from the Alderking in the bedrooms of Fairfold, he'd be set.

"All this rushing into danger isn't like you," Hazel said, finally, because she had to say something.

Ben nodded, giving her an odd look. "Finding our prince is different."

She pushed herself up from the kitchen table. "Well, if you have any brilliant ideas, wake me. I'm heading to bed."

"Night," Ben said cheerfully—maybe a little too cheerfully—and started for the living room. "I'm going to check the local news. See if they're sticking to the vandal story."

Climbing the stairs, Hazel resolved to try to stay awake as long as she could, hoping to catch whatever had called her from her bed the night before. She'd heard stories of people so enchanted that they slipped out of their houses to dance with faerie Folk on full-moon nights, heard stories of people waking up at dawn with raw feet, lying in rings of mushrooms, with a yawning chasm of yearning for things they could no longer recall. If she was going to be used by the Folk, she wanted to know about it.

Of course, there was the possibility that, having used her for whatever service was needed, she wouldn't be summoned back for a long while, but it was better to be safe than sorry.

In her room, she knelt down and slid an old wooden trunk from underneath her bed. The wood was cracked and warped in places. When she was very little, Ben would hide in it and pretend he was Dracula in his coffin, and then the prince in his. When she was even littler than that, Mom had put her toys and baby blankets inside. But now it was the place where her old sword rested, along with a bunch of mementos of her childhood. Rocks with shining mica she'd loved and pocketed on walks through the woods. The silver gum wrapper

Jack had folded into the shape of a frog. Her old, makeshift green velvet cape, which was supposed to be part of a Robin Hood costume. A daisy chain so brittle from drying that she didn't dare touch it or it would fall to pieces.

Those were the things she expected to find when she opened the box. She'd thought she could take out the black-painted sword and stuff it between the mattress and box spring.

It wasn't there.

The wooden trunk was empty except for a book and a folded-up tunic and pants—ones made from a light silvery-gray material she'd never seen before—and beside them a note in the same eerily familiar hand that wrote the message inside the walnut: 241.

She took out the book. FOLKLORE OF ENGLAND, the spine read. She flipped to page 241.

It was the story of a farmer who bought a stretch of land that came with a big, hairy, troublesome boggart who'd claimed the land for himself. After some argument, they decided to split the land. The boggart demanded everything that grew above the ground and told the farmer he could have anything below. But the farmer got the better of the boggart by planting potatoes and carrots. At the harvest, the boggart got only the useless tops. He was furious. He raged and shouted and stamped his feet. But he'd made the bargain, and, like all faeries, he was bound to his word. The next year, the boggart demanded whatever was below ground, but again the farmer got the better of him. He planted corn, so that the boggart was left with only stringy roots. Again the boggart raged, more terrible and angrier than before, but again he was bound to his word. Finally, in the third year, the boggart demanded that the farmer should plant wheat, but they would each plow the field, keeping what they harvested. Since the farmer knew the boggart was much stronger, he lighted on the idea of planting iron rods in the ground on the boggart's side of the field, so the boggart's plow became blunted again and again, while the farmer plowed merrily away. After hours of that, the boggart gave up, saying that the farmer could have the field and good riddance to it!

The words *carrots* and *iron rods* had been circled by a muddy finger.

Hazel frowned at the book. The story didn't mean anything to her.

Confused and frustrated, she busied herself by pulling the muddy linens from the bed and stuffing them into the hamper. Then she grabbed a clean, but wrinkled, bottom sheet and an old blanket from the hall closet. Finally, she changed into rocket ship–print pajamas, flung herself down, picked up a paperback off the side table at random, and opened it, trying to distract herself, trying to convince herself that she needed an old sword about as much as she needed a Robin Hood costume.

The book turned out to be one she'd read before, where zombies chased around a brother-and-sister reporting team. After a few pages and the wash of words, she put it down. She couldn't concentrate. None of it seemed as real as her memory of a mossy stone house with an elf-wrought knife lying on a worn wood table. None of it seemed as real as her sore hands, muddy feet, and missing night.

None of it seemed as real as Jack's having a double life. She knew you had to be careful around faeries, no matter how beautiful or clever or charming, but somehow Jack had always been the exception. Now, though, thoughts of his silvery eyes and the odd way he'd spoken wouldn't leave her. Somehow that and the memory of their kiss became tangled, and she felt like a fool.

So she rested, eyes shut, pretending to sleep, until she heard the creak of floorboards. Someone coming up the stairs and down the hallway. Ben coming to bed? Or was Ben already asleep and something else was creeping toward her? Hazel sat up and reached for her cell to check the time: two in the morning.

As she slid out of bed, she heard someone bang back down the stairs.

Shoving her feet into her wellies, clutching her phone, she followed as stealthily as she could. If the Folk could have drawn her from her bed, it stood to reason that they could draw Ben, too. He might not owe them anything, might not have bargained with them, but that only meant they had no right to him. They took lots of things they had no right to.

She found Ben already outside by the time she got her coat and made it out the door. He walked toward his car purposefully. She started to panic, indecision halting her in the shadows underneath an oak tree. There was no way she was going to be able to follow him on foot. She considered racing to the passenger-side window and tapping on it. If he was bewitched, that might snap him out of it.

But what if he wasn't? What if he was going out to look for the horned boy alone? It wasn't as if he had to take his tagalong little sister everywhere he went.

Ben pulled his car out of the driveway slowly, without turning on his lights.

Coming abruptly to a decision, Hazel went to the shed and yanked her old bike out from among the cobwebby tools. With shaking hands, she ripped off the reflective discs attached to the spokes, hurling them into the dark. Then she hopped up onto the seat and pushed off, pedaling fast. By the time she made it to the street, his headlights were on and he was making the first turn.

She braked gently, trying to stay out of his line of sight without losing the Volkswagen. Speed limits on the back roads were cautious, which made things easier, but there was no way she could keep up if he disobeyed them and gunned the gas.

The wind whipped her hair behind her, and the moon was high in the sky, turning everything to silver. She felt like she was pedaling into a dream landscape, a hushed world in which everyone but her and her brother was asleep. The last of her tiredness burned away as her muscles worked and she got into such an efficient leg-pumping rhythm that for a moment she didn't notice he was pulling over. She stopped short, the bottom of her boots scraping against the road. Then she eased the bike off into the trees, where she dropped it among vines and felled branches.

A cold sweat had broken out along her back. She'd guessed where he was going: to the remains of the glass casket.

She followed Ben on foot, creeping along as slowly as she could.

She hoped the snap of twigs wouldn't betray her. Whether she was still good at moving silently through a forest or Ben was just distracted, he didn't so much as glance in her direction.

It was a lot like hunting, except that it was her brother she was after.

The night was damp and chill enough for Hazel's breath to cloud in the air. Creatures rustled in the underbrush and called to one another from the misshapen limbs of trees. An owl peered down at her with its clock face. She wrapped her coat more tightly around herself and wished that she'd bothered to change out of her pajamas before she'd left the house.

Ben stopped near the fallen trunk of an oak tree. He seemed to be reconsidering whatever had brought him all the way out here, pacing back and forth, kicking the leaves of a fern bush. Hazel wondered again if she should say something, call out and let him know that he wasn't alone.

I followed you because I thought you'd been enchanted, she imagined herself saying. *But now I realize that you're probably not enchanted, because enchanted people don't suddenly get confused about what they're doing out in the middle of the woods in the dark. Sorry. I guess I probably shouldn't have followed you after all.*

That would go over well.

But then Ben resumed marching through the forest, feet kicking up leaves, and Hazel resumed following him. They walked until he came to the grove where the prince had slept, a grove they'd been to a hundred times. Broken glass and crushed beer bottles shimmered in the moonlight. But all the vegetation, from the trees to the shrubs to the thorny vines, was blackened and dead. Rotted, as though winter had come early. Even the evergreens had withered away.

And the coffin had been shattered. Everyone knew it, but it was different to see—a sacrilege, as though the casket had turned out to be no more magical that a car window someone smashed to get to a radio. Destruction had made it ordinary.

Ben walked over to the glass case and ran his hand over the metal edge, then he pushed the remains of the lid back, tinkling pieces of crystal breaking off and falling. His hand went inside—maybe touching the fabric—then he paused and looked toward where Hazel was, as though maybe she had stepped wrong and made too loud a sound.

What was Ben looking for? What had he come to find?

She made a silent vow that if her brother tried to climb into the coffin, she was going to step out of the shadows, no matter how mad it made him.

He didn't, though. He circled it, as if he was as amazed by the ruin as she was. Then he bent, a frown on his face. When Ben stood, he had something cupped in his hand, something he'd taken from inside the coffin, something that flashed in the moonlight, something he was looking at in astonishment. An earring. A cheap green enamel hoop that Hazel hadn't even noticed was missing from her ear.

Immediately, excuses sprang to mind. Maybe Hazel lost it the night of the party—though that wouldn't explain the positioning:

inside the case, under chunks of glass. And she was pretty sure she remembered putting them back on the next day. Okay, better, maybe another girl had the same earrings and *she'd* lost one.

Hazel had guessed she might have had something to do with the horned boy's being loose, but some part of her had resisted believing it. Now, though, she had to believe. No explanation she came up with explained away the evidence.

She started trembling, panic rolling over her. Hadn't she scolded herself for running straight into trouble every chance she got? For leaving no stone unturned, no bad idea unembraced, and no boy unkissed? No scab unpicked? No sorrow unnumbered? No hangnail unbitten and no stupid comment unsaid? Certainly no stupid bargain unmade. Apparently, that was still the case, even if she couldn't remember it.

After a few minutes, Ben started back toward his car, swearing under his breath. Hazel crouched down and pressed her shoulders against a tree until he passed. Until she could get her breathing under control. She still wasn't sure what she was going to tell Ben, but at least she'd have until morning to figure it out.

Hazel walked back to her bike. It was where she had left it, obscured by a clump of pachysandra that seemed to swallow the frame. She stood it up, pushed toward the road, and began to pedal, following the distant taillights of Ben's car.

He seemed to be heading in the direction of home, so she no longer worried about keeping up. Instead, she concentrated on what she was going to do.

It was to the Alderking that she'd sworn her seven years. Maybe if she went to the hawthorn tree on the full moon and waited, she could make another bargain for answers. Or maybe she'd find the Alderking's revel and ask him directly what he was intending to do with her.

She was pedaling faster, imagining what she might say, when she saw the body in the ditch. A girl's body—pale legs splayed in the dirt, brown hair lying in a puddle. Someone was leaning over the body, someone with brown hair hanging in front of his eyes, some of it pushed back over his long, curving horns.

She startled, her whole body freezing up.

She lost her balance. The bike spun out from underneath her. It happened so fast that she didn't have time to react, to correct herself. One moment she'd been speeding along, and the next she was slamming into the road.

The horned boy watched her crash, his expression unreadable in the moonlight.

CHAPTER 9

She hit the pavement. Her hands, thrown out to protect her face, hit first, skidding along the road. Her breath was knocked out of her. She rolled sideways, skinning her elbows and scraping the back of her head. Everything felt raw and awful. For a moment she stayed there, dirt in her mouth, waiting for the pain to ebb.

She could hear the wheels of her bike spinning and something else—the horned boy coming toward her. His footfalls on the asphalt sounded as loud as snapped bones.

He knelt down, looming over her.

His skin was pale, seemingly bleached by the chill. He was still wearing the fine embroidered blue tunic he'd had on for generations, the fabric darkened by rain, ivory boots spattered by mud. His horns rose up over his temples and curved back behind his sharp ears, close to his head and ending in points just past his jawline, so that, to someone at a distance, they might appear like thick braids. Even his bone structure—the planes of his cheekbones, height of his brow— seemed subtly different from a human's. He seemed overall more finely wrought, like a crystal wineglass revealed to someone used to coffee mugs. His eyes were a mossy green that made her think of deep pools and cool water, and he looked down at her with those otherworldly eyes as though puzzling something through.

He was every bit as monstrously beautiful as he'd ever been. You could drown in beauty like that.

"What did you do to her?" Hazel asked, trying to push herself up. Blood was seeping from both of her knees and along her arms, making her pajamas stick to her skin. She didn't think she could run; her muscles were too stiff and too sore.

He reached for her, and she realized that she was going to have to run anyway. She got up, lurched three steps, and saw that the girl lying in the ditch was Amanda Watkins.

Her skin was white—not pale or even sickly, but white as a sheet of paper is white. The only pinkish parts were along the very tips of her fingers and around the inside of her eyes. Her lips were slightly apart, and the cup of her mouth was filled with dirt, a few vines curling out from the corners. She had a high heel on one foot, but her other foot was bare and mud-covered.

"Amanda?" Hazel called, staggering toward her. "Amanda!"

"I know you. I know your voice," the boy said, sounding hoarse, as if he'd been shouting for a week. He grabbed her arm and, when she whirled on him, stared at her with glittering, hungry eyes. "You're the very girl I sought."

She felt as if she'd waited her whole life for him to wake up and say those words to her. But now that he had, she was absolutely terrified. She tried to pull away. His fingers held her in place, as chill as if they'd been plunged into ice water, seeming to reach through her skin. She opened her mouth to scream, but all that came out was a strangled sound.

"Quiet," he said, his voice harsh. "Be *quiet*. I know who you are, Hazel Evans, sister of Benjamin Evans, daughter of Greer O'Neill and Spencer Evans. I recognize your voice. I know all your foolish desires. I know you and I know what you've done and I *need* you."

"You . . . you what?" She imagined her nine-year-old self whispering to him through the glass and blushed a hot, shameful red that went all the way down her throat. Could he really have heard all the things they'd said to him, all the ridiculous things that had been said *around* him, for all the time he was there?

"Walk." He pulled her along the road. "We must go. We're out in the open here."

She struggled against his grip, but he pulled her along, squeezing her wrist tightly enough to bruise.

"What about Amanda? We can't just leave her!" she shouted.

"She sleeps," he said. "My fault, perhaps, but I cannot alter it, nor is it of much consequence now. Things will be worse for her and for everyone else if you don't tell me where it is."

"Where what is?"

"The sword." He sounded exasperated. "The one you used to free me. Do not play at ignorance."

Dread turned Hazel's stomach. She thought of the nearly empty trunk underneath her bed. "A sword?"

"Return Heartsworn. Things will go better for you if you simply do as I ask. If you trifle with me, I will have to show you why that is unwise."

"Ask?" Hazel snapped automatically. "You call what you just said 'asking'?" As soon as the words were out of her mouth, she regretted them. She urged herself to *think*. It was disorienting to stumble along, aware that he might be taking her somewhere to kill her and at the same time, confusingly, embarrassed that he was going to kill her while she was wearing her pajamas and wellies. If she'd known she was going to die at his hand, she would have dressed up.

His lip curled into an almost smile, and he jerked her arm. "Asking in the nicest way I know."

"Want my help?" she said. "Then tell me what you did to Amanda." As she spoke, she fumbled in the pocket of her coat for her cell phone. He might be a magical creature, a real knight, but he'd still been asleep for a hundred years. She bet he didn't know shit about modern technology.

"I? You are much mistaken if you think it was I who did that. There are worse things than me in these woods."

"What kinds of things?" Hazel asked.

"You have perhaps heard of a creature who was once one of the Folk and is now something else. A creature of mud and branch, moss and vine. She hunts me. It was she who set upon your Amanda. No blade but Heartsworn could even scratch her, so you can see it would be in your own best interest to *give me the sword.*"

Oh, Hazel thought, a little bit dazedly. No big deal. Just the monster from the heart of the woods, the creature of legend. She tried to keep her fingers steady as she typed to Ben without looking at her phone, grateful for a lifetime of texting during class: HELP AMANDA HURT ON GROUSE RD!!! MONSTER!

"You've freed me." He looked back at her—and for a moment she thought that underneath all his cold fury, there was something else. "And you are likely to pay for your kindness in most grievous coin. Why did you do it?"

"I don't know. I didn't even know for sure I was involved until tonight. You said you heard my voice—was there anyone else there? Anyone giving me orders?"

He shook his head. "Only you. But by the time I came awake— truly awake—the sky was bright and you were gone."

"I don't remember that. I don't remember going anywhere last night."

He sighed. "Try to remember. Consider the fate of Amanda Watkins, who, by the way, I know you didn't like. Still, the next victim might be someone you do care about."

She startled at his saying that. He was a stranger, yet the way he spoke and the press of his fingers against her arm were oddly intimate. She'd imagined a scene so very like this so many times that to walk beside him in the dim woods had become half nightmare and half fantasy, all unreal. Hazel felt dizzy, as though she might faint. She kind of wanted to faint, so she didn't have to deal with any of it. "Just because I don't like her doesn't mean I want her to die."

"Well, then," he said, as though that settled everything. "Perfect. She's not yet dead."

He didn't even glance in her direction. He just kept walking.

They left the road, wading through the brush. Her heart felt as if it were going to thud its way out of her chest.

The phone in her pocket buzzed, but she couldn't risk looking at it. She felt better knowing that Ben must have received her message, that someone was going to find Amanda.

"We left you some food and stuff," she said, trying to fill the scary silence of their walk and disguise the sound of her phone, which buzzed again. Ben must be calling her. "My brother and I, we're on your side."

He didn't need to know she had doubts about his story.

A pained expression flashed across the horned boy's face. "I am no hob or hearth spirit, to be obligated by gifts."

"We weren't trying to *obligate* you," she said. "We were trying to be nice."

Given the Folk's obsession with manners, she wondered if he might feel at least a little bit bad about dragging her through the forest. She hoped he felt awful.

The horned boy bowed his head slightly, a thin smile on his face that she thought might be self-disgust. "You may call me Severin," he said. "Now we are both nice."

Which was as close to an apology as one of the Folk was likely to give, given that they prized their own names highly. Maybe he really did feel bad, but Hazel got the sense that it wouldn't matter. Whatever drove him, its hooks bit deeper than courtesy.

Time slipped by as they walked, her stumbling and his walking beside her, catching her arm if she moved too far or too fast, her body still sore from crashing her bike, her mind buzzing. They plodded on until they returned to the grove.

Severin let go of her and went to the remains of the casket. "Do you know what this was? Not glass," he told her, sliding his hand inside, running his fingers over the lining. "Nor is it crystal. Nor is it stone. It's made of tears. Almost impossible to shatter. Made by one of the finest craftsmen in all of Faerie, Grimsen. Made to hold a monster."

Hazel shook her head numbly. "You?"

He snorted. "No one tells the old stories anymore, do they?"

"What are we doing?" Hazel asked him.

He took a deep breath. "You need to recall who has Heartsworn. Who gave you the blade and guided your hand? Who told you how to break the casket and end the curse?"

"I can't—"

"You can," he said softly. He brought up one hand to her cheek. His fingers were cool against her hot skin, brushing back hair from her face. She shuddered. "For all our sakes, you must."

She shook her head, thinking of the sword she'd found beside Wight Lake all those years ago, the one that had disappeared from beneath her bed. "Even if I had the first idea where the sword was, what makes you think I would tell you?"

"I know what you want of me," he said, coming closer. Everything else seemed to melt away. He lifted her chin, canting her face toward his. "I know every one of your secrets. I know all your dreams. Let me persuade you."

And, pressing her back against the blackened trunk of a tree, he kissed her. His lips were hot, his mouth sweet. And inside her, a warm, numb darkness flooded her thoughts, making her skin shiver.

Then Severin moved back from her, leaving her to smooth down the front of her pajama top.

"Benjamin Evans," he called into the darkness. "Come out. Don't worry about interrupting us."

"Get the hell away from her!" Ben's voice, shaky but determined, came from the other side of the grove.

It was the worst thing about being a redhead, Hazel thought, the way blushes splashed up onto her cheeks and down her neck until she practically felt as if her scalp were burning.

Ben stepped farther out of the shadows, looking flushed, too. He was carrying an ax their mom used sometimes to chop kindling for the stove in the art studio. "Hazel, are you okay?"

Her brother had come to save her, like in the old days. She couldn't quite believe it.

The elf knight smiled, and there was an odd light in his eyes. He stalked toward Ben languorously, spreading his arms wide in invitation. "Going to split me open as though you were a woodsman in a fairy tale?"

"Going to try," Ben said, but there was a quaver in his voice. He was tall and gangly, all loose limbs and freckled skin. He didn't look dangerous. He didn't even look like he could heft the ax without straining.

She felt a hot wave of shame that Ben had seen the horned boy kiss her, when for so long he'd been something they'd shared between them.

"Ben," Hazel cautioned. "Ben, I'm okay. If anyone's going to fight, it should be me."

Her brother's gaze flickered to her. "Because you don't need anyone's help, right?"

"No, that's not—" She took a step toward him, before Severin drew his golden knife.

"It would be better if neither of you fought me," Severin said. "You've got the range and your weapon may bite deeply, but I'll wager I'm faster. So what are you to do? Will you run at me? Will you swing wildly and hope for the best?"

"Just let her come home," Ben said. His voice shook a little, but he hadn't backed down, not an inch. "She's scared. It's the middle of the night and she's not even dressed. What do you think you're doing, grabbing her like that?"

Severin slid a little closer, moving as lightly as a dancer. "Oh, you mean instead of grabbing *you*?"

Ben flinched as though he'd been slapped. "I don't know what you think you're—"

"Benjamin," Severin said, his voice dropping low. His face was inhumanly beautiful, his eyes as cold as the sky above the clouds, where the atmosphere is too thin to breathe. "I have heard every word you've ever said to me. Every honeyed, silver-tongued word."

Ben's mortified blush deepened. Hazel wanted to call to him, to say that Severin had tried the same thing on her, to tell him the same thing had *worked* on her, but she didn't want to be a distraction. Ben and Severin had begun to circle each other warily.

"I'm not going away without Hazel," Ben said, bringing his chin up. "You can't *embarrass* me into leaving my own sister."

He was going to get himself killed. He was no longer quick-fingered, no longer carrying a set of pipes hanging around his throat on a dirty string. He couldn't play, and he'd never fought with a blade. She had to do something—she had to save Ben.

Hazel hefted the biggest stick she could find. The weight was oddly comforting in her hand, and the stance she went into was as automatic and easy as drawing breath. As soon as the fighting started, she was going to rush Severin and hopefully catch him off guard. It might not be honorable, but it had been a long time since she played at knighthood.

"Don't be foolish," Severin told her brother. "I was trained to a sword when I was a child. I watched my mother butchered in front of me. I have cut and I have killed and I have bled. You can't possibly win against me." He glanced at Hazel. "Your sister at least seems to know what she's about. Her stance is good. Yours is abysmal."

So much for catching him by surprise. She was just going to have to hope for dumb luck.

"If you're going to kill me, then do it," Ben told him. "Because if you want to take her, that's what you're going to have to do."

For a frozen moment Severin brought up his blade. Their gazes caught, snagged silk on a thorn.

Hazel held her breath.

With a snort, the elf knight sheathed his knife. He shook his head, looking at Ben oddly. Then he made an elaborately formal bow, his hand nearly sweeping the ground.

"Go, then, go, Hazel and Benjamin Evans," Severin said. "I release my claim on you tonight. But our business is not done; our affairs are far from settled. I will come for you again; and when I do, you will be eager to do as I wish." With that, he turned from them and walked deeper into the woods.

Hazel looked at Ben. He was breathing fast, as though from a physical fight. The ax slipped from his fingers onto the forest floor, and he regarded her with wild, wide eyes. "What just happened? Seriously, Hazel. That was insane."

She shook her head, equally baffled. "I think you impressed him with the sheer force of your stupidity. How did you find me?"

A corner of his mouth curled up. "When you weren't on Grouse Road, I tracked the GPS in your phone. You were close enough to the casket that I thought you might be headed there."

"What is that quote?" Hazel said, walking to him, too glad he'd come to object to the danger he'd put himself in. "The Lord protects fools, drunks, and dumb-ass ax wielders?"

He touched her shoulder gently, running his fingers against the fabric of her pajamas and sucking in his breath, as if he was imagining how much all her scrapes had hurt. She realized she was covered in dirt from her fall—dirt and blood. "Are you really okay?"

Hazel nodded. "I crashed my bike when I saw him and Amanda. I'm okay, but I don't think she is."

"I called the sheriff's department, so they must have sent someone over by now. Are you going to tell me what you were doing on Grouse Road?" Ben asked.

Following you, she wanted to say, but the words stuck in her throat. If she told him that, he'd ask her about the earring and then ask all the questions that inevitably followed.

She got into his car instead, resting her head against the dashboard. "I'm really tired. Can we just go home?"

Ben nodded once and walked over, squatting down beside her, inside the open door, visibly swallowing his questions. His blue eyes were black in the moonlight. "Are you sure you're okay?"

She nodded. "Thanks to you."

He grinned and pushed himself upright. One hand moved to smooth down her hair. "Our prince really was something, huh?"

Hazel nodded, thinking of Severin's mouth against hers. "Severin," she said. "Our prince's name is Severin."

Once, Ben had told Hazel a tale about a great wizard who took his heart and hid it in the knothole of a tree so that when his enemies stabbed him where his heart was supposed to be, he wouldn't die. Ever since Hazel was small, she'd hid her heart in stories about the horned boy. Whenever someone hurt her, she comforted herself with tales of him being fascinating, a little bit awful, and desperately in love with her.

Those stories had kept her heart safe. But now, when she thought about Severin, when she remembered his moss-green eyes and the horrible, shivery thrill of his words, she didn't feel safe at all. She hated him for waking up and being real and stealing her dreams of him away.

He wasn't their prince anymore.

CHAPTER 10

On the car ride home from the woods, Ben had a barely contained nervous energy that caused his hand to tap against the steering wheel and to fiddle with the radio. They'd passed Grouse Road and saw the flashing lights of the sheriff's car and an ambulance, shining in the dark with reassuring steadiness. Someone had come to fix things, to fix Amanda, who Severin had claimed was still alive.

"We have to stop," Hazel asked. "What if she's—"

"Are you really going to tell them what happened?" Ben asked, eyebrows raised, turning the wheel to take a different route home.

In her mind's eye, Hazel saw Severin circling her brother, a hungry expression on his face, a shining blade in his hand. And then a shudder went through Hazel when she thought of the awful sprawl of Amanda's pale limbs in the patchy grass. Amanda had not seemed alive. No, Hazel wasn't sure she knew what to explain to the police, even in a place like Fairfold.

"Go ahead and stop," she said. "I don't know what I'm going to tell them, but I have to tell them something. My bike's there."

She had no idea if they'd believe her or not. But when Ben showed up with the ax in his hand, she was reminded of all the reasons he had stopped hunting years ago. He'd understood how dangerous it was and how vulnerable they were back then, even if she hadn't.

She didn't ever want to put him in that position again. Just because he'd gone looking for the prince didn't mean he wanted to get dragged back into danger.

Looking at her like she'd gone crazy, Ben pulled up several feet behind the ambulance. Hazel got out. Paramedics were bent over Amanda's body.

An officer looked over at her. He was a young guy. She wondered if he'd grown up in Fairfold. If not, she was about to really freak him out. "Excuse me, ma'am," he said. "You better get back in your car."

"I saw Amanda earlier tonight," said Hazel. "With the horned boy. You've got to look for him—"

He walked closer, blocking her view of the stretcher and the paramedics. "Ma'am, get back in your car."

Hazel got back in Ben's car, slamming the door behind her. Her brother shook his head at her as the officer shone his flashlight inside. "Please roll down your window. Who's in there with you?"

She cranked down the passenger-side window.

"I'm her brother," Ben volunteered. "Benjamin Evans. You were talking to Hazel."

The policeman looked at them like he didn't quite know what to make of the situation. "You both have identification?"

Ben handed over his driver's license. The officer looked at it for a long moment and then handed it back.

"And you say you saw someone?"

"The horned boy. With Amanda. She was already unconscious, but he was here. And now he's out there, and if he did this, then we're all in a lot of danger."

The cop looked at them for a long moment. "You two better get on home."

"Did you hear me?" Hazel demanded. "We're in a lot of danger. Fairfold is in danger."

The policeman stepped back from the car. "I said, you better get on home."

"You're not from around here, are you?" she asked him. "I mean you weren't born here."

He looked back at her, uncertainty in his face for the first time. Then his eyes hardened and he waved them on.

"At least tell me if Amanda's okay?" Hazel called after him, but he didn't answer.

Ben drove home with the sun rising in the east, gilding the tops of trees.

As they pulled onto their street, he turned to her. "I didn't expect you to do that."

"It didn't work," Hazel said.

"Tonight," he said, keeping his voice light and conversational with clear effort, "kind of got out of control, huh? Everything about it was unexpected."

"Yeah," she said, leaning her cheek against the coolness of the window, her hand on the latch of the car door.

He pulled the car into their driveway, the tires crunching over gravel. "I'm your older brother, you know. It's not your job to protect me. You can tell me stuff. You can trust me."

"You can tell me stuff, too," Hazel said, opening the door and stepping out. She expected him to take the earring out of his pocket and confront her with it, demand an explanation. But he didn't.

For all that they'd claimed they could tell each other stuff, they told each other nothing.

Hazel walked into the house. It was entirely dark. Even the lights in the outbuilding were off. She began to climb the steps.

"Hey, Hazel?" he called softly in the upstairs hall, and she turned. "What did he kiss like?" There was a confusion of emotions on his face—longing and maybe a little jealousy and a whole lot of curiosity.

She snorted a surprised laugh, her bad mood dissolving. "Like he was a shark and I was blood in the water."

"That good?" he asked, grinning.

She'd known he'd understand. Brothers and sisters had their own language, their own shorthand. She was glad to be able to share the weird, ridiculous impossibleness of it with the only person who knew all the same stories, with the person who'd made up those stories in the first place. "Oh yeah."

Ben went to her, slinging an arm over her shoulder. "Let's get you fixed up."

She let him lead her to the upstairs bathroom, where he sat her on the edge of the tub and then doused all her cuts with peroxide. Together, they watched the liquid hiss and froth over her skin before it swirled down the drain.

Then, kneeling awkwardly on the cracked beige floor tiles, he wrapped her legs and arms in gauze, the stuff they'd called "mummy bandages" when they were little. The old phrase rested on the tip of her tongue, making her remember times they'd come in here after a hunt, cleaning their skinned knees and binding up wrists or ankles.

The house was usually full of people back then, so it was easy to slip in and out. People were always dropping by, come to pose for a piece or to borrow some canvas or celebrate someone booking a job with a bottle of bourbon. Sometimes there wasn't any food but a weird, boozy trifle left out on the counter, or a can of cold ravioli, or cheese that smelled like feet.

Over the years, her parents grew up and got more *normal*, even though they wouldn't admit it. Hazel wasn't sure if their memories of those days were as much a blur of people and music and paint and confusion as hers were. She wasn't sure if they missed the way things had been.

What she did know was that normal was a lot more tempting when it was out of reach.

Once normal had been a heavy, smothering blanket she feared being trapped beneath. But now normal felt fragile, as though she could unravel it all just by teasing out a single string.

When Hazel finally collapsed in her bed, she was so tired that she didn't even bother to pull her comforter up over her body. She fell asleep like a flame being extinguished.

———

That morning, Hazel dreamed that she was dressed in a tunic of cream wool, with chain mail on top of it. She was riding a horse at night, through the woods, fast enough to see only a blur of trees and flashes of hooves pounding ahead of her.

Then the leaves seemed to part, and by the light of the full moon, she found herself looking down at humans kneeling in the dirt, surrounded by milk-white faerie horses. A man, a woman, and a child. The humans were dressed in modern clothes, flannel, as though they'd been camping. A tent, slashed and sagging, rested beside a dampened fire.

"Shall they live or shall they die?" one of the Folk asked of his companions. He was speaking carelessly, as though it truly didn't matter either way. His horse snorted and pawed the ground. "I bet they came out here to glimpse sweet little faeries gathering dewdrops. Surely, that's enough reason to cut them down, no matter how they cringe and beg."

"Let us see what talents they possess," said another, leaping off his steed, silver hair flying behind him. "We could let the most amusing one go."

"What say we give the big one ears like a fox?" shouted a third, a woman with earrings that chimed like the bells on her horse's bridle. "Give his mate whiskers. Or claws like an owl."

"Leave the little one out for the monster," said a fourth, making a face at the child. "Maybe she'll play with it for a while before she gobbles it up."

"No, they've ventured into the Alderking's woods on a full-moon night, and they must have the full measure of his hospitality," Hazel heard herself say as she swung to the ground—was that her voice? She spoke with such authority. And the humans were looking at her with just as much fear as they'd looked at the others with, as though she were a faerie, too. Maybe in her dream, she was. "Let us curse them to be rocks until some mortal recognizes their true nature."

"That could take a thousand years," said the first one, the careless one, with a lift of one brow.

"It could take far longer than that," she heard herself say. "But think of the tales they'd tell if they ever did win freedom."

The human man began to cry, pulling his child to his chest. The man looked anguished and betrayed. He must have loved faerie stories to have sought the real thing. He should have read those stories more closely.

The silver-haired rider laughed. "I should like to see other mortals picnic upon them, all unknowing. Yes, let's do that. Let's turn them to stone."

One of the humans began to beg, but Hazel looked up at the stars above her and began to count them, instead of listening.

⌒

Hazel woke, covered by a thin sheen of sweat.

Her alarm played tinny music beside her ear. Turning, she shut off her phone and pushed herself out of bed. She should have been disturbed by her dream, but instead it kindled in her a long-forgotten desire for a blade in her hand and sureness of purpose. She'd barely gotten any sleep; she should have been far more exhausted than she felt. Maybe adrenaline was an even better drug than caffeine.

After her shower, Hazel got dressed in a loose gray T-shirt and black leggings. She felt stiff and sore. Even the knuckles of her fingers were scraped. As she pulled her hair into a rusty ponytail, memories scattered her thoughts. Flashes of the horned boy—of *Severin*—kept distracting her. His expressions, the feel of his fingers on her skin, the heat of his mouth. In the bright light of day, it seemed impossible, unreal, but she'd felt the realness of it, all the way down to her traitorous gut. And then her brother, ax held high in shaking hands, face flushed, red hair blowing over his eyes. She hadn't seen Ben like that in years, brave and mad and anguished. She'd been terrified for him—more scared than she'd been during her own stumbling walk through the forest with the horned boy pulling her along.

She wondered if that was how Ben had felt all those years ago, when it had been Hazel out in front, blade clutched tight, facing down faeries.

⸺

Mom was making smoothies in the kitchen when Hazel came downstairs. Kale and ginger, kefir and honey were all lined up on the counter. Mom had on one of Dad's ratty, checkered bathrobes, her short brownish hair sticking up at odd angles, paint still under her fingernails. On the radio, an old song about shiny boots of leather was playing.

Ben was sitting on the counter, dressed in rumpled green corduroy pants and a baggy sweater, rubbing his eyes, yawning, and drinking his smoothie out of a quart jar. A tiny square of kale was stuck to his upper lip.

"Morning," he said, sounding as though he was still half asleep. He raised his mason jar in salutation.

Hazel grinned. Her mother handed over a mug of coffee. "Ben and I were just talking about the Watkins girl. She got hurt last night, a couple of blocks from here. Something about it was just on the radio—along with a warning to stay inside after dark."

Hazel imagined what the emergency services people had seen—Amanda's body, arms folded over her chest, eyes closed, dirt in her mouth, hair spread out like a cape.

"What were they saying about her?" Hazel asked dully.

"She's in a coma. There's something wrong with her blood. With tonight being a full moon, you both better get home early. Call if you have to be somewhere, okay? I'm going to let your father know, too, in case he decides to drive home sooner than he planned."

Ben pushed off the counter. With his long legs, it was barely any drop at all to the floor. "We'll be careful," he said, answering what Mom hadn't asked.

Mom poured a glass of greenish liquid from the blender and handed it to Hazel. "Don't forget to wear your socks inside out, too. Just in case. And put some iron in your pockets. There's a bucket of old nails in the shed. You can grab one from there."

Hazel gulped down her breakfast. It was a little gritty, as though the kale hadn't been quite pulverized enough.

"Okay, Mom." Ben rolled his eyes. "We know."

Hazel hadn't done any of that stuff, but she appreciated Ben acting as if she had. They went out to the car together. On the drive to school, he looked over at her sleepily. "Later today you're going to tell me all the parts of last night that I don't know, right?"

Hazel sighed. She should have been grateful he was at least giving her some time to figure out how to answer him, but all she felt was dread.

"Okay," she said.

Reaching into his pocket, he fished out a necklace with a chip of rowan wood drilled through so that it hung from a chain. "Wear this for me, okay? Mom's not wrong."

Rowan wood. Protection from faeries. All the kids in their school had made pendants like this in kindergarten, along with four-leaf-clover pins, and most had hung on to them—or made new ones—to wear every May Eve. Hazel stroked her thumb over it, touched that he'd give her a necklace she was sure he'd made more than a decade before. She lifted her hair and hung it around her throat. "Thanks."

He didn't say anything else, but he glanced over at her several times, as though he was trying to learn something from her expression, as though he hoped to discover something he hadn't ever thought to look for before.

School was strange. Hushed and a little deserted, as though more than a few kids had been kept home by parents. People whispering in the halls instead of shouting, standing around in knots of close friends. Hazel noticed that lots of them had charms tied around their wrists or hanging around their throats. Red berries, dried and strung on silver cord. A gold coin. Herbal oils wafted up off their skin, making the hallway smell not unpleasantly like a head shop. When Hazel began to unpack her bag into her locker, a walnut rolled out, bouncing twice on the linoleum floor.

Leaning down to pick it up, she saw that it was tied with rough string.

With shaking fingers, she opened it. Another rolled-up piece of paper was inside. She unfurled that to read a new message in the same scratchy hand: *Full moon overhead; better go straight to bed.*

No way. She wasn't taking orders from some mysterious faerie. Not anymore. Not if she could help it. Crumpling up the note, she tossed it back into her bag.

Leonie sauntered up to Hazel's locker, smelling of cigarette smoke. She had on a long, ratty flannel shirt over her white T-shirt, with a gold chain around her neck. She'd strung it with a key ring, and—in addition to her house keys—it had half a dozen charms hanging from it. Her dark curly hair was pulled up into two buns on top of her head. They were wet, like she'd put them up right after a shower. "So," she said. "I guess you heard, right?"

"About Amanda? Yeah." Hazel nodded.

"Last person to see her was Carter. Everybody's saying one of the Gordon boys had something to do with what happened." Leonie shrugged, to show she wasn't necessarily agreeing, but since she was spreading the rumor, she probably didn't consider them entirely innocent.

"I thought whatever happened to her was magical." A shudder went through Hazel, remembering the dirt in Amanda's mouth and the vines.

"Well, that's only one of the Gordon boys, then. And that's the one most people are blaming."

"Jack had nothing to do with this!" Thinking of the night before made her recall the shock of Severin's mouth against hers. Just two days after she'd kissed Jack, as though the universe was conspiring to give her everything she'd ever wanted and punishing her at the same time.

When her thoughts returned to Amanda, lying in the ditch, she felt even worse about the kisses.

"Well, it's all just a rumor," Leonie said airily. "It's not like I believe it or anything."

"Well, it's *crazy*. And you shouldn't be repeating it."

"This shit is crazy," Leonie said. "This is not normal Fairfold weird. Not tourist weird. It's actually fucked-up-and-not-okay weird. Amanda's family's always lived here; she's supposed to be protected. People are freaking out. And I'm repeating the rumor because I thought you'd want to know. I'm not broadcasting it all over school."

Hazel took a few calming breaths. Snapping at Leonie wasn't helping anything. "Sorry. It's just that none of the stuff that goes on in the woods is okay, not the tourist stuff, not any of it. And I don't see what Amanda's being unconscious has to do with Jack at all."

"Well, I think it comes from two facts: Firstly, Jack's one of *them*. And secondly, Amanda broke Jack's heart, which is tragic because it means that even a supernatural hottie has the same generic taste as every other idiot in this school. I think he liked her even more than he used to like you, and that's saying something. But it does give him a motive."

Hazel rolled her eyes. "Me? You must be thinking of someone else. Jack Gordon was never into me."

Leonie shook her head. "Whatever, the point is, he's not human and people know it. Remember when he broke Matt's nose?"

"I guess," Hazel said, slamming her locker shut. She was having difficulty with the whole staying-calm thing. "Matt is supernaturally annoying, if that's your point."

The bell rang and they both started down the hallway in the direction of their first-period classes. They had about five minutes before the second bell. Hazel wondered if Jack or Carter knew about the rumors. If they did, she hoped they stayed home from school until all this blew over. Everyone was just scared, that was all, and Jack made a convenient target. No one would ever believe Carter had anything to do with this, not for long. And they'd get over thinking it was Jack, too, just as soon as they thought things through.

At least Hazel hoped they would.

"I was there," Leonie said. "The fight with Matt got weird. The kind of weird that people remember."

Matt Yosco was about three years older than Hazel and Leonie, handsome, with jet-black hair and a constant sneer. Matt had been Leonie's worst habit, worse than cigarettes or weed, worse than any wastrel any of the rest of them had ever dated. He'd been the kind of cruel that insinuated itself into your head, making you doubt yourself, and Hazel had hated him. He was one of the few cute boys in town she'd never even considered kissing. Despite being so awful, when he moved away for college, Leonie had cried for a week straight.

"Weird how?" Hazel asked. They were standing in front of her American History room, but she wasn't ready to go inside. Her heart was racing. It felt as though Severin's being released from his casket had been the first domino to fall, but she still didn't know the pattern its falling produced. And if Severin *wasn't* the first domino, then she knew even less.

"Jack didn't punch Matt." Leonie glanced to one side, as if she was afraid of being overheard. "Matt was being his usual awful self, then Jack—well, Jack smiled this really weird smile, leaned over, and whispered in his ear. The next thing we knew, Matt was hitting himself. Like, really going to town, slamming his fist into his own face, until his lip was cut and blood was streaming from his nose."

Hazel had no idea what to say to that. "How come you never—"

"Said anything? I don't know. Later, Matt seemed to remember it like it was a fistfight, so I just went along with that. It seemed easier. Other people were there, though, and even if they didn't say anything before, they're going to talk now. And that can't be the only time Jack slipped up. There's stuff about him that he's not exactly forthcoming about, I guess is all I'm saying. He has secrets. He can do things."

The bell went off, making Hazel jolt.

"I should have told you before," Leonie said softly.

"Ms. Evans," Mr. DeCampo, her balding teacher, called. "Standing directly outside my door and gossiping with your friend is not the same as being in class, so I suggest that you get to your desk immediately. Ms. Wallace, you are beyond late. I suggest that you run."

"You're a good friend," Hazel told Leonie.

"I know," Leonie said, making a face in Mr. DeCampo's direction. "See you at lunch."

At her desk, Hazel opened a notebook. But instead of taking notes on the major domestic issues of the Federalist era, Hazel began to list what she knew. She liked lists. They were comfortingly straightforward, even when they were full of crazy stuff, like:

WARNINGS:
SEVEN YEARS TO PAY YOUR DEBTS.
MUCH TOO LATE FOR REGRETS.
AINSEL → name of faerie
enchanting me?
The weird story about the farmer
tricking the boggart.
FULL MOON OVERHEAD; BETTER GO
STRAIGHT TO BED.

OTHER INFO:
Jack has magic he's hiding.
Severin is loose and super scary.
I'm the one who freed him.
Even scarier monster is hunting for
Severin and maybe put Amanda into an
enchanted sleep.
Severin knows all the stuff we said
in front of him.
Someone (the Alderking? because of
bargain?) is making me do stuff I don't
remember after I go to sleep. (Or did
at least once.)
Severin needs a magic sword
called Heart-something for unknown

*and possibly sinister reasons. (To kill
the thing that put Amanda to sleep? To
fight back against the Alderking? To
kill us all?)*

*My old sword is gone → same
sword???*

Then she stopped. The idea that the sword she'd found all those years ago was the one he'd been looking for had occurred to her before, but she hadn't really let herself dwell on it. If so, either someone took the sword or she'd handed it over to someone. Maybe to the person who'd left her the notes. Maybe the mysterious Ainsel?

Had she made a second bargain with the Folk? One that she could no longer recall? Was her forgetting part of the condition of the bargain? She pressed her pen against the page so hard that the shaft started to bend.

She needed answers. To get them, she needed to find someone with more information, which, unfortunately, meant one of the Folk. She thought of her dream from the night before and of the full moon that was going to rise that night, which meant a revel. Maybe Jack, with all his secrets, would know the way there. And then all she had to do was survive the revel, get the information, make a plan, and then survive the plan.

No problem.

She shifted on the hard plastic chair of her desk, figuring out what she could say to Jack to persuade him to tell her about the revel. After class, she waited at his locker, but he didn't show; and when she went by his next-period class, he wasn't there. She was too distracted to take a single note; and when she was called on in Language Arts, she gave the answer to a trigonometry question from the period before, making everyone laugh.

It took Hazel until just before lunch to find him.

Jack was walking down the hall with Carter. She wasn't close enough to hear much of what he was saying, but Carter sounded angry. She caught the words *with me last* and *suspect*. Jack was hunched over, looking exhausted. There was a purpling bruise coming up along his cheekbone. She wondered how much today had already sucked for him.

She wondered how much worse she was about to make it.

"Jack," Hazel called, before she could lose her nerve.

He turned, and his smile was real enough that she felt somewhat better. At least until she saw how red and watery his eyes were, as though irritated by all the charms and oils, because any protection from faeries must work against him. Then she saw how raw Carter's knuckles looked. Blood was drying across them. There must have been a fight.

"Can I talk to you for a second?" she asked, weaving her way to Jack through the tide of the hallway.

Carter gave him a playful shove in Hazel's direction. "Go on, then. Don't keep the girl waiting." Hazel wondered what she'd done to get on Carter's good side.

Jack looked a little embarrassed. "Yeah, sure, whatever."

They matched their steps to each other's. He had on a striped cardigan over a worn Afropunk festival T-shirt. Heavy silver hoops shone in his ears. He tried to hold on to the smile for her, but it sat in odd contrast to the rest of his expression.

"You okay?" she asked, clutching her books to her chest.

He sighed. "I just wish Carter didn't have to deal with this. You probably heard it all already, but just in case, he didn't do anything to her."

Hazel started to protest that she already knew that.

He shook his head. "And I didn't, either. I swear it, Hazel—"

"Listen," she interrupted. "I really do know it wasn't him. Or you. I saw Amanda last night with the horned boy."

"What?" His brows went up, and he stopped looking eager to convince her of Carter's innocence. "How?"

"I told the police, but I don't know if it matters," she said. "And I'm sorry to have to ask you this on top of everything else, but I need to know where the Folk hold their full-moon revel. Can you help me?"

"That's what you wanted to talk to me about?" Jack asked her, his expression becoming remote. "That's why you stopped me in the hall?"

"I really need to know."

"Yes," he said softly. "I know where it's held."

She soldiered on. "Have you been there?"

"Hazel," he said, cautioning her.

"Please," she said. "One way or another, I'm going to go."

Jack tilted his head in a way that made her newly aware of how the planes of his face weren't quite like Carter's, of how his cheekbones were higher, his face longer. And she was aware, too, of the subtle points at the tips of his ears. For a moment, as when he delivered the warning to her and Ben, his familiar face was made strange.

She thought of Leonie's story about him whispering in Matt's ear, about Matt slamming his own fist into his own face, over and over again.

"I've got to get to class." He started to walk away, then seemed to feel bad about it and turned back to her. "I'm sorry."

She grabbed hold of his arm. "Jack," she said. "Please."

He shook his head without looking at her. "Did you know there are different names for different moons? This month it's going to be the Hunter's Moon, but March has the Worm Moon and the Crow Moon. May has the Milk Moon, July the Mead Moon. February has the Hunger Moon and late October the Blood Moon. Aren't they lovely names? Aren't they something, Hazel? Aren't they warning enough?"

"How many times have you been there?" she asked in a whisper. If Jack's mother even suspected, it would break her heart.

"Lots," he said, finally, in a strangled voice.

"I'm going with you," she said. "We're going together tonight to the Blood Moon or the Hunter's Moon or whatever name you want to call it—the Head-Chopping Moon, for all I care."

Jack shook his head. "It's not safe for you."

"Did you not just hear me say I don't care?" Hazel said. "Someone is using me and I need to know who and why. And you need to clear Carter's name—and yours, too. We need to know what's really going on."

"Do not ask me for this," Jack said, with odd formality. Hazel wondered if he was worried about betraying his other family. She wondered if *his* Fairfold was a Fairfold that Hazel couldn't even imagine.

"I'm not *asking*," she told him, as firmly as she could. "I'm going, even if I'm going alone."

He nodded once, inhaling shakily. "After school. I'll meet you on the kids' playground." Then he turned and sped off down the hall. A few stray students, late to class or sporting hall passes, slid away from him as though he were contagious.

CHAPTER 11

Changelings are fish you're supposed to throw back. A cuckoo raised by sparrows. They don't quite fit anywhere.

Jack grew up knowing he was strange, without, at first, knowing why. He wasn't *adopted*—he could see that. He looked just like his brother, Carter. He had the same dark skin as his mother and the same tight brown curls and the same slightly-too-long first toes. But something was wrong. He might have his father's amber eyes and his father's chin, but that didn't seem to stop Dad from glancing at him with a worried, nervous expression, an expression that said, *You're not what you seem.*

His mother rubbed him with coconut oil after his bath and sang him songs. His grandmother held him and told him stories.

There was a village near the Ibo River, one story began, a story passed down to his grandmother from her Yoruban ancestors. In it, a woman named Bola had a son who grew too large to carry on her back to the market, so Bola waited until he was sleeping and went without him, latching the door behind her. When she returned, he was still asleep, but all the food in the house was gone.

She wondered whether someone could have snuck into the house. But the door had not been forced and nothing but the food was missing.

Soon after, a neighbor came to Bola and asked her to repay a string of cowrie shells. Bola hadn't borrowed money from her neighbor and told her as much. But the woman insisted, explaining that Bola's son had come to her house, saying that he was on an errand for his mother, who needed the cowries to buy more food.

Bola shook her head and brought the neighbor into her house. The child was napping on a woven mat.

"See," she said. "My baby is very little, far too small to walk and talk. How could he have come to your door? How could he have asked to borrow cowries?"

The neighbor stared in confusion. She explained that the boy who'd come to her door looked much like the sleeping child, but was far older. When Bola heard this, she became greatly distressed. She didn't doubt her neighbor and believed that her child must have been possessed by an evil spirit. When Bola's husband came home that night, she told him everything, and he became troubled as well.

Together, they made a plan. Her husband hid himself in the house while Bola went to the market, leaving the baby sleeping behind a latched door, just as before. Her husband watched as the child stood, his body stretching as he grew to the size of a ten-year-old. Then he began eating. He ate yams, locust beans, ripe mangos, pawpaw, and savory plantains, washing it all down with water from a calabash. He ate and ate and ate.

Finally, his father, recovering from the shock of what he'd witnessed, stepped from his hiding place and called the child's name. At the sound of his father's voice, the boy shrank down to a baby again. In this way, Bola and her husband determined that their child was, indeed, possessed by a spirit. They beat the child with rushes to drive the spirit out. Finally, it fled, leaving them with their own sweet baby again.

Jack hated that story, but it didn't stop his grandmother from telling it.

Years later, when Jack heard how he had come to be part of the family, he remembered the folktale and understood the reason his father looked at him the way he did. He was neither his father's son nor his mother's nor chosen by the family; he'd been foisted on them. He was wearing borrowed skin, watching them with borrowed eyes, and living with them in the life he'd almost stolen from Carter.

And, like Bola's child, Jack was always hungry. He ate and ate and ate, fresh cheese and loaves of bread, jars of peanut butter and gallons of milk. Sometimes, when one of his parents took him to the grocery store, he would swallow a dozen eggs behind a turned back. They would slide down his throat, shells and all, filling up the aching emptiness inside him. He picked sour apples off the summer trees and gulped down cotton balls soaked in water when he was too embarrassed to ask for a fifth helping of dinner.

The first time he met Hazel Evans, he thought that she might be a creature like him. She looked wild enough, her hair clumped with mud and face smeared with berry juice, running through the woods in bare feet, sword strapped to her back. Ben Evans had come running behind her, nearly as wild.

They stopped short at the sight of him.

"What are you doing?" he asked.

"Hunting monsters," Ben said. "Seen any?"

"How do you know I'm not one?" Jack asked them.

"Don't be stupid," Hazel said. "If you were a monster, you'd know it."

Jack wasn't so sure. But they'd shown him how to find black-berries and how to make a sandwich of dandelion leaves, wild onions, and fiddlehead ferns. More than anyone he'd ever known, Hazel was herself. Not scared of anything. Not scared of him.

And Ben understood about having magic. He understood all the ways that magic *sucked*.

Which was one of the reasons Ben was an awesome friend. They got tight after he came back from Philadelphia, in part because they made a pact to tell each other all the stuff they couldn't tell anyone else. Ben confessed that his music alternately tempted and terrified him. He told Jack stories about the ways his parents were screwups. In turn, Jack told Ben about the magic sparking inside him and how hard it was to hide sometimes. He told Ben about the hunger and the loneliness.

"So the riders came again?" Ben asked one afternoon, after a full-moon night. They were walking home from school, past the glass coffin, where Ben would go on his lunch breaks to talk with the sleeping prince. Jack thought about teasing him, but Ben's crush on the horned boy was only *slightly* more ridiculous than Jack's own crush.

He nodded, torn.

"Does your mom suspect?"

Jack shrugged. "She never says anything, but she's always rubbing the lintels with Saint-John's-wort to keep the Folk out—or me in. Hangs a garland of marigolds over the doors on May Eve."

"That sucks," Ben said, looking up at the sky. "But it sounds like it could just be her standard operating procedure. If she knew, she'd say something, wouldn't she?"

"Maybe. Just the other day, she made Carter carry dried holly berries in the pocket of his jacket. He got mad and chucked one at me. They sting like a bitch."

Ben winced. "I bet."

Jack remembered the way his skin had hurt for an hour after, as if from a spider bite. Fairfold was full of protections. People wore them around their necks, smeared them on their doors, hung them from the rearview mirrors of their cars. The stupid Saint-John's-wort made him itch. So did cold-shaped iron, when it was near him, although it burned where it actually touched his skin. Pockets full of oatmeal or grave dirt made him sneeze. Some amulets made his head hurt;

others made his head swim. None of it was deadly, not just from being close by, but the constant discomfort was a reminder of how little he belonged among the people of the town.

Jack picked up a dried-out stick, turning it in his hand. "It would almost be better if she *did* know."

They'd come for the first time two months before, on a full moon. Three of them, dressed in silvery gray, on three horses—one black, one white, and the third red. Jack had woken from a sound sleep to music—music that made him feel an intense longing for the forest and the wind in his face and the casting-off of mortal things. When he went to the window, he saw them on the lawn, riding around the house, eyes flashing, hair streaming like pennants. Seven times they circled and then the riders paused, looking up as though they'd spotted him in the window. They were achingly beautiful and absolutely terrifying, black-eyed and red-mouthed. One wore a face familiar enough that it seemed to him that this must be a dream. He knew, without any speech, that they wanted him to follow. He shook his head, staying where he was, framed by the window, fingernails digging into the wood. After a few moments, they turned one by one and rode off.

In the morning, when Jack woke, the window had been thrown wide, despite his mother's anointing of the lintel. Leaves were scattered all around his room.

"Creepy riders are creepy," Ben said.

"Yeah, creepy," Jack echoed, but even to his own ears, he didn't sound sincere.

"You're not going away with them next time, are you?" Ben asked, voice teasing.

"Shut up." Jack chucked the stick at Ben, but he ducked and it flew past him.

Ben stopped walking and stopped smirking, too. "Wait, you are?"

"You don't understand what they were like. How I felt. You can't understand." Jack spat out the words before he considered them, unwilling to tell Ben that he *had* gone that last time. He'd regretted not riding alongside them ever since they'd come on the first full-moon night. When he refused them a second time, it nearly broke his heart. The third time he was helpless to resist the call. He went, and after, he feared he could not summon up the strength to resist them again.

Maybe Ben saw something of what Jack felt in his expression, because he grew serious. "Sometimes I wonder about Kerem," he said. "I worry that the music made him like me. And even knowing that doesn't keep me from wanting to play again. That's why I broke my hand. Otherwise, I'd play. Every time I wanted something bad enough, I'd play."

Jack blinked, shocked. "How come you never said that before?"

Ben snorted. "Saving it for a special occasion, I guess. A special occasion where I could make you feel less crappy by telling you something awful about myself. But if you don't want to go with them, you're going to have to lash yourself to the bed like sailors who lashed themselves to masts to avoid jumping into the sea with Sirens."

Ben might have understood more than Jack had thought, but he still couldn't possibly have known what it was like to ride with them through the night or plunge into a moonlit pool. He couldn't have understood what it felt like to dance until the force of his steps seemed to crack open the earth itself, to be among creatures who had never been human and could never be human, to be one of them. And Ben couldn't have known the shame that Jack felt after, when, sweat cooling on his skin, he promised himself that when they came for him the next time, he wouldn't go.

A promise that he'd never keep.

✦ CHAPTER 12 ✦

Instead of going to lunch, Hazel went to the bathroom to splash water on her face, studying her freckles in the mirror, looking past eyeliner and eye shadow to the blue of her iris. She hoped to see someone who knew what she was doing staring back. Someone she could believe would get her out of this. No such luck.

Jack might take her to the revel, but once there, she was going to need to figure out the right questions to ask, the ones that would make them think she knew more than she did, the ones they would answer without knowing they were giving anything away. The girl in the mirror didn't look like a master of deception, though. She looked as if she was already in over her head.

If she couldn't trick them, then it would be good if she had some-thing to trade, because with the Folk, nothing was ever free. If she'd been Ben, she could have played a song for them and, even broken-fingered, she would have been so good that they would have granted her any boon. If she'd been like Jack, they would have told her stuff because she was one of them.

But she was Hazel. She had no magic. Which meant she needed to be on her toes, thinking fast and paying attention to everything. With a sigh, she took one of the paper towels from the dispenser, wiped her face, and went into the hall.

A freshman boy came around the corner so fast he nearly knocked into her. His face was wet. Lourdes's little brother—Michael, she thought that was his name. Tears streamed over his blotchy cheeks. A choking sound came from his throat.

"What's wrong?" she asked. "Did something happen?"

"I can't," he managed through the tears and ragged breaths, wiping at his face furiously. "I can't stop. She's coming. She's almost here."

That's when she heard it—sounds of crying coming from inside the classrooms around her. Thin wails that rose to shrieks.

The door to a classroom to Hazel's right flew open, and seniors flooded into the hall, eyes wild with terror and wet with tears. Megan Rojas fell to her knees and began to tear at her clothes in an orgy of grief.

"Please," Franklin sobbed, turning his face to Hazel, his anguish so raw she barely recognized him. "Please, make it stop. Kiss me. Make it stop."

Abruptly, she remembered Jack's warning: *Something even more dangerous than your prince walks in his shadow.*

Hazel backed away from Franklin, from his terrified, upturned face. There was a scent in the air like turned leaf mold and vegetal rot.

"It's so sad," Liz was saying, over and over, words muffled by tears. "So sad. So very, very sad."

Hazel had to do something—she had to find Ben before whatever was happening to them happened to him. She started to run, past lockers and closed doors, turning a corner into the art-room hallway. Light streamed in from a bank of windows facing a grass-covered courtyard. One of the freshman Language Arts teachers was locking a door. A burst of laughter came from another classroom. It was as though she hadn't just come from a hallway full of weeping students.

"Did you come from some kind of assembly?" Ms. Nelson asked. "I heard a lot of noise."

Hazel began to speak, stammering over words, when, above their heads, a loudspeaker crackled to life. Someone on the other end seemed to be crying. The sound of it stuck in Hazel's head like taffy.

Ms. Nelson looked puzzled. "Someone must have hit the button in the office without realizing it."

Hazel could hear the weeping in the liquid drum of her heart. In her every breath. It pricked the back of her eyes. It was so much—so sad, as though all the sorrow she'd ever felt woke in her at once.

Ms. Nelson stumbled, her hand going to the glass. Her breath hit the window, fogging it. Her eyes filled with tears. And then Hazel noticed blotches of something greenish, like mold or moss, creeping across the glass. Outside, black crows began landing on the branches of a tree, cawing to one another.

"We've got to get out of here," Hazel whispered in a tear-slurred voice. She stumbled away and heard a body hit the floor, heard the sound of soft, muffled weeping.

Hazel had to think. Her eyes were already filled with hot tears, her throat already thick with them, and everything she'd ever lost was crowding her head. She remembered looking down at Adam Hicks's half-rotted body and feeling utterly helpless. She thought of being sick during one of her parents' parties, having eaten a big chunk of cake before she realized it had been soaked in rum. Dizzy, she'd looked for her mother, but everyone had seemed to be a stranger. She'd thrown up in the bathroom for what felt like hours, until some of her throw-up was streaked with blood and a man she didn't know brought her a glass of water from the tap. Hazel thought of that night and other nights, thought of her brother's broken fingers, of the way his nails blackened and fell off, one by one. Of all the boys she'd kissed and how the names she remembered first were of the ones who'd hated her after, because she remembered things that hurt more easily than anything nice. Hazel wanted to lie down on the sticky linoleum floor, curl up, weep forever, and never rise again.

It seemed pointless not to give in, to keep standing, but she kept standing anyway. It seemed pointless to cross the hall, but she crossed the hall anyway.

Go over there and pull the fire alarm, she told herself.

She didn't think she could.

You don't have to believe you can, she told herself. *Just do it.*

The sound of weeping grew louder, nearly crowding out all other thoughts.

Her fingers closed on the red metal lever. Throwing her weight against it, she brought it down hard.

Immediately, the alarm sounded, louder than the crying, louder than the keening and the shrieking and the cawing of crows. Hazel's head pounded, but she could think again. After a moment, students started shuffling out of classrooms. Their cheeks were wet, eyes red-rimmed, and faces ashen. Normally the hall would ring with shouting, with gossip, with friends calling to one another. Right then, it was as quiet as a procession of the dead.

"Liz?" The Industrial Arts teacher came over, crouching near Ms. Nelson's body. "Evans, what happened out here? What's happening?"

"I don't know," Hazel said, looking up at the loudspeaker. Moss was spreading up the wall in patches, thickening like fur. If it kept growing like that, it would eventually smother the alarm.

He blinked at her, as if he hadn't quite processed what he was seeing yet, as if he was still making up excuses in his head.

Ms. Nelson blinked and started to push herself up. "What's going on?" she asked, voice hoarse. "Is that the fire alarm?"

The shop teacher nodded. "Some kind of emergency. Come on, let's get you outside."

A tiny crack started in one corner of the wall. Hazel watched it spread, watched it split into two cracks as vines seeped through.

"There's a fire?" a sophomore boy with a shaved head asked, coming from another hall in gym clothes.

"Outside!" commanded the shop teacher, pointing toward the exit. "You too, Evans."

Hazel nodded, but she wasn't ready to move. She was still staring at the moss and at the looping, pale vines poking through the growing fissures like fingers pushing free from a grave.

Students flooded around her, on their way to line up outside. On their way to wait for the fire department to declare this a false alarm, maybe a prank. Hazel leaned against the windows, taking several shaky breaths.

That was when she saw Molly coming down the hallway, moving against the stream of bodies. She was walking strangely, as if she was half dragging herself along, as if her limbs had become unfamiliar to her. Her expression was blank, her gaze seeming to slide over everything until it fell on Hazel.

Molly's lips looked blue at first, but the more Hazel stared at them, the more she realized they were stained green, stained from the inside, as though she had been eating sour apple Laffy Taffy.

Hazel stayed still, a hideous chill starting at the base of her spine. She'd been scared when she saw the other kids crying, but the revulsion she felt at the way Molly moved was entirely new. Hazel knew that she might be looking at Molly's body, but Molly was no longer looking out through her eyes.

"Stay back," Hazel said as whatever it was got close, throwing up a hand automatically, stopping just short of knocking the girl to the floor.

A syrup-sweet voice came from Molly's mouth, speaking in sing-song. Her head tilted to one side. "I loved him and he's dead and gone and bones. I loved him and they took him away from me. Where is he? Where is he? Dead and gone and bones. Dead and gone and bones. Where is he?"

With every word, clumps of dirt fell from her tongue.

"What are you doing to Molly?" Hazel asked shakily. The hall was nearly empty. The alarm was still ringing, but somehow the voice coming from Molly's mouth carried easily over the sound.

"I loved him and I loved him and he's dead and gone and bones. I loved him and they took him away from me. Where is he? Where is he? Dead and gone and bones. Dead and gone and bones. My father took him. My brother killed him. Dead and gone and bones. Dead and gone and bones. Where is he?"

Molly had been Hazel's best friend for two years, the one she'd stayed up late instant-messaging about boys, the one she'd trusted to trim her bangs. When she and Molly walked through the halls, Hazel had felt like there was nothing wrong with normal, as if maybe she could just focus on having fun and not worrying too much about what came after. Molly didn't care about faeries in the woods; they were just stories to her. She thought that all the tourist stuff was a scam and that the tourists themselves were boring, desperate for someone to tell them they were special. Seeing Fairfold through Molly's eyes was like seeing an entirely new place. After Molly dumped her, Hazel sometimes thought she missed seeing the world that way even more than she missed Molly.

Now Molly would have no choice but to believe in the Folk. The thought made Hazel furious.

"You can't have her," Hazel said, fumbling for her necklace, the one Ben had made her wear. She pulled the chain strung with rowan wood from around her throat. When the creature didn't react, Hazel thrust it over Molly's head, letting the amulet settle at Molly's throat. "See? So go! Go! You're not welcome here!"

Abruptly, Molly's eyes rolled upward, until Hazel saw only the white of her sclera.

Hazel's heart thundered. Then Molly collapsed to the floor, her whole body going limp at once. Her head hit the linoleum, making a horrible, hollow sound.

"Help!" Hazel called. She knelt down, fumbling for Molly's wrist, meaning to take her pulse, before she realized she had no idea how to do that. Over and over she screamed the word, and over and over nobody came.

Then Molly opened her eyes, blinking wildly, coughing so hard it was half choking. When she looked at Hazel, the expression that washed over her face was some commingling of embarrassment and terror. It was an entirely human expression.

"Hazel," Molly croaked, spitting out dirt and what appeared to be leaves.

Sweet, incredulous relief made Hazel lean against the wall. "You're okay?"

Molly nodded slowly, pushing herself into a half-sitting position, wiping at her chin. Her black hair, usually gelled into spiky precision, was a mess. Blood dribbled from a shallow cut where her head had struck the floor, turning the collar of her white shirt red. "I saw it. The monster. It's made of old, knotted branches grown over with moss, and it has these horrible black eyes."

Hazel scooted closer and reached out to take Molly's hand. Molly squeezed hard.

The alarm was still going, a siren wailing into the emptiness of the halls.

"You always knew this was all real, didn't you?" she asked, anguished. "How can you stand it?"

Hazel was trying to formulate a reply when Molly's eyes closed. She shuddered once and collapsed like a marionette with its strings cut. Hazel shouted and shook her by her shoulders, but Molly's body was as limp as Amanda's had been.

The monster was no longer content to wait in the heart of the forest. It had come to the center of Fairfold in the middle of the day, and Hazel wasn't sure if it could even be slain.

Whether it had come for Severin, because someone had summoned it, or for a reason beyond Hazel's comprehension, she had to focus.

She needed to get out of that hallway and she needed to get Molly out, too. Carrying Molly over her shoulders would be possible, but not ideal. Hazel wouldn't be able to fight and she wouldn't be able to move fast, either.

"Stay right there," Hazel said to Molly softly as she got up. She passed the widening crack in the wall, from which tendrils of ivy spilled into the room like snakes, and she went down the hall toward the art room just as two people came barreling around the corner. It was Carter, with a phone in one hand and a hockey stick in the other. Robbie Delmonico was beside him, brandishing a baseball bat. He yelped at the sight of her, stumbling back into a bank of lockers, making them rattle like chains.

Hazel found her hands balled into loose fists. "What the hell?"

"Relax. We were looking for you," Carter said. He was wearing the rib pad from his football uniform and knee plates. Hazel had never before noticed how much football gear was like armor. With his broad shoulders and excellent jawline, he looked like Sir Morien from the Round Table. "Emergency services people won't let anyone back into the school. Ben and Jack got stuck out in the parking lot, so they've been lecturing me over texts on where you might go." He gestured vaguely toward the front of the school.

"There's some kind of thing," Robbie put in. "We found three freshmen under one of the tables in the cafeteria. They were out cold—or at least I thought they were, but one of them opened her eyes and told me something super creepy—something about bones. Then she passed out again. We carried them to some EMTs through an open window, but figured we'd stay inside until we were sure everyone else got out."

Hazel nodded. She was forcibly reminded what a good guy Robbie was and why she'd kissed him in the first place, before things had gotten weird. The hardest thing about being wanted was the hardest thing about wanting—wanting badly enough that it gave you a stomachache, wanting in the way that was partly about kissing and partly about swallowing whole, the way a snake gulps down a mouse or the Big Bad Wolf gulps down Red Riding Hood—wanting turned someone you felt like you knew into a stranger. Whether that person was your brother's best friend or a sleeping prince in a glass prison or a girl who kissed you at a party, the moment you wanted more than just touching your mouth to theirs, they became terrifying and you became terrified. "Dead and gone and bones," she said.

He lifted his bat higher, eyes widening. "Not you, too!"

Hazel shook her head, sighing. "Molly said that, before she passed out. She was—I don't know—possessed or something like it."

"Molly Lipscomb?" Carter looked past Hazel, down the hallway, and stiffened at the sight of Molly's body. "Did you see the monster? Was it here?"

Hazel shook her head. "We've got to move her, though. I'm getting a chair." She turned to Robbie. "Try to find rope or yarn or something we can tie her with."

"Yeah, okay." Robbie nodded, starting toward one of the classrooms.

"Jack says..." Carter seemed to realize he was talking to himself more than them and bit off the thought with the shake of his head. "I'll stay by Molly. You guys get whatever you think you need."

Hazel found a swivel chair behind the teacher's desk in the second classroom she entered and rolled it into the hall, while Robbie managed to discover a spool of heavy bright blue string in one of the closets. Hazel lifted Molly, while Robbie braced the chair so her weight didn't send it flying suddenly backward. Then Carter helped them tie her in place, as if she were a prisoner about to be interrogated or a fly stuck in a spider's web. Head lolling to one side, eyes shut, Molly was soon held fast to the chair by layers and layers of crisscrossed string.

Then Hazel went back for a weapon. She found a pair of heavy scissors in the desk and slammed them down until the two pieces came apart and she had made herself twin daggers.

"Jesus, that was loud," Carter said, hands on the back of Molly's chair. "Come on."

They walked down the empty hall together, peering into abandoned classrooms, where jackets were still draped over the backs of chairs and desks still had papers and pens and books lying on them. Whiteboards had been left with math problems half solved, carried ones floating above unadded numerals. A documentary about genetics still played on a projection screen. A few desks in the back of one room were entirely covered in a spreading tide of moss.

The shadows lengthened as they made their way past the gymnasium. Hazel stepped in, her scissors gleaming in the flickering overhead lights. Ivy dripped down from the ceiling, knotting around the cables. Her heart pounded in her chest hard enough that it felt like a fist. Hard enough that her insides felt bruised from it. The gym had never seemed ominous to her before, with its slick, shining floor and the skeletal metal scaffolding of bleachers, but now she was acutely aware of all the places a monster might rest, folded up, looking like nothing more than a pile of mats, long fingers creeping out to grab hold of an ankle....

"Do you see anything?" Robbie asked from behind her.

Hazel's muscles tensed. She shook her head, glad not to have otherwise shown how much he'd startled her.

"You don't have to help us look for stragglers," Carter said. "Take Molly and head for the front. Your brother is worried about you. *My* brother is worried about you."

In the flickering light, the boys seemed different. Robbie looked sallow and a little frantic, the hollowness under his eyes made prominent. Carter looked more like Jack than ever, his face sharpened by shadows. If she tried, she might have been able to pretend he was his brother. For a horrible moment she understood why someone might do what Amanda did. It would be like kissing Severin's casket. It wouldn't be real. It couldn't hurt.

"Why don't *you* get out?" she asked him, not particularly nicely, since she didn't appreciate being condescended to and she didn't like where her thoughts were going.

"Guilt, mostly. I was the last one to see Amanda—everyone's saying it and it's true."

"What happened?" Hazel asked. They were moving through the literature and history hall, toward the principal's office and the main doors, passing by the auditorium, where the curtained stage lurked. One of the wheels on Molly's chair hung up a little, making a small squeal of protest, over and over, as it rolled.

Robbie pushed, flinching over and over at the noise.

There were echoes in some of the rooms, sounds that Hazel couldn't place. In her mind they became the crawl of the ivy, the slide of a monster's foot, its nails dragging against a wall. She'd hunted through the woods and knew how magnified noise could become through hyperalertness and adrenaline. She knew how convinced you could be that you'd heard something when it was only your own breathing. And yet she knew how dangerous it was to dismiss your instincts. But at least in the woods she had experience identifying the rustlings and breezes and footfalls. At school, she was lost. Every movement made her teeth grit and the hair along her arms stand.

Carter spoke again, softly, his voice pitched so Robbie might not hear. "We had a fight. Me and Amanda. She said some stuff about Jack that was—ridiculous. Like that he wasn't even a person. Maybe she was just trying to rile me up, but, well, it worked. I kicked her out of the car, even though she was wearing these huge, dumb heels, and figured she could just walk.

"I got about three blocks before I realized I was being an asshole. Mom would *kill* me if she found out that I took a girl on a date and then left her someplace, all by herself, with no way home."

"And?" Hazel asked.

"Amanda wasn't there when I went back. I didn't see her again, and her parents won't let me visit her in the hospital." He raised his voice slightly. "Hey, Robbie, what about you? How come you're sticking around, trying to be a hero? Why don't you get out of here?"

Robbie gave them a lopsided grin. "The one thing I know from movies is never to split up. Besides, you two would be lost without me."

"True enough," Carter said amiably, even though that didn't seem even a little bit true.

"Hey, Hazel, how come you—" Robbie began, but he never got to finish. A scream split the air.

They took off running toward it, the thud of their footfalls pounding against the floor, the shrill squeak of Molly's chair loud in their ears. The screaming was coming from the girls' bathroom.

Hazel charged ahead, slamming her shoulder against the door, scissor daggers poised to strike.

Leonie stood near the sinks, water streaming from one of the faucets to puddle on the floor. At the sight of Hazel, she screamed even louder. The room seemed empty, but Hazel's heart was beating so fast and Leonie seemed so scared that she wasn't sure. She kicked open the first stall, but there was only the toilet, with three burnt cigarette stubs floating in it. She kicked open the second: empty. She was about to kick open the third when Leonie grabbed her arm.

"What are you doing? Stop!" Leonie said. "You're freaking me out."

"*I'm* freaking *you* out?" Hazel shouted. "You were the one screaming."

"The thing—I saw it," Leonie said. "Jesus—I thought it was safe to go out into the hallway, but then it was there. Oh god, what happened to Molly?"

"Did you get a good look at it?" Carter asked from the doorway. He and Robbie were standing at the threshold, as though, even now, the idea of putting one foot into the girls' bathroom, with its Pepto-Bismol tile and ancient tampon machine on one wall, was forbidden.

Leonie shook her head. "I saw something. It was horrible—"

"We're almost to the exit," Robbie reminded them, shuddering visibly. "Let's just get out."

"What if it's waiting?" Leonie demanded. "It's somewhere nearby."

"That's why we've got to go," Robbie said louder, as if he'd forgotten why they'd been whispering earlier, as if he'd forgotten that they'd stayed inside to get more people out, to be honest.

For a single moment Hazel contemplated walking away from all of them, walking deeper into the school and waiting for the monster there, daggers drawn. She'd imagined fighting it so many times when she was a kid—it was the embodiment of the forest, the embodiment of terror. In her mind, fighting the monster was like the boss battle in a video game. In her mind, if she'd faced it and won, all the other terrors would stop.

Her instincts pushed her toward a fight. Her fingers gripped the scissors more tightly, her blood pumping. She wanted to find the monster and slay it.

"Okay, everyone, shut up!" Carter yelled. "Hazel, what do you think? Should we get out of here or keep looking for more survivors?"

"What are you asking *her* for?" Robbie demanded.

"Because I know what I think and I know what you think and it doesn't matter what Molly thinks. And because—" Carter bit off the words and spun. There was a strange sound, as though someone was dragging a dead body through the halls. Abruptly, one of the rods glowing overhead burst into a shower of sparks, and moss began to boil from the sinks. Spots of mold dotted the mirror. Carter pushed Molly's chair farther into the room, her head lolling to one side, hair over face. Robbie slammed the door closed behind them. Carter slid his hockey stick through the handle and braced to hold the door shut since there was no lock.

No one spoke. Hazel sucked in her breath and held it.

The patterned glass showed a shadow of something move on the other side of the door. It was huge, easily over seven feet in height, and looked roughly human in shape, if a human could be made from branch and vine and soil. It had a hunched back, and the top of its head seemed to twist into a gnarled stump. Impossibly long twig fingers hovered in the air.

It paused a moment, as though it could hear the hammering of their hearts, as though it was listening to their caught breaths. Then it moved past, thudding down the hall.

Hazel counted in her head. *One one thousand. Two one thousand. Three one thousand. Four one thousand. Five one thousand.*

"I vote we go," she whispered. "I vote we go *now.*"

Carter opened the door of the bathroom, and they raced for the front of the school, Molly's chair wheeling faster and faster as Robbie pushed it, Leonie's sneakers squeaking as they pounded against the hallway floor. Hazel brought up the rear, glancing over her shoulder again and again as she ran. She kept expecting the creature to grab them from the shadows, horrible hands lifting them, dirt choking them. She was swept along by panic and the thwarted urge to fight. It wasn't until they were through the front doors and gulping down lungfuls of cold, autumn air that she realized they'd made it out of the school.

From the trees all around, cawing crows went to wing in a rush of black feathers, like blackflies rising off a corpse.

The parking lot was lit with the flashing lights of cop cars and an ambulance. A few other cars, too, knots of students beside them, but it seemed as though the majority had already gone home. Those remaining had their faces tinted with stroking blue and red, turning them ghostly.

"Is anyone else in there?" one of the emergency-service people asked as they descended the steps.

"A monster!" Leonie told him. In the clear afternoon light, Hazel could see the way her eye makeup had run, as though she'd been crying.

"There was a gas leak," he said, looking confused and a little alarmed. "You might have breathed in some."

Not bothering to answer, Leonie rolled her eyes and walked past him. Carter heaved up Molly's chair, carrying it, at the same time Ben ran up the steps and hugged Hazel. Her arms went around him, hands still gripping her scissor blades as she pressed them against his back.

"Are you crazy?" he whispered into her hair.

Her eyes went past him, to Jack, seated on the hood of Ben's car, watching them with his silvery eyes. *Three times I will warn you, and that's all I am permitted*, he'd said. Had he known about this, but been forbidden to say?

"You know I'm crazy," she whispered back.

After Hazel had been checked over by a very solicitous volunteer with the ambulance team, she was told she could go home, but to go to the hospital immediately if she experienced any light-headedness.

Ben was waiting for her by his car, talking with Leonie in low voices. But as she started toward him, Jack caught her arm. When she turned, startled, his gaze made her feel suddenly self-conscious.

"I think the playground meeting is off," he said.

"You better not be about to tell me you're not taking me tonight. Not after what just happened," she said. She tried to keep her voice steady, but it didn't quite work.

Jack shook his head. The bruise on his cheek looked worse, the swelling more pronounced, turning the skin around his eye the color of a Concord grape. "Come by my house around sundown, but don't come inside, okay? I'll sneak out and meet you in the backyard. We can walk from there."

"Okay," Hazel said, surprised she hadn't had to argue even more—surprised and relieved and, despite herself, a little afraid. "So what do I wear?"

His eyes lit with wickedness. For the first time that day, something had amused him. "Anything you like or nothing at all."

———

On the way home, Hazel described to Ben the monster she'd seen through the distorted glass and the way the vines and moss had crept over the school. In turn, he explained how Jack had hustled him outside after the first students collapsed. Jack had been about to go back in for Hazel and Carter when several of the teachers had stopped him, forbidding his going inside in a way that made it plain they blamed him for everything that was happening.

"This has got to blow over," Ben said, sighing. "They have to see he's got nothing to do with any of this. We all know him."

Hazel nodded, but she remembered the way people had shrunk back earlier that day, remembered the fresh bruise on his face and the story Leonie had told, the one she'd been keeping to herself for years. How many other people had a story like hers? How many people had seen his mask slip and never quite forgotten?

"And we still have to talk—you and me," Ben reminded her as he parked his car in front of their house. "About Severin and what happened the night he got free."

Hazel nodded, even as she hoped she could avoid doing that until after the revel.

Inside, their mother was sitting at the kitchen table, smoking a cigarette. Hazel hadn't seen her smoke in years. When they came through the door, Mom ground the lit end into her plate and stood. "What is wrong with you? Neither of you picked up your phones. I've been freaking out, calling people, trying to figure out what was going on. The school called, but none of their explanations made sense. And now there's a curfew. I think we should talk about going to stay with your father for a while, in the city—"

"A curfew?" Ben echoed.

"It was announced over the emergency broadcasting thingie on the television," she said, waving toward it. "Everyone's supposed to stay inside unless absolutely necessary, and no one is supposed to go out after six tonight under any circumstances."

"What are they saying the reason is?" Hazel asked.

"Inclement weather," said her mother, raising her eyebrows. "What really happened today?"

"Inclement weather," Hazel said, and took the stairs two at a time.

Once in her room, she crossed over to her closet and opened the door. Lots of vintage dresses, worn pairs of jeans, and sweaters with holes in them, some hanging, some in a pile on the floor, covering another pile of shoes. Nothing seemed quite right for a faerie revel. Nothing that would make them believe she was someone to be reckoned with.

After all, the news promised a storm.

✦ CHAPTER 13 ✦

J ack had said to come at sunset, but it was almost full dark by the time Hazel got to the foot of his driveway. She'd snuck out of her house as soon as she was dressed, walking straight through the front door while her brother and mother were in the living room, quiet and steady so they wouldn't notice. She left her cell phone on her bed along with a note, so Ben would know he couldn't get hold of her and hopefully wouldn't worry too much. She'd be back by dawn and then—*then*—she would tell him everything.

Jack was in the backyard, tossing a ball to the Gordon family dog, a golden retriever named Snickerdoodle. The porch light illuminated a narrow pool of grass where they ran. In that moment, Jack looked every bit like a normal human boy, unless you noticed the points of his ears. Unless you believed the stories. Then he looked eerily like something playing at being human. When Hazel got close, Snickerdoodle began to bark.

"Time to go inside," Jack told the dog, with a glance at the woods. Hazel wondered if he could see her in the dark.

She waited, wishing she'd brought a jacket. The autumn air grew colder as the orange glow on the horizon tipped down into night. She occupied herself by gathering up horse chestnuts from where they'd fallen and picking off their spiky coverings. It hurt a little where the husk got under her nail, but it was immensely satisfying to feel something come apart in her hands.

It seemed as if she were standing there at the edge of the woods for ages, but it was probably only about fifteen minutes before a window on the second floor opened and Jack climbed out onto the roof.

Inside, she could see the television in the living room—a splash of moving color—could see Mrs. and Mr. Gordon sitting on opposite couches. He had his laptop open, and the pale glow of it made the shadows outside seem deeper.

Jack stepped off the roof and onto the bough of a tree, sidling along it, before jumping to the ground. She braced herself for the noise, for his parents' heads turning, for Snickerdoodle to start barking again, but Jack landed nimbly and quietly. There was only the sound of the leaves rustling when he leaped from the branch—and that sounded only like wind.

Hazel met him at the edge of the woods, shivering slightly and trying to be brave. "Hey," she said, letting the chestnut she'd been holding fall. "So what now?"

"You look nice," he said, his eyes silver in the dark.

She smiled, feeling a little awkward. She'd put on the only thing that seemed to look right—a pair of jeans and a green velvet top she'd discovered in the very back of her closet. In her ears she'd hung silver hoops, and on her feet were her favorite boots. She hoped it would be fancy enough for Faerieland.

"This way," he whispered, and began to walk. She followed. In the moonlight, the woods were full of shadows and secret pathways that seemed to open before them, and it quickly became clear that Jack saw much better than she did in the dark. She tried to keep up, tried to keep from stumbling. She didn't want to give him any excuses to decide she should be left behind.

After they got a ways from his house, Jack turned. "I should warn you about some stuff."

"Always be polite," she said, reciting what she'd been told a dozen times by concerned adults who didn't want any of the local kids acting like tourists. "Always do what they ask you, unless it contradicts one of the other rules. Never thank them. Never eat their food. Never sing if you suck at singing, never dance—and never brag, ever, at all, under any circumstances. That kind of stuff?"

"That's not what I was going to say." Jack took her hand suddenly, his skin warm. There was a rough intensity in his voice that shivered over her skin. "I'm ashamed of going; that's why I've been hiding it. I know how reckless it is—how *stupid* it is. I don't mean to and then I hear it, like a buzzing in the back of my head, when there's going to be a revel. It's like someone whistling a song far off and I can barely hear the music, but I'm leaning forward, straining to hear it better. So I go, all the while telling myself that I won't go the next time, but when the next time comes, I do the very same thing all over again."

He dropped her hand. The words seemed to have cost him something.

Hazel felt awful. She'd been so busy worrying about her own puzzles that she hadn't thought about what she was asking of him. The last thing she wanted was to hurt Jack. "You don't have to come with me. I didn't know. Just tell me the way and I'll go on my own."

He shook his head. "You wouldn't be able to keep me from the revel—no one could. That's the problem. But I wish that you'd go home, Hazel."

"And you know I won't," she said.

He nodded. "So here's the rest, then. I don't know how to protect you from them, and I don't know what they might try to do to you. What I do know is that they hate to be reminded of my human life."

"And you think I'll be a reminder?" she asked.

"To them—and to me." He started walking again. "Be careful. Ben would never forgive me if anything happened to you."

The words stung. "Yeah, well, Ben's not my keeper."

"Then I'd never forgive *myself*."

"Will you . . ." She hesitated and then forced herself to ask. "Will you *look* different there?"

That startled a laugh out of him. "I won't. But everything else might."

Hazel pondered what that meant as they made their way through the woods. She could tell he was trying to slow down so she could keep pace, but she could also sense his eagerness, his hunger to be at the revel.

"Tell me a story," he said, pausing to look up at the fat, full coin of a moon as she clamored over some rocks, then back at her. "Tell me what you know of the horned boy and Amanda."

"After what happened at school, I'm not sure I know much," Hazel admitted. "He said the monster was hunting him, and you said the Alderking was after him. Do you think the Alderking is controlling the monster?"

"Mayhap." Jack smiled as he said the word, exaggerating its oddness. "But you know better. You're the one he spoke with."

"He was looking for a sword," Hazel told him. "He said that was the only way he could defeat the monster."

This was deeper in the woods than she'd ventured since she was a child, and back then she'd done it with the knowledge she was crossing into dangerous lands. The trees here were old, their trunks massive, and the tangle of their branches overhead was thick enough to blot out the stars. The first rash of fallen leaves crackled beneath Hazel's feet, like a carpet of brittle paper.

Jack looked over at her. "There was something else you said— about them using you."

"You remember that, huh?" she asked.

"Hard to forget," he said.

"I've been—I've been losing time. I'm not sure how much." She'd never said anything like that out loud before.

He studied her for a long moment. "That's ... not good."

She snorted and kept walking. He didn't say anything more. She was glad for his silence. She'd been afraid he'd push her for answers; in his place, she might have. But apparently, he was going to let her decide what she wanted to tell him and when.

They came to the swell of a hill, ringed in thornbushes that grew in a gnarled circle, creating a thick tangle chasing steps that rose to the top of the hill, where the foundation of an old building rested among tall grass. The steps were cracked and worn, with moss oozing from the gaps and flowing up to an archway. There was a sound in the air, faint music and laughter, flickering in and out, as though blown in by the wind.

Suddenly Hazel knew where they were, although she'd only ever heard of the place before.

This was the meetinghouse one of the town founders had tried to build before he discovered this was a hill sacred to the Folk. According to the story, whatever was built during the day was dismantled at night; whatever land was cleared became overgrown before dawn. Shovels snapped and accidents left men with cracked bones and bruised bodies, until, finally, the town center of Fairfold was moved miles to the south, where the first meetinghouse was constructed without incident.

Faerie hills are hollow inside, she'd once heard Mrs. Schröder say. *Hollow like faerie promises. All air and misdirection.*

Hazel shuddered at the memory.

Jack walked toward the looping vines of thorn. Scarlet roses grew there with a velvety nap on their petals, heavy and thick as fur. Stems slithered, curling up to make a path, slowly, so that if you didn't watch closely, if you looked away and looked back again, it might seem as if there had always been a way through. He tossed her a grin, raising his eyebrows.

"Did you make that happen?" Hazel asked in a whisper, without really knowing why she was whispering. "Will the path stay open for me?"

"I'm not sure. Just stay close," he said as a sharp tangle spiraled behind him.

And so they climbed, with her hand on his back, keeping close enough that the briars let her pass, up the steep incline.

Jack skipped up steps and then, at the arch, tapped his foot three times against the ledge and spoke: "Lords and ladies who walk unseen, lords and ladies all in green, three times I stamp upon the earth, let me in, green hill that gave me birth."

A chill went through Hazel at the words. It was a scrap of a poem, almost like the sort of thing they would have made up while playing in the woods as kids, but it sounded far older and of uncertain origin. "Just like that?" she asked.

"Just like that." He grinned, wide and wild, almost as if he was daring her. "Your turn." Then, stepping through the arch, he let himself fall backward.

Hazel didn't even have time to cry out. She ran forward, to see if he was okay, but he was gone. Disappeared. She saw the rest of the hill, the rest of the foundation of the old building, saw the silvery carpet of long grass. Not sure what else to do, she leaped through the arch, hoping it would take her, too.

Hazel landed in the grass, losing her footing and falling to her knees painfully, brambles tearing at her jeans and the velvet top. She hadn't fallen through into another world. She was exactly where she'd been before, and she was alone.

A breeze made the thorns shiver, bringing with it tinkling laughter.

"Jack," she shouted. *"Jack!"*

Her voice was swallowed up in the night.

Just like that, he'd said. But the thorns hadn't parted for her, and the poem was unlikely to work. The words weren't right. The green hill wasn't where she'd been born. She wasn't one of the Folk. She didn't have any magic.

Was this some kind of test? Pushing to her feet, Hazel climbed the stairs again. She wasn't very good at rhymes, but maybe if she altered the poem a little, maybe then the hill would open for her? It was a terrifying sort of magic. Stomping three times on the ledge, she took a deep breath and spoke:

"Lords and ladies who walk unseen, lords and ladies all in green, three times I stamp upon the earth...." Hazel hesitated and then gave the only reason she could think of why the Folk might grant her entry to their revel. "Let me in for the sake of mirth."

Squinching her eyes closed, she stepped through the archway. She fell, just as before, but this time she fell *into* the grass, the earth beneath her opening up. She struggled, the rich, mineral smell of dirt all around her, her nails scraping at the tiny rocks, at the weeds, digging in, trying for purchase. She took one last breath, one last shuddering gasp, and then there was only darkness closing over her.

A scream came unbidden to her lips. Her stomach lurched. She spiraled in the air once, the world below her a blurry streak of mad sights and sounds. Then she was caught, suspended in a net of roots, pale and long and hairy. Below her was the revel, lit by tiny moving lights and leaping fires. There were dancing circles and banquet tables; there were faeries covered in furs, in armor, in great swirling gowns. A few looked up, pointed, and laughed, but most didn't notice her hanging above them like a living chandelier. And then she saw, resting on huge tiles of gray stone, a throne that seemed to be shaped from the rock itself. It was covered in pelts, and a man in armor was seated upon it. A page whispered in his ear, and he turned to look Hazel's way. He didn't so much as smile.

She'd come to the Alderking's court on a full-moon night. She couldn't possibly have done anything more foolhardy if she tried.

Hazel pushed with her feet, trying to get her bearing on the roots and, maybe, to begin to climb. But as she did, the roots let go. Hazel fell again, this time hitting the ground hard. After a moment of nerving herself to do more than blink up at the domed ceiling, she pushed herself to her knees. A hand on her arm steadied her.

"Thanks," Hazel said automatically, opening her eyes.

Then she realized her mistake. *Never thank them.*

A monstrous creature stood in front of her, its black eyes wide, a look of disgust on its face. Pale fur grew from the top of its ridged nose and the tips of its cheekbones to a crest above its head, fur that dusted over its shoulders and midriff. It was clad in an asymmetrical leather piece stretching across its waist. It let her go as though it had been touching something foul and strode off, leaving her stunned and blinking after it.

"Sorry," she called, not sure if that made what she'd done better or worse.

The revel was like nothing she had imagined, not even her dreams of where the horned boy had come from. It wasn't the way stories told in town had made it seem. Music rang through the air with an aching sweetness. She was left breathless and reeling.

Creatures spun on the earthen floor, some with long-limbed, liquid grace, others tromping or gamboling. Small faeries flitted through the air on tattered moth wings, baring their teeth at Hazel. Short folk in heath-brown clothes, with hair that stuck up from their heads like the pistils of flowers, played at dice games and drank deeply from ornately blown glass goblets and wooden cups alike. Tall beings, shining in the gloom as though they were lit up from the inside, whirled in their dresses of leaves, in cleverly shaped corsets of bark, in exquisite silvery mail.

Other creatures, far less human-looking, walked among them on stilt-like legs or loomed over them with faces as gnarled as the knots of trees.

They were terrifying and beautiful and horrible, all at once. All of them.

In their midst, seemingly oblivious to the danger, were people she recognized. People from Fairfold. Ms. Donaldson, who taught kindergarten, dancing barefoot with an owl-faced creature. Smiling Nick, a long-haired guy who did odd jobs like sharpening knives door-to-door, stumbled among the throng, dressed in black silk scarves streaming behind him. Beside him was a young guy whose name Hazel didn't know but whom she'd seen before. He worked at the general store in town, mostly stocking shelves. She had once seen him juggling apples in the produce aisle. Not many humans, but here and there she spotted human clothes, even if she couldn't see faces in the crowd.

Were they really human, though? Or were they faeries who went among humans and wore their shapes? And if they were human, did they know they were here, or would they wake with muddy feet, as Hazel had, and no memory of the night before?

It wasn't just humans she recognized; she knew one of the creatures, too. Sitting in a corner, overgrown with hair and munching on golden beetles, was an ogre called Rawhead. She'd heard of him, heard of his taste for human flesh, and even figured out where his lair might be, back when she was a little girl with a big, sharp sword. Rawhead grinned in her direction with his red smile as if maybe he recognized her, too.

Move, she told herself. *Don't just stand there gaping. Move.*

Hazel started walking in a random direction, just putting one foot in front of the other, propelling herself along without any sense of quite where she was going. She didn't see Jack yet, but he had to be somewhere close by—and as frightening as it was to move through the revel without him, as shaky and scared as she felt, she had to find out what she could about the horned boy and the monster and the mysterious messages from the mysterious Ainsel. Otherwise, all the terror and danger were for nothing.

Trying to stay far from the dancing, she made her way through the hollow hill. Gillyflower, roses, and sage scented the air, making her dizzy as she went.

"Will you take a drink?" asked a small, long-nosed creature with a stubby tail and eyes that were black as a crow's. It held up a small tray of tiny, carved wood cups with some liquid inside, barely a thimbleful in each. "I swear by the corn and the moon that you'll never taste a sweeter drop."

"No, tha—" She stopped herself from *thanking* another one of them, shaking her head instead. "I'm okay."

It shrugged and kept moving, but the encounter had given her the jitters. Hazel knew all the rules, but obeying them was turning out to be hard. It was so easy to do the wrong thing automatically, way easier than she could have ever guessed.

A laughing woman with thick plaits of russet hair paused as she went past with a goat-headed companion. "Didn't you sketch me once?" the woman asked Hazel, surprising her.

For a moment Hazel didn't know what she could possibly mean. Then suddenly the old story came back to her, the one that had always been about Ben. "You're thinking of my mother."

The woman frowned, looking puzzled. "Can it really have been so long? Why, you must be my musician, then, grown! Will you give me a song in recompense for my blessing?"

Hazel shook her head. "That was my brother. I wasn't born yet and I'm awful at music. You wouldn't want me to sing." She wondered if she should tell the faerie woman how little joy Ben had gotten from her gift, but Hazel suspected that would violate those rules about politeness. "But, um, I'll tell Ben I saw you."

"Do," she said. "Tell him to come and play for Melia and I'll make rubies fall from his tongue."

That sounded more like a threat than a promise, but Hazel nodded and, not sure what else to do, made a little bow before backing away. Then she walked fast, elbowing through the merry crowd; past pipers and fiddlers; past stick-thin faeries with powdery wings; past willowy green women with black mouths and tongues, wearing dresses fine as mist; past long-fingered girls with crowns of twigs woven into the nimbus of their loose hair; past sneering boys with the feet of lions; past crow girls laughing all together; past large, misshapen creatures with moss growing on their massive limbs and mouths full of teeth that appeared to be more cracked rock than bone.

Someone grabbed her arm. She wheeled around with a cry, pulling against his grip, before she realized who was holding her.

"Hazel." Jack looked out of breath and a little panicked. "I didn't know where you were."

"You left me." Her voice came out more sharply than she'd intended.

"You were right behind me," he insisted. "I thought you'd just follow me through the way you'd followed me up the path."

"Well, I couldn't," Hazel said.

Someone was with Jack: a tall and spindly faerie woman with skin the silvery brown of bark. Her eyes changed color, lustrous gold igniting with green.

She couldn't be anyone but Jack's elf mother. Her eyes were just as they'd been in the stories.

"Red hair," she said, turning Hazel's head from side to side, observing her. Plucking up a lock, the elf woman gave her hair a sharp tug. "They used to say that meant you were a witch. Are you a witch, child?"

"No, ma'am," Hazel told her, remembering, at least, the value of politeness.

"And what brings you here? Or should I ask who?"

"Ainsel," Hazel said, hoping the name would mean something.

"Well, aren't you a wit?" the elf woman said, scowling.

"So you know who that is!" Hazel exclaimed, barely able to breathe for eagerness. "Please, tell me."

"How can it be that you don't recall?" Her frown seemed to signal Hazel to silence. Then she turned, pointing a long finger at Jack. "And I think that this is the boy who brought you. This boy, and this boy alone. He was very wrong to do so. Whatever you're looking for, this is no place for you."

Hazel wasn't sure how to answer that without referring to

Fairfold, when Jack had warned her against it, not sure how to direct the conversation back to Ainsel. "Jack? Sure, he brought me, but..."

The faerie woman circled them both, and Jack moved close to Hazel, as though ready to impose his body in front of hers if the woman grabbed for Hazel again. His mother's voice rose. "*Jack?* Is that what *she* calls you? Jack of what? Jack of Hearts? Jack of Diamonds? Jack of Weeping? Jack of Woe?"

"I don't bother with all that fancy stuff—I just go by Jack, these days," he said, and Hazel laughed—a short, awkward bark that she instantly regretted. It had just been such a surprise, his casual, quotidian response to her anger.

"Why should I care if he wishes to idle time away in Fairfold? If he wants to play at being a human child, what is it to me? He can eat mortal food and sleep in a mortal bed and kiss a mortal girl, but he will never be human. He will always be playing." She was directing her speech to Hazel, but the words were clearly for Jack's benefit. Hazel wondered how many times they'd had this conversation.

He grinned. "You've got to grow where you're planted." It was a human saying if Hazel had ever heard one, but it had an odd resonance right then.

His elf mother's attention didn't waver. Her eyes stayed on Hazel. "So have you come to pull him down off his white horse like in a ballad? Have you come to save him from us?" the woman asked, long fingers gesturing out at the vast knotwork of roots across the domed ceiling. "Or is he here to save you?"

"Stop," Jack said, putting an arm in front of Hazel. "Enough, okay? Stop talking to her that way. It's enough and more than enough."

"Just remember, blood summons blood," she said.

One of the tall knights in shining silver armor—one with shoulder plates crafted to look like screaming faces picked out in shaped gold—approached them with a shallow bow and turned his gaze toward Hazel. "The Alderking would greet her."

Jack's elf mother nodded and cut a look at Jack. "He honors you," she said, but her tone belied the words.

Hazel had heard stories of the Alderking, of course. Each solstice, townsfolk left special offerings out for him. When the weather was bad, they said he must be angry. When the seasons didn't turn fast enough, they said he must still be asleep. She'd never quite imagined him as real. His power seemed great, and he seemed too distant for her to imagine him as anything but a legend.

"Lead on," Hazel told the knight.

Jack made to come with her, but his mother grabbed his arm, twig fingers digging into his skin. Although she tried to hide it, there was genuine terror in her voice when she spoke. "Not you. You remain with me."

He turned to her, head held high, and even in his human clothes managed to convey some of the haughtiness of his lineage. "Marcan here isn't exactly known for his fair dealing with humans." His gaze went to the knight. "Are you?"

"No one requested your presence, changeling." The knight smirked. "Besides, Hazel doesn't mind coming with me. We've crossed swords before."

Hazel wasn't sure what he meant. Maybe he'd had something to do with one of the creatures she'd fought when she was a child? Whatever it was, Jack looked ready to object. His hand slid into the back pocket of his jeans as if he was reaching for a weapon.

"It's okay," Hazel said. "Jack, it's fine."

Jack's elf mother leaned her long body toward him, to press a kiss to Jack's forehead. Hazel had never thought of her as longing for her lost son, never wondered if there was another side to the story of how Jack came to live with the Gordons, but she couldn't help wondering then.

"Mortals will disappoint you," she told him, almost a whisper against his skin.

Jaw set, fury in his eyes, Jack stepped back and allowed Marcan to lead Hazel across the earthen floor of the underhill.

The Alderking was seated on the great stone throne she'd glimpsed when she'd hung above the revel. Horns like those of a stag rose from a circlet at his brow, and he wore a shining coat of mail shaped from small bronze scales, each one tapering to a point, all of them overlapping like how she might have imagined the scales of a dragon to be. He had green eyes so clear and bright that they made you think of poisonous drinks or maybe mouthwash. On every finger of his hands, he wore a different, intricately shaped ring.

Across his lap was a golden sword with an ornate cross guard. For a moment she thought it was her own missing blade and took a half step toward it before realizing that her sword had a plainer hilt. All his knights wore similar swords—forged from bright metal, they gleamed like polished sunlight in their obsidian scabbards.

Resting at the Alderking's feet was that pale and naked creature she had bargained with so long ago, the pale catlike one with crimson-tipped skin. It regarded her lazily, through half-lidded eyes. Then it waved a long-fingered hand, all claws.

Her careful questions about memories and monsters flew from her head. She went down on one knee. As she did, she saw something shimmer among the intricate tiles of the floor, like a dropped coin catching the light.

"Sir Hazel," said the Alderking, leaning forward and peering down at her with those startling eyes. As handsome as any fairy-tale prince, he was beautiful and awful, all at once, despite the cruel twist of his mouth. "I do not remember commanding you to come here."

Hazel looked up at him, baffled. "No, I—"

"In fact, I have explicitly told you *never* to come to a full-moon revel. And last night, though you were most grievously needed to hunt with us, you ignored my summons. Have you forgotten our bargain so quickly? Defy me to your peril, Hazel Evans. Have I not given you the deepest, dearest wish of your heart, an unasked-for boon? Have I not made you one of my company? Know that I could take it from you just as easily. There are far more unpleasant ways to serve me."

"I—" Hazel opened her mouth to speak, but no words came out.

Suddenly the Alderking began to laugh. "Ah," he said, looking not unlike the faerie woman upon realizing she'd mistaken Hazel for her mother. "You're not my Hazel, are you? Not my knight. You're the Hazel Evans who lives by day."

CHAPTER 14

Hazel thought that maybe she should stand, but she felt rooted in place. The party seemed to fade to a buzzing in her ears.

Sir Hazel, the Alderking had called her.

Jack's elf mother had asked Hazel an odd thing, too. *So have you come to pull him down off his white horse like in a ballad? Have you come to save him from us? Or is he here to save you?* She knew the ballad where someone got pulled down off a white horse. It was *Tam Lin*, where a human knight was forced into the service of a queen of Faerie and saved by a brave mortal girl, Janet. Tam Lin was a human knight.

Hazel thought of the message in the walnut. *Seven years to pay your debts. Much too late for regrets.* And there was the odd thing the knight had said to her when he'd brought her over, that they'd crossed swords before.

Words deserted her.

"How..." she forced out anyway.

"You do not remember the bargain you made?" The Alderking leaned toward her, the horns on his circlet tipping forward.

"I promised you seven years of my life. There's no way I could forget that." Hazel took a deep breath. She was getting her nerve back. Pushing herself to her feet, heart pounding, she steeled herself for a battle of wits. Here, in some fashion, were the answers she needed. She just had to ask the right questions in the right way. "But—you're saying I've been paying my debt to you? I don't remember—I don't remember doing so."

He smiled patiently. "Am I not generous to take those memories from you? Every night, from the moment you fall into slumber until your head touches your pillow again near dawn, you're mine. You are my knight to command, and your own daylight life is unaffected. You always had potential—and I have guided that potential. I have made you into one of my number."

Hazel was pretty sure that people who went without sleep for weeks died. *Years* was ridiculous. And it was equally incredible to think that she'd been trained by the knights here under the hill—trained to be like them. She glanced to the three who stood to one side of the Alderking's throne, looking as though they'd stepped out of paintings from a time that never was. "That doesn't seem possible."

"And yet," the Alderking said, gesturing to the air as though that was all the explanation needed. Magic as both question and answer. "We came to your window and carried you through the air to our court, evening after evening. You are the knight you always dreamed of being."

Breathe, Hazel told herself. *Breathe.*

She remembered the tiredness that had come over her in Philadelphia, a lassitude that had never quite left her. Now, at least, she knew where it had come from—not puberty, as her mother had believed. "I never dreamed of being your knight."

"Indeed?" drawled the Alderking, as though he knew the truth of her heart better than she ever could. "I forbade you from telling your day self about our arrangement, but there is no small pleasure in seeing you so astonished."

Hazel was speechless. She felt as though she didn't know herself. As if she'd betrayed her own ideals in some vast and profound way, but she wasn't yet sure how deep that betrayal went. She remembered her dream of riding beside other knights, of punishing humans with a grin on her face, and shuddered. Was that the person she'd become?

He laughed. "Well, Sir Hazel, if you haven't come here as my knight, why have you come?"

She had to think fast. She had to push away thoughts of her other, untrustworthy self.

He must not know that she'd been the one to smash Severin's coffin. Since she'd been awake all the night before, following Ben through the woods, her other self wouldn't have shown up, couldn't have been interrogated, couldn't have revealed anything. And since the Alderking hadn't wanted her to know about her night self, he wasn't the mysterious Ainsel. Which meant her knight self might have an ally in his court, someone whom she was working with.

Hazel's gaze went to the creature lying at the Alderking's feet. This was the being to whom she'd rendered a promise, and while it had accepted her vow in the Alderking's name, maybe it had power over her still.

"I came here because there's a monster in Fairfold. I wanted to know how to slay it."

His smile was cold as his hand went to lift a silver-chased goblet and bring it to his mouth. A few of his courtiers laughed. "Sorrow, she's called. A great and fearsome creature, her skin hardened to bark tough enough to bend even faerie metal. You cannot slay her—and before you ask, the only antidote to the sleeping sickness she brings, to the moss that seeps into your veins at her touch, is her sap-like blood. So how about I make you another bargain, Hazel Evans?"

"What kind of bargain?" Hazel asked.

"The monster hunts for Severin. After all these long years, I discovered a means to control her. She obeys me now." He raised his hand to show off a bone ring.

He spoke on, not noticing her grimace. "Bring me Severin, and I won't use her might against Fairfold. I will even keep my people in check. Things will return to the way they once were."

Hazel was so surprised she laughed. "Bring you Severin?" He might as well have asked for her to bring him the moon and the stars.

The Alderking didn't look particularly amused. He looked impatient. "Yes, that's the order I intended to give my Hazel, but last night passed without her arrival. That's two nights you've cost me her service, counting this one. She is to hunt down the horned boy—my son, Severin—who's escaped his confinement. She is to kill anyone he is in league with and drag him before me to face my wrath."

Bring him Severin. His son. Her prince. A very real prince.

Am I actually capable of doing that? Hazel wondered. She was a little worried she was going to laugh again. It all seemed so impossible. "Why me?" she managed.

"I think it would be appropriate if it was a mortal who defeated him," the Alderking said. "Your better self would know not to trifle with me, but in case you have some romantic idea of warning my son, let me explain why you ought not do that. You think I have done your people such grievous wrongs, but allow me to demonstrate what I could do without any effort at all." He turned to one of his knights. "Bring me Lackthorn."

A few moments later, a fierce-looking goblin with grayish skin and pointed ears came before the Alderking, holding a dirty hat in his hands.

"What pleasures do I allow you in town, Lackthorn?"

The goblin shrugged. "Only a few. I steal the cream and break some dishes. When a woman threw dirty water on me, I drowned her. Nothing more than you said I might do."

Hazel was astonished at the casualness with which he listed awful things. But no one else seemed surprised. The Alderking was looking down on him as though these were normal faerie caprices. Maybe to him, they were. "You didn't always let them go so far, though, did you?"

"I have allowed more leeway as I have come to see what a blight you mortals are. But attend closely. Lackthorn, if I gave you leave to do what you'd like, what would you have done?" The Alderking cut a glance at Hazel.

"What would I have done?" The little goblin laughed in such a gluttonous, awful way that the sound shivered up Hazel's spine. "I'd set fires and burn up their houses with them inside. I'd pinch and pinch them until they ached to their very bones. I'd curse them so they'd pine away, then I'd gnaw on what was left. What would I do if you gave me leave? What wouldn't I do?"

"Did you know that the meat of the hazelnut was once thought to be the repository of all wisdom?" the Alderking said. "Be wise, Hazel. Lackthorn is one of the least dangerous of my troop. Imagine the answer the Bone Maiden might give. Or Rawhead. Or my splendid, monstrous Sorrow. Do not test my goodwill. Bring me Severin or I will harrow Fairfold. I have plans afoot and I would not like them to be interrupted. Sorrow hunts for him now, but I need her for other things."

Hazel felt as though she couldn't quite get her breath. Music still played in the background, people still whirled around, laughing and dancing, but it all went a little blurry and odd in her peripheral vision. She seemed to have been robbed of her power of speech. He'd made a threat so vast and terrible she couldn't quite believe she'd heard it right.

Hazel could tell from the Alderking's expression that he no more expected Hazel to speak than he expected a toad to turn into a toadstool, but she had to say something.

Clearing her throat, she spoke. "If you set Sorrow on the town, I'll stop you."

He had a cruel laugh. "You? Like a wren stops a storm? Go now, Sir Hazel, and delight in the revel. Tomorrow is soon enough to begin your hunt. I will give you two days and two nights."

The knight with the screaming faces on his shoulder plates stepped to her elbow. A lutist began playing. Lackthorn made a bow and disappeared into the crowd. Hazel knew she was dismissed.

"Oh," the Alderking said, and she turned back to him. "One more thing. My son has a sword—a sword he stole from me. Bring it here and I will forgive your seven-year debt. Now, aren't you pleased that I've given you this task?"

"How long have I served you?" Hazel said. "I made that vow when I was almost eleven. I'm sixteen now. That's five years, give or take."

"But you've only served me half that time," said the Alderking. "You owe me all your daylight hours yet."

Numbly, she began to move through the crowd. Finally, she found Jack, standing near a table set with golden plates piled high with ripped-open pomegranates whose ruby beads clung to the fruits' wet, membranous skins; dusky plums; and grapes so purple they were black.

These are his people. She'd known it intellectually, but really seeing, really *believing*, had taken until that moment. This was all familiar to Jack, this hidden, terrifying, beautiful, awful place. These terrifying, cruel people.

But even knowing that, he was still the only familiar thing in a sea of strangeness.

"What did he say?" Jack asked, looking puzzled but not displeased when she took his hand. "Did you find out anything?"

Hazel shook her head. She didn't want to tell him then and there, with all the eyes and ears around them. Anyway, she reminded herself, it was just one more secret, one more thing she couldn't say, just one more thing she was going to have to figure out how to fix.

Step one: Figure out if her nighttime self was a villain.

Step two: Find out who was leaving her notes. Figure out if it was the same person who'd gotten her to smash Severin's coffin. Figure out if that was the same person who had her sword.

Step three: Figure out whether Ainsel was a friend or another enemy.

Step four: Figure out how she was supposed to bring Severin to the Alderking.

It was enough to make her want to sit down on the ground and start to cry. It was too much. But there was no one else, so it couldn't be too much. It had to be exactly enough. It had to be what she could handle, and she had to handle it.

"You want to do something before we go back?" Jack looked impish and oddly relaxed. "We could dance."

"No dancing," she said with a forced grin. "That's one of the rules."

He took her hand and drew her across the floor of the hollow hill, seeming to step outside the Jack she'd known most of her life, the Jack who was her brother's best friend, the Jack who was safe and entirely off-limits. "I won't let you dance until you wear the leather on your boots through. I won't even let you dance until dawn. Now, isn't that a handsome promise?"

The revel was as beautiful as it was awful. Maybe he wanted to show the beauty to her, to someone from his other life. There were so many things she couldn't be honest about that she understood the allure for him to be able to be honest about this.

She rolled her eyes, but after the Alderking's threats, she craved a distraction. "Promises, promises."

A shadow passed over his face. Then he grinned and pulled her toward the music.

As they got closer, the songs crept deeper into her mind. The ache she'd first felt when she came to the revel returned, pulling at her, sinking down into her bones, and making her body move of its own volition.

The airs were sweet and wild, full of reckless stories of bravery and honor and chance that she'd lived on when she was little. A jolt of fierce joy shivered through her, and she spun toward the other dancers. The music caught her up and bore her along, leaving her feeling giddy and a little scared and then giddy again. Jack's hand was in hers, then trailing over her waist, and then gone. She looked for him, but there were too many others dancing, all of them whirling and turning in a circle around the fiddler at their center. A girl with a crown of braids, a heavy brow, and upturned features laughed in a way that was almost a shriek. A boy with clawed hands dragged them over another boy's shoulder. Above them, the curve of the hill seemed as distant as the night sky, a canopy of roots and glowing, darting lights. Beside her, Jack's body moved in parallel, occasionally crushed against hers, warm and strong and not at all out of reach. Hazel danced and danced, until her feet were sore and her muscles ached, and still she danced. She danced until all her cares were swept away. She danced until an arm closed around her waist and pulled her from the circle.

They collapsed together on the packed earthen floor. Jack was laughing, his brow wet with sweat. "It's good, right? Like nothing else."

She felt abruptly dizzy and also as though she had suffered a terrible loss. She crawled back toward the whirling faeries. It seemed to her in that moment that if she just joined them again, she would be okay.

"Hey, whoa!" He grabbed her again, pulling her farther from the dance, causing her to have to stagger to her feet. "Hazel, don't. Come on, sweetheart, time to get going. I'm sorry. I didn't think it would get you so bad."

Sweetheart. The word hung in the air, pulling her halfway out of her fugue. But, no, he couldn't have meant anything by it. *Sweetheart* was what you called lost cats and adorable toddlers and dames in old-timey movies. Hazel blinked at him, her head starting to clear.

He laughed again, this time a little uncertainly. "Hazel?"

She nodded, embarrassed. "I'm okay now."

He slung his arm around her shoulders, giving her a half hug. "Good."

At that moment, a girl ran up from the dance and grabbed hold of his collar. As Hazel started to object, the girl pressed her lips to Jack's.

His arm slid free of Hazel, his grip going slack, his eyes fluttering closed. The girl had a wide red mouth, a bluish tint to her skin, blue roses braided into her messy brown hair, and the kind of unearthly beauty that caused sailors to steer straight for the heart of storms. Hazel had no idea *how* they knew each other or even *if* they knew each other, but watching the muscles of his throat move, watching the faerie girl's hand travel across the bottom of his shirt, fingers sliding underneath, made shame heat Hazel's cheeks. She didn't know what to feel and desperately wanted to stop feeling entirely. Jack broke the kiss, looking toward Hazel, clearly dazed.

Cups of what appeared to be amber wine were passing by, carried by a creature in golden armor. The girl swept one into her hand, put it to her lips, and drank. Then she turned to Hazel.

And kissed her, full and deep. Startled and amazed, Hazel didn't pull away, didn't draw back. She felt the softness of the girl's lips and the coolness of her tongue. A moment later Hazel tasted wine as the girl tipped it into Hazel's mouth from her own.

No food or drink. That was one of the important rules, one of the big ones—because after you have their food, anything else tastes like dust and ashes. Or you go mad and wind up wearing a giant mushroom for a hat, running through town, believing that you were being chased by an army of grigs. Or possibly both at once.

So it wasn't like Hazel didn't know how foolish she'd been. Or how screwed she was.

It tasted as though starlight were slipping down her throat. She smiled stupidly at Jack. Then there was a great roaring in her ears and nothing more.

CHAPTER 15

B en stood in the doorway of Hazel's room, looking in disbelief at the note on his sister's bed, a ripped piece of notebook paper with scrawls in ballpoint pen:

> Don't get mad at Jack. I made him take
> me. I just want you to know I'm okay and
> I'm not alone.

He punched the wall with his bad hand, wincing at the impact, frowning at the flakes of paint that chipped off onto his fingers. Ben was furious—at her, at himself, at the world.

He didn't understand why Hazel wasn't *boasting* to him about freeing their prince, why she'd let Ben tromp through the wet woods, making a fool of himself, instead of telling him what she'd done.

Maybe she was trying to protect his feelings. Which made him unbearably pathetic.

Hazel was bigger than life; she always had been. Always trying to protect people—protect the town, protect their parents from having to confront that they'd let a lot of stuff slide, protect him from having to face his own cowardice after he'd quit hunting. While something was attacking the school and everyone else was panicking, she'd been inside, helping Molly. He remembered how she'd come through those doors with that familiar swagger, the one that said she didn't need magic, didn't need any faerie blessing.

Ben told stories. Hazel became those stories.

She was brave. And she was an idiot, too, running off like this.

"Ben?" his mom called from downstairs. "Is everything okay? Did you hurt yourself?"

"I'm fine," he called back. "Everything's fine."

"Well, come down here. And bring your sister."

Mom was in the kitchen, wearing one of Dad's big, paint-covered shirts, pulling old stuff out of the fridge to throw away. She looked up when he came in, a plastic container of moldy yogurt in one hand. "Your father called. He wants us to come up and stay with him in Queens for a couple of days."

"What? When?"

She chucked the yogurt into the bin. "As soon as you and your sister are ready. I really don't like this town sometimes. The stuff that's been going on gives me the creeps. Where is Hazel?"

Ben sighed. "I'll find her."

"Pack light. Both of you."

For a moment Ben wanted to ask her if having the creeps meant she was *scared*. He wanted to know how she managed to pretend bad stuff wasn't really *that* bad, managed to pretend it so hard that sometimes Ben thought he was crazy for remembering.

He went outside. Not really knowing what to do, he sat on the steps for the better part of an hour, picking foxtails and knotting their stems until the weeds snapped, staring up at the moon in the still-bright sky. It was his obligation as a sibling to cover for Hazel, but there was no way Mom wasn't going to find out she was gone. Finally, he banged back through the screen door.

"Hazel's not here," he said.

Mom turned toward him. "What do you mean?"

"What do you think I mean?" he said. "She's gone. She's not here. She left hours ago, probably trying to figure out what's actually going on in town."

Mom looked at him as though he wasn't making any sense. "But that's dangerous."

Ben snorted and started up the stairs toward his room. "Yeah, I know."

He tried Jack's cell phone, but it went straight to voice mail. Hazel's was in the next room. Ben flopped down onto his bed, exhaustion overwhelming him. He'd been up all night the night before. He had no idea what to do. Lying there, pondering, it was easy for his eyes to drift closed. And then he was asleep, on top of his bed, clothes still on.

When he woke, it was because of a cool breeze coming through the open window. He blinked stupidly at the darkness outside. He had no idea how long he'd been sleeping, but he knew the gnawing at the pit of his stomach was instinct kicking in. Something was nearby. Adrenaline and dread and the kind of excitement that turns skin to ice flooded his veins.

When he'd gone to sleep, the window had been shut.

He remembered feeling that way in the old days, when he and Hazel were out in the woods, the hairs on the back of his neck rising to alert him that even if he couldn't see a monster, in all likelihood, a monster could see him.

Then he heard a voice near his ear. "Benjamin Evans."

Struggling to sit up, Ben saw the boy standing by the bed, illuminated by the full moon. A boy wearing his clothes. For a moment Ben just blinked. The hood of the sweatshirt shadowed the boy's face, but he knew the garment. He'd left it in the woods, folded up on a worn wooden table for an elf prince to find.

"Hi," Ben squeaked, barely getting the word out. He knew he had to do better than that. He had to say something that showed he wasn't afraid, although he was. "Decided to kill me after all?"

Severin pushed back the hood. Sable hair curled around his cheeks, and Ben saw the very points of his horns beneath his ears. His expression was impossible to read.

He was crushingly, heart-stoppingly beautiful. And he belonged to Hazel. It was Hazel who'd freed the prince, so he was fated to love her. Hazel, whom he'd kissed. Probably his first kiss in a century. Hazel might not love him back right away, but she'd come around in the end. That was how fairy tales worked.

Ben was a sap. Ben would have loved him instantly.

"I have come to tell you a story," said Severin, and his voice was soft. "You've told me so many. My turn for a tale."

"Why?" Ben asked, still not really able to process the fact that Severin was there, in his bedroom. "What do you want?"

Even without the lights on, he was aware of the silly posters on his wall, the jeans on his floor where he'd kicked them off and never bothered to pick them up. His hamper was full of dirty clothes, and beside his dresser, tacked to a corkboard, was a tattered photograph of the horned boy, asleep. Everything about his room was embarrassing.

"What do I want? Many things. But for now, only to talk," Severin said. "I find your voice to be...steadying. Let us discuss sisters."

"Sisters," Ben echoed. "You want me to tell you about Hazel?"

"You misunderstand me," said Severin. "I wish for you only to listen."

Ben remembered what Severin had said just before he'd kissed Hazel. The words felt as though they were burned on his skin. *I know every one of your secrets. I know all your dreams.*

If he knew Hazel's secrets, then certainly he knew Ben's even better. It was Ben who'd gone out to the coffin nearly every day, Ben who'd talked to the boy in the coffin like he was talking out loud to himself. He'd confessed to Severin that he'd drank too much cheap André champagne last New Year's Eve and vomited in the bushes outside Namiya's party; he'd admitted to Severin exactly how dangerously good it felt the very first time a boy had touched him; he'd explained who at school hated each other and who pretended to hate each other but really didn't. Maybe Hazel was right not to tell Ben anything important.

Severin took a breath and started to speak. "It is mostly solitary fey who dwell in deep forests like those that surround Fairfold, and solitary fey are not well liked by the trooping gentry from faerie courts. They are too wild, too ugly, their violence too unrefined."

"Solitary fey?" Ben asked, trying to keep up.

"Tricksy phookas. Green ladies who will strip a man's flesh from his bones if he steps into the wrong bog," Severin said. "Hollow-backed women who inspire artists to heights of creativity and depths of despair. Trow men, with long, hairy tails and large appetites. Prankish goblins; homely hobs; pixies with their iridescent, stained-glass wings; and all the rest. Those of us who make our homes in the wild or at a mortal hearth. Those who do not live at courts, who do not play at kings and queens and pages. Those who are not gentry like my father."

"Oh." The word *mortal* struck Ben powerfully. It was such an odd, old-fashioned word. Mortal things were things that died.

Severin brought his fingers to Ben's cheek, cool against hot skin. The faint smell of dirt and greenery came to him as Severin's fingers lifted a piece of hair and tucked it behind Ben's ear.

Ben's whole body seemed to seize up at the touch.

Severin went on, hand moving away, leaving Ben to wonder what the touch had meant, if it had meant anything at all. Severin's eyes seemed brighter than ever, shining with intensity. "Sorrel, my sister, was born to a court lady before our father's exile. Father stole her away with him when he fled, along with seven magical blades—including the one I seek—and the smith who forged them, a creature named Grimsen, who could craft anything from metal. Father came to Fairfold with his retinue and called himself the Alderking, for the alder tree is known as the king of the woods. But *Alderking* has a more sinister meaning, too. Perhaps you've heard this before: *Mein Vater, mein Vater, jetzt faßt er mich an! Erlkönig hat mir ein Leids getan!*"

Ben shook his head. It sounded like German.

Severin moved away from Ben, away from the bed. He leaned against the windowsill, shoulders against the glass.

Abruptly, Ben felt as though he could breathe again. His lips were dry and he licked them.

"My father, my father, he grabs me fast. For sorely the Alderking has hurt me at last." Severin's hands clenched into fists, rings still glimmering on the fingers, contrasting with the shabbiness of the borrowed jeans and hoodie. "It's one of your human poets, writing about a man whose child dies in his arms because of the Alderking. Pain is the Alderking's meat, and suffering, his drink. He ruled over the solitary fey here in Fairfold and even got a son on one of them.

"A son who looked enough like his father's people, although the horns that rose from his brow were all his mother's. My mother was one of those wild fey—a phooka. Which means that though my father's blood runs through my veins, I am no true heir for him. I am too much made of trees and leaves and open air. Maybe if my father liked me better, it would have spared my mother."

The horned boy really was a prince, Ben thought. He recalled what Severin had said about his mother before, about her being cut down in front of him. Because of his father?

Severin kept talking. He was a good storyteller, the cadences of his voice rising and falling like the movements of a song. "Though I wanted our father's approval, and Sorrel cared nothing for it, he favored her all the same. I would listen as he spoke of his plans to defeat the queen, Silarial, who'd exiled him, for neither his ambition nor his rage had cooled with time. My sister would tell him that fate had brought him to this place and he should delight in it. She loved the woods and she loved the town. Which was well enough until she also fell in love with a mortal boy."

The way Severin said the words, he made it sound as though his sister had come down with some kind of deadly disease.

"That's bad, then?" Ben asked. He wished Severin would come back to the bed, and then he didn't. He felt like an idiot.

The elf's eyebrows rose. "To my father? There was little worse she could have done."

"And you agreed with him?" Ben wondered just how loathsome he was to Severin.

"Oh, I did. The boy was called Johannes Ermann, pale-haired and broad-shouldered, who liked to take long walks through the woods, daydreaming and composing odes to dank ponds and patches of wildflowers, which he would recite to anyone who'd listen. I didn't like him much at all," Severin said. "In fact, I killed him."

Ben couldn't help it; he laughed out loud. It was right out of a fairy tale, crazy and terrifying.

Severin grinned, as though he was a little amused, too. Maybe at Ben's reaction, maybe in recalling how funny the murder had been. His smile made him even more beautiful, so beautiful that it was suddenly easy to remember that he wasn't human and that Ben would be very foolish to imagine he was likely to behave like a human.

"I didn't kill him right away; perhaps if I had, things would have gone differently. My sister became his wife, putting aside gowns woven from moonbeams, putting aside the wild pleasures of the woods. She allowed herself to be clad in a heavy, old-fashioned, ill-fitting silk dress from Germany, lent to her by the groom's mother, and to go to one of their churches and make their vows."

Ben tried to imagine it. Whispering through the glass of the coffin had felt a bit like screaming to a musician up onstage, like swooning over movie stars. But what happened if you were chosen from the crowd? What happened if you were summoned to the after-party? He wondered whether that was how Johannes had felt when he brought a faerie wife home.

"My father allowed Sorrel to marry only if her new husband would submit to a geas. Do you know what that is?"

Ben didn't. "Like a quest?"

Severin shook his head. "It's a taboo, a prohibition. A thing you must or must not do. My father said that if my sister wept three times because of Johannes, he would never see her again. Johannes, besotted, agreed.

"Sorrel was a dutiful wife, making supper and mending clothes, tending to a garden and attending church on Sundays. She tried to create a welcoming home for her husband, but her strangeness was obvious, no matter how she tried to fit in. She stitched fanciful roses and leaves onto the cuffs of a sober coat. She made a pet of a blue jay. She added herbs to her jams and jellies as she sang bawdy songs. But she adored Fairfold—and that was what I never understood. No matter that the townsfolk looked at her askance, she loved them. She loved to play games with the children, loved to laugh at the gossip. And, for all I sneered at him, she loved Johannes.

"You must understand. We do not love as you do—once won, our love can be terrifyingly constant. After they were married, Johannes changed toward her. He became more afraid of her strangeness, no matter that she remained his loyal wife."

"So he was a jerk?" Ben asked, propping himself higher against his headboard. There was something disturbingly intimate about sitting in bed and talking about this stuff, even if the story ended in tragedy. "Was she sorry she married him?"

"We love until we do not. For us, love doesn't fade gradually. It snaps like a branch bent too far."

To Ben, love was the flame in which he wanted to be reborn. He wanted to be remade by it. He understood why Sorrel had run away to start over. And for the first time, he understood what a bad plan it was. "Is that what happened?"

"I fear not." Severin rose and turned a little, fingers against the window, profile blurred in the moonlight. Ben suspected that Severin didn't want him watching his expression shift as he spoke. "Maybe Johannes didn't remember the geas or didn't consider the consequences, but my sister wept because of him. The first time, it was because Johannes reprimanded her in public for her wildness. The second time she wept was because he remonstrated her for not keeping the Sabbath. The third time she wept, it was because he struck her. There would be no fourth.

"Of the seven magical swords my father brought from the Court in the East, two were special. Heartseeker and Heartsworn, they were called. Heartseeker never missed its mark. Heartsworn could cut through anything, from rock to metal to bone. My father gave me Heartsworn and told me to kill Johannes. I was angry enough and I despised humans enough and I wished to please my father badly enough. While Sorrel was out gathering herbs, I went to her house and struck Johannes down."

"You killed him? In cold blood?" It was a nightmare story, the kind that kept kids up, listening for movements in the dark.

"His blood was hot enough," Severin said, looking out into the forest. "And mine, too. I was so angry that I didn't consider what Sorrel would feel."

"Because she was still in love with him, right? Her feelings hadn't snapped like a branch or whatever yet."

The elf shook his head. "I suppose that was an insufferable thing to say. Maybe we don't love any differently than you do; maybe everyone loves until they don't—or maybe everyone loves differently, humans and faeries alike. Forgive me. I grew up on my father's boasting about the superiority of my people, and although I have listened to your kind for decades upon decades, it still hasn't chased out all my worst habits of presumption."

Ben, who'd been perfectly serious when he'd asked about Sorrel's feelings changing, was mortified that Severin thought he'd been implying anything else. "No, I—"

"I didn't understand," Severin said. "I thought because Johannes was human, his life didn't matter. How could his death matter? It seemed ridiculous that my sister could love such a creature, no less be hurt by him. If he wasn't good to her, why not merely get another? I had no idea how long a single day could be. I didn't know that the span of a single mortal life would seem interminable as I lay unmoving in that case. I didn't know."

Without quite deciding to do so, Ben slid off the bed. Although it was clearly the worst idea in the world and he thought he might faint or die, Ben put his hand on Severin's back, feeling the corded muscles under his fingers, the brush of silken hair at the nape of the boy's neck.

Severin tensed and then let out a long, shuddering sigh. "Maybe envy moved my hand, for Sorrel was my confidante at court. She took my side against our father. She made up silly songs for me when I was sad. Without her, I was alone and I wanted her back. We are all capable of great self-deception when it serves us."

Ben was still touching him, not sure what to do with his hand— it seemed bizarre to leave it where it was, but incalculably daring to move it over to Severin's shoulder or down to his chest. Ben inhaled the crushed-grass smell of him, took in the warmth of his skin.

Once, Ben had brought a boy out to Severin's casket and made out with him on top of it, pretending it was the horned boy he was kissing.

He'd told Severin that, too. And it wasn't even the most humiliating thing he'd told him. Ben didn't move his hand.

After a moment, Severin spoke again. "She grieved, endlessly did she grieve for her dead husband. She abandoned her home, lying in a patch of moss in the woods and weeping. So terrible was her grief that beetles and birds, mice and stags, all wept with her, rotting away to fur and bone in their misery. Rocks and trees wept with her, cracking and shedding leaves. I went to her and begged her to put aside her sorrow, but she hated me for what I had done and would not. I threw away Heartsworn and begged her to revenge herself on me, but she would not listen even to that. Her grief transformed her. She became a monster, a nightmare creature of grief and sorrow, all because of me."

"Your *sister* is . . . the *monster*?" Ben stammered.

"Yes," Severin said. "The creature loosed on your town was once my sister. That's the story I came to tell you. And you must understand that if I can save her, I will. But you should also understand the danger you're in."

Ben understood about sisters. And he understood about stories. But he didn't understand what he'd done to merit being told this one.

"So you came to *warn* me?"

"When I heard your voice that night, I recognized it instantly. It's a voice I know better than I know my own. For countless years, I have not spoken aloud. Now I can. It's you I would speak with. You to whom I owe a great debt."

"A debt?" He felt like a particularly stupid parrot, repeating the last thing Severin said.

"You know, it nearly drove me mad to listen to so many voices, a cacophony of sound, of words I didn't know piling up, of time slipping in skips and jumps. And then you, speaking to me—*to* me. I started to know the length of a day in the interval between your visits."

The blush started on Ben's skin. It was all too much. He realized that Severin was going to hurt him worse than he'd ever been hurt before, because Ben had already set the blade to his chest, had already wrapped this stranger's hand around the hilt.

He loved Severin and he barely knew him.

Severin told him the rest, how his father was troubled by Sorrel's monstrous form, but yearned to find a way to harness her power. How he ordered Grimsen to craft a casket that would hold her until he could find a way to have control of her. Severin described the making of the casket, the forging of the metal frame from blood-quenched iron, and the crystal spun from tears. And he explained how he stood against his father, refusing to let the Alderking lock her away. The Alderking had railed at him, telling him that he wished Severin and Sorrel had never been birthed, swearing that should he beget another child, he would cut its throat rather than have it grow to betray him as they had. Severin would not back down, no matter how his father shouted. He would not let him put his sister in the casket.

But then the Alderking drew his magical sword, Heartseeker, the blade that could never miss. And since Severin had thrown Heartsworn away, he was screwed. He got trapped in the casket instead of her, and there he remained until Ben's sister effected his release.

Ben tried to focus on the story, tried to focus on the words and figure out what it all meant, but all he could think of was how he was lost.

CHAPTER 16

"Wake up," Jack was saying, his voice floating somewhere above Hazel, his hand on her cheek. He sounded hoarse, as though he'd been shouting. "Please, please, please. Please, wake up."

She struggled to open her eyes. It was as though they had been glued shut. When she finally managed to blink, she found Jack looming over her, looking angrier than she'd ever seen him. He punched the ground and closed his eyes for a long moment, drawing breath.

"What were you *thinking*?" he shouted, voice echoing off the trees. It was then Hazel realized that they were still in the forest, that there was a bed of grass and moss underneath her, and that the sky overhead was the pale gray of dawn.

She tried to sit up, but she was too dizzy. "I don't know," she said miserably. "I was—I don't know. I'm sorry. What—what happened?"

"You mean before or after you tried to drown yourself in an underground lake?" Jack paced the carpet of pine needles, resting his head against the trunk of a tree and looking up at the clouds as though he couldn't quite believe he'd been saddled with such an enormous burden. "Or how about how you recited prime numbers instead of speaking words? Or how you threatened some hulking, hairy grim with a knight's sword, a sword, by the way, that I have literally no idea how you swindled away from him? Or how you passed out and I couldn't wake you up and I was *really worried*, because there's a lot of that going around right now?"

"I'm sorry," she repeated, faintly, because she honestly couldn't think of anything else to say. She didn't remember much past the press of the elf girl's mouth, past her lips parting and the taste of honey and wine. Everything else was blank blackness.

"Don't apologize," Jack told her, scrubbing his hand over his face. "I'm not—I'm not myself. Don't listen to me right now."

Hazel pushed herself up into a sitting position and looked around. Her dizziness and blurriness were receding a little. "How did we get here?" she asked, not recognizing the stretch of forest. "Did we walk?"

"I carried you," he said with a lopsided smile.

She must have been horribly heavy, like a sack of flour with the ability to drool. And although she hadn't imagined she could be more humiliated, it turned out that no matter how far you fall, there's always a lower place.

"Thanks," she said, trying not to cringe. Then she remembered the Folk didn't like being thanked. She'd never thought of Jack as someone to whom their rules applied before, but after the revel, she was forced to think differently. "Sorry." That was the third sorry, and she was tempted to follow it up with a fourth and a fifth, a litany of sorrysorrysorry.

"Hazel," he said with a vast sigh. "I'm not mad, okay?"

"Okay." She didn't believe him, but there was no point in arguing. She flopped back down.

Her feet were wet, her boots sodden. She couldn't remember how they got that way, but she could guess. Underground lake. She wanted to kick them off, but she also wanted to stay where she was, lying on her back and feeling sorry for herself.

Jack sat down on a root beside her. He'd lost his coat somewhere, and the front of his shirt was a little ripped, as though someone had pulled it too hard. "Not mad at *you*, anyway. I was pissed at myself."

"Why?" she asked, snorting with disbelief. "I knew the rules and I broke them."

"You acted the way every human acts when given faerie wine. *Every* human, since the world began. I should have stopped you. I saw what you were doing and what she was doing, and I was caught up in the moment and I didn't do a damn thing. Sometimes when I'm with them, I feel like a different person. A different creature entirely *from* a person. But you—you were supposed to be under my protection. I didn't behave well, and then yelling at you—well, I haven't behaved myself at all. Both of my mothers would have me beg your pardon. I'm sorry, Hazel."

A trace of the way they spoke was still in his voice. It made him sound, oddly, more like himself. It was the way that sleepy people sometimes slipped back into an accent they no longer possessed when fully awake.

Light was filtering through the trees, warming the ferns and grass around her. Overhead, birds were calling to one another, and beside her, the scents of crushed brambles filled the air.

Dawn was coming.

"I'm fine," she said, reaching out to tug at his hand. He flopped down beside her.

"No thanks to me," he said.

"Many thanks to you, and still, *fine*. I had an adventure." She sighed. "But the Alderking told me something. He said that I had to bring him Severin."

"Severin?" Jack echoed.

"The prince," Hazel said. "I've got two days. If I don't manage to do it, the Alderking said that he'd send his people against the town."

Jack raised his eyebrows. "When you spoke to him, you told me you didn't find out anything."

"I lied," Hazel said, with a twist of her mouth.

He didn't look angry. Instead, he seemed intrigued. "Why?"

Ask me no questions and I'll tell you no lies. What was that from? It echoed in her head, a bit of nursery rhyme logic. She took a deep breath and tried to be as honest as she could. "I didn't want to see the look on your face, because I was sure you'd be horrified—you do look kind of horrified now—and I'd have to admit how screwed we all are."

"You don't have to do this alone," Jack said, turning full onto his back and looking up at the lightening sky over the tops of the trees.

Hazel remembered what it had been like to have a partner, back when she believed there was nothing so terrible that Ben would back down from it, back when she thought her job was to be a knight. Ben's knight. The one who held the blade, who went out in front, keeping him safe so he could save everybody else and tell the tale. "You don't have to say that," she told him.

"If I *had* to say it, it wouldn't mean much." His grin was quick. "But I've been thinking. Why would the Alderking single you out? Why believe that you could bring him Severin? And why aren't you asking those questions, too? Hazel, what aren't you telling me?"

"What do you mean?" Hazel said, stalling. Her heart beat triple-time. Jack was clever, clever enough to figure out that she'd omitted things, maybe even to guess at *what* she'd omitted.

The idea that someone could see through what she wasn't saying, could guess at her secrets, tempted her to tell him everything. She was so tired of being alone. "I'm freaking out. My heart is beating a million miles an hour. Feel it. Here, give me your hand."

He shook his head, but then he seemed to relent, letting her take his fingers and press them against her skin. His palm opened, cool and careful over her heart.

"Anyone would be freaked out," he said. "That's normal."

"I never wanted to be normal," Hazel told him softly, and it was an ache in her to admit that to someone who'd probably never felt that way. Then, even softer, she said, "Distract me."

"Distract you?" He regarded her from beneath half-lidded eyes, hand still against her chest.

"What?" she asked, smiling without quite intending to. She couldn't read his expression, but she could read the way his body bent toward hers.

"You really want me to...?"

"More than anything," Hazel said, soft and sure.

Leaning over, not speaking, he brought his mouth to hers. For a wild moment she wondered if he wanted her. *Her* and not just *this*.

At first, the kiss seemed part of the night and the dancing, full of dreamy madness. Jack kissed her as though he could reassure himself she was awake and okay only so long as they were touching. He kissed her as though he thought she'd turn to smoke the moment he stopped.

She rolled toward him, and his arm came around her, pressing her closer, his fingers against the small of her back. Everything felt liquid and slow. As her hands fumbled with his shirt, trying to get it up and over his broad shoulders, as she pressed her cheek against smooth brown skin, and as he made a soft sound in the back of his throat that seemed to be his way of holding in check some other, less polite sound that Hazel desperately wanted to hear, she couldn't help thinking of how strange it was to be doing this with a friend.

She pulled back, looking at him, his mouth swollen, his breaths ragged. His eyes were closed.

"Hazel," he started to say, and she realized that whatever it was he was about to tell her, she didn't want to hear it. She didn't want apologies and she didn't want excuses and she didn't want to stop.

She kissed him, pushing him back against the ground, and then kissed him some more for good measure. His hands came up and under the back of her shirt, clever fingers sliding over her ribs. He looked obscene and filthy and gorgeous with his jeans undone and pushed low on his hips. With her hands splayed over his stomach and his hips canted toward her.

"Hazel," he said again, and this time he put his hands against her shoulders to keep her a slight distance from him. He said the words slowly at first, as though it was hard for him to concentrate, but once he began speaking, the rest tumbled out in a rush. "Hazel, I just want to say that I like you. And I mean…maybe I'm crazy, but I don't know if you'd do this with me if you knew that. I kind of think you wouldn't, so that's why I'm telling you. But if you want to keep doing whatever we're doing, then I am fully prepared to shut up now."

Hazel's face went blank; she could feel the momentary pause where her panic showed. And even though she tried to smile to cover it, it was too late. He knew her way better than she thought. Way better than she was comfortable with being known.

Jack nodded once, sliding his hands over her to try to zip up his pants.

"*You* like *me*?" she asked, needing him to say those words again, so she could be sure he meant them the way he had seemed like he did.

Weirdly, that made Jack put his hand to his face, rubbing over his eyes and cheek. "Yeah. You're surprised? I feel like everyone guessed. I mean, why do you think Carter is always giving you shit?"

"I don't know," Hazel said. "Not because of that!"

He looked at her with an expression she wasn't sure she'd ever seen on his face before, hungry and a little desperate. "I thought about kissing you so many times at parties. I imagined pressing you back against the bark of a tree, shoving aside those boys you didn't care anything about. I thought you might like the laugh of it, me being your brother's best friend and all."

"You think I want to hurt Ben?"

Jack shrugged. "I think both of you always want a little bite of whatever the other person's got, that's all."

It unnerved her, how not wrong he was. "So why didn't you, then? Why not kiss me?"

His laugh was a soft huff of breath. "The last thing I need is another thing to pretend about. I didn't want to act like I didn't have feelings for you when I did. But, I mean, I've liked you for a long while. My mother once—she showed me a girl wearing your face."

Hazel shifted away from Jack, so she could concentrate on what he was saying without the heat of his body clouding her thoughts. "Wearing my face?"

"Well, yeah. I mean, you know that my people can glamour themselves to appear in different forms. They were messing with me." He frowned. "Hazel? What's going on?"

Nausea twisted her stomach.

"Hazel?" Jack repeated, louder this time. He waved his hand in front of her face. "Look, I didn't mean to completely freak you out. We can forget about what I said."

"It's not that," she told him softly, putting her clothes back together. "I have something I need to tell you. Something I should have told you before."

He waited, shifting so she could sit upright.

He'd guessed enough about her that she hoped he'd understand why she'd hidden the rest. Before she could think better of it, Hazel started talking.

She told him everything. From hunting with her brother, to her bargain, to waking up with mud on her feet and shards of crystal in her palm, from the riddles to the monster to the whole of what the Alderking had said that night.

Jack was looking at her in amazement. "So he told you that you've been serving him this whole time? As a knight?"

She sighed. "I guess it sounds stupid when you—"

That was when Jack grabbed a long stick from the ground. With a howl, he leaped up and swung it at her.

Startled, she reacted without thinking. She kicked him in the stomach and wrenched the branch out of his hand in a move so fluid that it felt as though it was happening all at once. He went down in the dirt and leaves and pine needles with a groan. She took a step forward, turning the stick unconsciously, stopping herself just before she stabbed down at him with it.

Rolling onto his back, astonished, he started to laugh.

"Are you crazy?" Hazel yelled at him. "What were you doing? Why are you laughing?"

He shook his head, one hand on his stomach, the other propping him halfway up. "I don't know. I thought we'd figure out if maybe—ow, that really hurt. Obviously he was telling the truth. You've had some training."

She stuck out her hand to pull him to his feet. "Are you okay?"

"Bruised, but I deserved it," he said, staggering up. "What a brilliant plan that was, huh?"

"So you had no idea that I was his knight? That wasn't one of the things you were forbidden from warning me about?"

Jack shook his head. "If I'd known, I'd have told you. I'd have found a way. Hazel, I swear it."

Hazel smiled, despite herself. "I just—I'm afraid I ruined everything."

"That's not possible," he told her, squeezing her fingers. "Not everything's ruined, so you must not have ruined everything."

For a moment Jack looked like he was going to say something more, and she could see the moment he decided to say something else instead. "Come on, what we both need is some sleep. And if we don't go now, we're not going to be able to sneak into our houses."

"Yeah, you're right." Hazel had so much to puzzle through that sleep sounded enormous and good. Just turning everything off for a while was the best thing she could imagine.

They walked together until they got to the edge of the woods near Jack's house and crossed the lawn. Pale, buttery light was just beginning to filter through the trees in the east.

"You okay to get home?" Jack asked. The memory of touching him haunted her. The scent of him was in her lungs, and her fingers itched to brush over his skin again, to reassure herself that he'd still smile, that he still liked her. "I can walk you back."

Hazel shook her head. "I'll be fine."

He stepped away from her, hands in his pockets, with a final vague smile. "See you in a couple of hours."

Then the back door of the Gordon house opened, and his mother stepped out in a blue fuzzy robe. She was barefoot and had a silk scarf tied over her hair. "Carter! Get in here right—*Jack?*"

They both looked at her, too shocked to move, no less answer.

"Jack!" she said, walking across the lawn toward them. "I would have believed this of your brother, but not you. And *Hazel Evans*. What would your mother say about you spending all night out with a boy...." Her words trailed off as she got a better look at them.

Hazel's face heated.

"Where were you?" Mrs. Gordon demanded.

"You know," Hazel said quickly. "Like you said. Spending the night."

"In the woods? With a full moon in the sky?" She said the words more softly, as if speaking more to herself than them. Then she turned fully toward Jack. "You brought her to them? How could you?"

Jack took a step back, as though her words were a physical blow.

"Do you know what they're saying about you in town? That all this is happening because of you."

"But that doesn't make—" Hazel began.

Mrs. Gordon held up her hand, cutting off Hazel's words. "Enough, both of you. Jack, you get on out of here. You can't come inside right now. You're going to go off to the Evanses' or someplace you think you can stay for a while. And you're not to come back until I say so. Do you understand?"

Hazel never thought Mrs. Gordon would ever kick Jack out, not for anything. Ground him, sure. Make him do extra chores or take away his cell phone or dock his allowance, but not this. Not throw him out of her house like he'd never been her son.

There was a muscle moving in Jack's jaw and his eyes shone too brightly, but he didn't protest, didn't beg. He didn't even explain himself. He just nodded, once. Then he turned away and started walking, leaving Hazel to run after him.

"We'll go to my house," she said.

He nodded.

Together, without speaking, they walked, keeping to the edge of the road. The early-morning air felt good in Hazel's lungs, and although her legs still ached from dancing, it was reassuring to put one foot in front of the other on the asphalt. The sun was rising fast, hot on her back, but it was still too early for many cars to be out, so she veered to walk on the center line of the street. Jack kept pace with her, striding along as if they were gunfighters heading into a strange new town, looking for trouble.

✦ CHAPTER 17 ✦

Ben sat at his desk, watching Severin sleep. He just couldn't quite wrap his head around the fact that the boy he'd whispered to through glass was lying on his bed, head pressed against his pillow, one horn making a deep indentation in it—a pillow Ben had drooled on and cried into and shed skin on, which seemed kind of disgusting the more he thought about it. But that was part of what made Severin's being there so impossible. His room was such an ordinary place, filled with junk he'd amassed over seventeen years of life, and Severin wasn't ordinary at all.

They'd talked for hours in the dark. Severin had wound up on the floor, head tipped back, showing the long column of his throat, eyes drifting closed as it got closer to dawn.

"You're welcome to take the bed," Ben had said, shifting to the edge of it, rumpling the comforter. "I mean, if you want to rest."

At that, Severin's eyes opened. He blinked rapidly, clearly disoriented, as though he'd half forgotten where he was. "No. I ought not. I fear never waking."

Ben considered that. "Have you even slept since the curse was broken? Because that was more than two days ago. Forty-eight hours?"

Severin nodded vaguely.

"And you're not planning to *ever sleep again*?" Ben asked, raising his eyebrows in a slightly exaggerated manner.

A corner of Severin's mouth lifted. "You think I'm too tired to detect sarcasm?"

"That's not sarcasm," Ben said, grinning. "At least not sarcasm *exactly*."

With a groan, Severin levered himself up and spread out on Ben's vintage *Star Trek* coverlet, the one he'd told Hazel was ironic but secretly he just really loved. "Haven't I slept enough?" he asked, but the words became garbled at the end, his body stretching and relaxing into sleep. He looked as beautiful as he'd ever been, messy waves of dark hair curling around his horns, brows curving up, berry-pink mouth slightly parted. Now that he was no longer enchanted, he slept restlessly, his eyes moving beneath lids and his body turning on top of Ben's bed. Maybe he was dreaming for the first time since he'd been sealed in the coffin.

And so Ben sat like a lone and lonely sentinel until the sky was light outside and he heard a creak on the stair. He went to the door and cracked it open. His sister was in the hallway, Jack behind her.

Hazel looked as if she'd come from a party, in a green velvet top she hadn't been wearing yesterday morning. Her jeans were muddy and her shirt was ripped along one seam. Her hair was tousled and tangled with twigs. Ben watched as they went into Hazel's room.

"Are you sure you're not going to get in trouble, having me here?" Jack whispered. He sat on the edge of her bed.

Hazel shook her head and went to close the door. "Mom won't care. She likes you."

Where have they been? Ben stared at the closing door, wondering what exactly he was seeing. He'd figured that wherever Hazel had made Jack take her that night had something to do with how she'd been able to free Severin and whatever else she'd been lying about lately. But seeing them together, looking like they were about to sleep in the same bed, worried him for entirely different reasons.

He loved his sister, but she sure broke a lot of hearts. He'd rather Jack's not be one of them.

The hallway went dark again. A few moments later his sister left her room. Ben thought she was going to cross to the bathroom. Maybe he could catch her before she got there and find out what was going on. But she stopped, leaned against the wall, and started to sob.

Horrible, silent cries that made her bend double, curling around her stomach, as though it hurt to weep like that. Lowering herself to the floor, she crouched down, almost soundless. Tears ran over her cheeks and dripped off her chin as she rocked back and forth.

Hazel never cried. She was forged from iron; she never broke. No one was tougher than his sister.

The worst part was how quietly she wept, as if she'd taught herself how, as if she was so used to doing it that it had just become the way she cried. When Ben was little, he remembered how much he'd envied Hazel, free from expectations or obligation. If she wanted to teach herself how to swordfight with YouTube videos and books checked out of the library, their parents didn't tell her she should practice scales instead. She wasn't the target of Mom and Dad's lectures on how talent wasn't meant to be wasted, how gifts came with obligations, how art was important.

He saw now the ways in which they tried to be careful with each other, afraid of hitting those raw places where they might hurt each other almost without trying. But sparing another person is a tricky thing. It's easy to think you're succeeding when you're failing spectacularly.

After a few moments Hazel lifted her shirt to rub the velvet against her eyes. Then she got up with a last, shuddering sigh and went back to her bedroom.

Ben padded over and turned the knob. Jack was unlacing his boots while Hazel brushed the leaves out of her hair, her eyes red and a little puffy. They both froze.

"It's just me," Ben said.

"We weren't—I mean, not really—" Jack started, making gestures toward the bed that Ben thought meant "I am not trying to dishonor your sister, although it is possible that I am hoping to have sex with her," at the same time Hazel began apologizing for ditching Ben.

He held up his hand to stop them from talking. "I need one of you—ideally Hazel—to explain what's actually been going on, and I need that to happen right now, starting with where you were last night."

"We went to the faerie revel," she said, sitting down heavily on her bed. She looked exhausted, the skin under her eyes as dark as a bruise. Ben hadn't expected her to give in so easily after so much evasion. "It didn't exactly go the way I'd hoped, but I found out some things. The Alderking offered to trade the town's safety for the capture of his son. There's only one problem, which is that he's crazy. Okay, two problems, the second being that his idea of a safe town is bullshit."

Ben just stared at her. He'd seen the Folk, but only a few, and those had been scary enough. He couldn't imagine willingly walking into a gathering of them. Especially if he were Hazel, who'd killed at least three. Her daring always surprised him, but right then he was floored. "The Alderking wants you to bring him *Severin*?"

Hazel gave him a sharp look. "How did you know Severin was his son? He didn't tell us that the other night."

Ben shrugged. "I guessed. Well, who else could it be?"

Hazel shook her head. "You're a god-awful liar. You're still in yesterday's clothes. Obviously, I'm not the only one with secrets. So where were *you* last night?"

Ben let out a sigh and walked all the way into the room, closing the door behind him. "Nowhere. Here. Severin came here. He wanted my help."

Jack's eyebrows shot up, and Hazel went completely rigid, as though she thought she ought to do something, but had no idea what. Ben couldn't help but be a little bit pleased that he could occasionally be shocking, too.

"Is he—what did the horned boy say?" his sister asked.

Jack sat down on the chair in front of her vanity, looking deeply uncomfortable, as if he was afraid he was going to be asked to choose sides in an argument that hadn't happened yet.

"For one thing, he wants his magical sword back," said Ben.

"I hope you didn't promise it to him," Hazel said. "I don't have it. And before you ask, I don't know who does have it or where it's being kept—I was looking for clues at the revel."

"So what else did you learn?"

Hazel rubbed her hand over her face and glanced toward Jack. The look he gave her was expressive. "Not much," she said finally. "Could you get in touch with Severin again? Could you get him to meet us?"

"I don't know. You're not thinking of actually trying to hunt him down for the Alderking, are you? You're not going to hurt him."

"I'm willing to do whatever I have to," Hazel said, standing. A muscle in her jaw jumped, as if she'd been clenching her teeth.

There was a moment when Ben thought about not telling her, when he imagined himself going across the hall and not saying a single thing. But he thought about people being brought out on stretchers from the school, and he thought about what Severin had said about his own sister. "Will you tell me *everything*, all the stuff you've been hiding from me?"

Hazel glanced at Jack and he looked back at her, his eyebrows rising. She must have told him some of it, for them to share a look like that.

"I will," Hazel said. "I should have before. Just, do I have to tell you right now? Because I'm dead on my feet and there's a lot."

Although it sounded like another excuse, this time Ben believed her. She looked exhausted and oddly fragile. "Okay. But he's in my room."

"What?" Hazel pushed herself up off the bed and took a step toward the door. "Are you kidding me?"

"Oh no," Ben said. "No, you don't get to be angry, you who've been lying to me and hiding things from me. You who brought my best friend with you and made him complicit in the lie. You don't get to be mad!"

Hazel's face shuddered. "I was trying to protect you."

Jack looked as though he wanted to say something. He was clearly tired, too, bright-eyed and hollow-cheeked.

"He's asleep. I'm not going to wake him up to be interrogated." Ben's heart was hammering. Although he'd demanded she tell him the truth, after seeing her reaction, he was starting to suspect that whatever she'd been hiding from him was bigger than he'd previously thought. He was a little scared to hear it.

"You'll make sure he stays?" Hazel asked.

Ben had no idea how he was supposed to do that. "Yeah. When you get up, we'll figure things out."

Jack rose, as if maybe he'd remembered it was ungentlemanly to stay in a girl's room when he'd slept over in her brother's a million times.

"No, stay," Hazel said softly, catching his fingers.

Jack looked helpless to refuse her.

Which made Ben wonder if he'd been wrong about Hazel being fated for Severin. "Sleep tight," Ben said, backing out before Jack had time to reconsider. He wasn't ready to share Severin with anyone yet. He was just getting to know him, just getting to think of him as a person it was possible to know.

As he crossed the hall, Ben felt a flash of fear that when he opened the door and then he saw that Severin was no longer there. It was as though by speaking Severin's name aloud, by telling his sister about the midnight visit, he'd broken some spell. The window was open, curtain billowing and a few brown leaves resting on the floor where they'd been blown in from the trees outside.

Panicked, Ben climbed onto the slope of the roof, sending a loose strip of shingle flying to the ground far below. The sky was early-morning pale and bright, the dew still wetting everything.

Ben sucked in a breath of cool air. For a moment, he saw only trees and road. Then, a moment later, he spotted Severin sitting in a crook of the wide sycamore just past the gutters of the house.

Letting out a sigh of relief, Ben made his way slowly across the roof, trying not to slip. "Hey, are you—"

"I am not a thing to be fought over," the horned boy said. He had stripped out of Ben's hoodie and was in just the borrowed T-shirt and jeans, bare feet against the bark. But he looked entirely alien, shadowed by branches in the pale morning light.

"I know," Ben said, edging closer to the tree. "I'm sorry. I don't know what you heard, but I guess you heard some of it. She wouldn't hurt you, even if she could."

Severin smiled. "I have a sister of my own, you'll recall. I know what it is to not see our siblings for who they truly are. You've done me a good turn that I will not soon forget, Benjamin Evans. You've given me succor this night. Nothing more can be asked of you."

Ben climbed up into the tree, unsure of where to put his feet. For a moment he thought he was going to slip, but he managed to steady himself. "Hazel went to the revel. She saw your father. He spoke with her. We need to pool information, figure out next moves. Besides, I know you like Hazel, even if you pretend like you don't."

Severin took Ben's arm and hauled him deeper into the branches, where it was easier to balance. "Because I kissed her?"

"It's just that Hazel is so—people *like* Hazel. Boys like Hazel. She goes through this world as if nothing touches her, as if no one can reach her, as though she's focused on something bigger and better and more important that she's not going to tell you a single thing about. It drives people crazy. It charms them."

"And you're not charming?" Severin asked him. Ben wasn't sure if he was being mocked or not.

"I'm sure that when you kissed her, you noticed she wasn't some irritable, gawky boy." Ben felt ridiculous as soon as he said it. Feeling insecure was one thing; showing it was another.

Severin studied him for a long moment, then leaned forward and pressed his mouth to Ben's. It was a searching, hungry kiss. His hand wrapped around Ben's head, holding on to him instead of the tree.

Ben's hand fisted in Severin's hair, brushed over horn, rough and cold as the back of a seashell. A few moments later, when he pulled away, Ben was trembling with some combination of lust and anger and fear. Because, yes, he'd wanted that. But he hadn't wanted it thrown in his face.

"Is it wrong that I like that you tremble? That you flinch?" Severin asked.

Ben swallowed. "I'm pretty sure it's not ideal."

The horned boy raised both brows. "So what do you suppose I noticed when I kissed you?"

Ben sighed, looking down at the patchy lawn below. He wanted Severin to *tell* him. Wanted to know what he'd thought when his fingers had tightened on the skin above Ben's hip, wanted to know what he'd felt when he'd gasped into Ben's mouth. But he was being childish. "I get it, being jealous is ridiculous when you've got actual problems like a monster sister and a killer father."

Severin shifted, making the trees rustle. His eyes were green as deep groves and forgotten glens, his hair falling around his face. "My problems are yours as well. All of Fairfold is blessed with my problems, and they do not lessen your own. You and your sister are very dear to each other. To show your regard, you give each other lovely bouquets of lies."

"It's not like that."

"I know you, Benjamin Evans," Severin said. "Remember?"

Ben slipped a little, nearly losing his balance. He'd been thinking of Severin as cold, as a story, as a *faerie prince*—beautiful and distant.

He kept forgetting that Severin knew him, knew more about him than any person in the world.

"You said you loved me so many times," Severin told him softly, and hearing him say that made Ben flush hotly. "But maybe what you loved best was your own face reflected in the glass."

It wasn't fair that he knew Ben like that. It wasn't fair. It wasn't fair that Severin could play on all of Ben's petty insecurities, petty insecurities dating back years to deliver a series of swift surgical cuts so sharp and sure that Ben felt as though he might bleed out before he realized the depth of the wounds.

"I don't—it's not like that," Ben said. "But yeah, I wanted to be in love like in the storybooks and songs and ballads. Love that hits you like a lightning bolt. And I'm sorry, because yeah, I get that you think I'm ridiculous. I get that you think I'm hilarious. I know, I get that you're mocking me. I get how stupid I am, but at least I know."

In a fluid motion, Severin stepped off the tree and onto the roof. He held out his hand in a courtly gesture, offering to help Ben out of a tree as you might hand a lady in skirts down from a horse. "I know, too, Benjamin Evans. And you're not nearly as stupid as you think."

Ben reached out his hand and let himself be helped onto the roof. They were crossing to the window when a truck pulled into the driveway. It belonged to one of Mom's artist friends, Suzie, a heavily tattooed sculptor who made little green man faces for over the lintels of houses. She was wearing a skirt, and her hair was pulled up into a ponytail, as if she was going to church or something.

"That's weird," Ben said, waiting until Suzie was in the house before he moved. "I'm going to find out what's going on."

"And you wonder if I will remain," said Severin.

Ben nodded.

"I shall be just as you left me," the faerie prince said, sitting on the wheeled chair in front of Ben's computer desk and looking up at him with unfathomable moss-green eyes. Ben mentally cataloged all the embarrassing things Severin might see if he looked around and then realized there was nothing half as embarrassing as what Severin already knew.

Severin grinned up at him, as though reading his thoughts.

Ben went downstairs.

"Oh, good, you're awake," Mom said. She was dressed up more than usual—jeans without paint stains, her oversize flower-print top, and three turquoise-and-silver necklaces. Without the streaks of silver in her hair, from a distance, she could have been mistaken for Hazel. "I heard your sister come in this morning. Tell her to start packing. As soon as I get back, we can get on the road."

"Where are you going now?"

"There's a town meeting over at the Gordons'. About Jack."

"Jack?" Ben echoed.

"You know I like him. But some people are saying that he's been in league with the Folk. And others are saying that if he just went back to Faerie, then all these bad things that are happening would stop."

"But you don't believe that, right?" Ben thought of Jack, curled up beside Hazel in her bedroom, and felt a flash of pure fury at every single person in Fairfold who'd thought anything like what Mom said.

She sighed, reaching for a travel coffee mug and her old brown leather purse, the one with birds stitched on it in blue thread. "I don't know. I don't think he's in league with anyone, but he was *stolen* from them. Maybe they do want him back. Maybe they want revenge, too. At least I might, if I were his mother."

"What's happening isn't Jack's fault."

"Look, nothing's decided. We're just sitting down with the Gordons to talk things over. And when I get back, hopefully we can all leave town for a while."

"Mom," Ben said. "If you let them do something to Jack, I will never forgive you. He's just like us. He's as human as any human."

"I just want you and Hazel to be safe," Mom said. "That's all any of us ever want for our children."

"Then maybe you shouldn't have raised us here in Fairfold," Ben told her.

Mom gave him a dark look. "We came back here for you, Benjamin. We could have stayed in Philadelphia, and you'd be well on your way to doing something most people can only dream of. You're the one who couldn't stand leaving Fairfold. You're the one who gave the chance at a different life up, who couldn't be bothered to practice after your injury."

Ben was too stunned to say anything in return. They never talked about Philadelphia, at least not that way—not in a way that acknowledged bad things had happened. They never talked about any of the big, looming, awful stuff from Ben's childhood. They never talked about the dead body Hazel found in the woods or the way Mom and Dad had let them roam around alone out there in the first place. He had always assumed that was the family compact, that they each got their own well of bitterness and they were supposed to tend to it without bothering anyone else.

Apparently, not anymore.

Walking to the door, Mom looked back at him, as if she was taking his measure. "And tell your sister to pack, okay?"

The screen slammed closed, but instead of immediately following her out, Suzie crossed the foyer to put her hand on Ben's arm. "You say he's as human as the rest of us. How can you be so sure? How can anyone really know what's in their hearts?" Before he could answer, she headed off after his mother. A few moments later he heard the truck tires roll over the driveway gravel.

Ben put his head down on the counter, his thoughts a tangled mess. Then, not knowing what else to do, he got down four mugs and started pouring coffee into them.

Everybody had to wake the hell up.

✦ CHAPTER 18 ✦

Hazel had never slept in the same bed with a boy who wasn't her brother. She figured it would highlight all the things about relationships that she wasn't good at. She imagined she'd toss and turn, steal blankets, kick in her sleep, and then feel guilty about it. What she didn't count on was how it would feel to pillow her head against Jack's arm. Or how warm his skin would be or that it gave her a chance to drink in the smell of him—forests and glens and deep drowning pools—without his noticing. She hadn't known how solid he'd feel. She couldn't have guessed how he'd run his hand over her back, lazily, as if he didn't know how to stop touching her, or how she'd shiver when he did.

For the first time since he'd said the words, Hazel allowed herself to luxuriate in them. *I just want to say that I like you. I like you,* he'd told her just before she'd informed him she'd been in the Alderking's service. *I like you*, just before she admitted she had not told him a ton of stuff about herself. It had all happened so fast and it had been so hard to believe.

Which meant that she'd never told him she liked him back.

She could tell him now—wake him up and say something. Or maybe he was half awake, the way she felt half asleep. Maybe she could whisper in his ear. While she was puzzling that over, she heard footsteps on the stairs.

Her brother came into her bedroom without knocking, carrying three mugs of coffee. Behind him, lounging in the doorway, holding a mug of his own, was the horned boy. Severin, in Ben's clothes, looking as comfortable there as he ever had in the woods. Severin, whom she was supposed to hunt. Severin, whom she'd freed. Severin, who gave her a wicked smile.

Hazel pushed down blankets, yawning. Sliding out of bed, she grabbed a hair chopstick off her dresser and pointed it at him, as though it were a blade, then used it to bind up her hair.

Severin saluted her with his cup of coffee. "I see you still haven't found my sword." He raised his brows, a small smile on his face, and took a sip from his cup. Despite everything, she blushed.

Ben walked across the room and held out a cup of coffee to his sister like a peace offering.

She took a deep sip, but her exhaustion was beyond the reach of caffeine. Still, the liquid was warm, clouded with soy milk, and it washed the taste of crying out of her mouth. She sat down hard on the chair beside her mirror. "What's going on?"

"There's some kind of town meeting at your house," Ben told Jack. "About how Amanda and the stuff at school have something to do with not returning you to Faerieland. About how they want to give you back. We've got to get you out of here—we've got to get you someplace where they're not going to find you."

"What?" Jack's eyes went wide. He ran a hand over his face, over his hair. "My mom thinks that?"

"He's not a pet that you can just rehome," Hazel said.

"I don't think your parents have anything to do with this," Ben said. "I think it's a bunch of scared people being stupid."

"That's why she sent me away." Jack said the words softly, as if he wanted them to be true but was afraid of being wrong. "It wasn't because she didn't want me in the house. It was because she knew everyone was coming. But she's—but they're going to blame my family if I'm not there." He started shoving his feet into his shoes.

"Jack, everyone in town is going to be there," Hazel said. "You know this isn't your fault. This has nothing to do with you. Nothing."

"That's what I'm going to tell them," he said, and started out of the room and down the stairs.

"I'm going, too." Hazel grabbed her boots, not bothering to put them on. She turned to Ben. "You keep him here. You have to keep him here until we get back."

She ran down the stairs, Severin's voice following her. "I think

I'd rather come. I tire of people talking about me as though I am still asleep." ·

But by the time she got out to the lawn, she saw Jack starting her brother's car. He must have known where Ben kept the spare key. She barely had time to get in on the passenger side before he pulled out onto the road.

⎯

The Gordon house—cream with white trim and no peeling paint anywhere—was a shingle-style colonial in perfect condition. It sat on a slight hill, overlooking smaller and shabbier houses. It was big, old, and lovingly restored—big enough to entertain half the town, which was good because, from the look of it, half the town was inside.

Cars parked along the side of the driveway had dug tire trenches in Mr. Gordon's grass. She'd seen Jack's dad out there all through the summer, mowing and watering and seeding, the skin of his brow shining with sweat. No one crossed his front lawn, not the mailman, not Carter's or Jack's friends, not even the dog, who knew to stay in the backyard if he wanted to run. Muddy grooves slashing up all of Mr. Gordon's work unsettled Hazel. It was as though the rules had suddenly changed.

Jack's hands curled into loose fists as he walked—faster and faster.

Yanking open the front door, he stepped into the hallway. Inside, all the woodwork was painted a crisp, shiny white. It gleamed in the sun-filled rooms where people stood around or sat on folding chairs, balancing Styrofoam cups of tea on their laps. Ottomans and chairs had clearly been brought from all over the house to accommodate the sheer number of people. No one seemed to have noticed their entrance.

Mrs. Pitts, who worked at the post office, was shaking her head at Jack's mother. "Nia, it's not as though anyone prefers things to be this way. We can't help thinking that—well, what you did, it strained our relationship with the forest people. It's not a coincidence that they got worse around the time you stole Jack from them."

Was that true? Hazel had been a child herself then, barely born. When people said things used to be better, that the Folk had once been less bloodthirsty, she thought they'd been referring to decades back, not the short length of her life span.

When had things started to go bad?

"We need to put things right," said the sheriff. "In the last month, something has been going on in the woods. Some of you might have heard about a few incidents that didn't make it into the paper, and probably everyone heard about what happened at the school. Amanda Watkins wasn't the first person we found in a coma. There was a drifter kid near the edge of town a month back. The place was overgrown, vines so big they practically covered his car. And Brian Kenning two weeks later, while he was playing in the woods behind his family's place, found curled up in a pile of leaves. They're moving against us, the faeries, and if anyone hoped that the horned boy waking up meant he was going to save us, I think it's clear by now that he's not."

Hazel thought of the Alderking's promise—if she brought him Severin, things in town would go back to normal, would be *the way they once were*. As if that were a generous offer. She'd believed she knew how bad things were in Fairfold; she'd believed that she knew all its secrets. But it turned out she'd been far from right.

What would I do if you gave me leave? the little faerie had said. *What would I do if you gave me leave? What wouldn't I do?*

"We can't trust the changeling," said Mr. Schröder. "Even if they don't want him back, I don't want him here. It's too dangerous."

All through the summer she worked at Lucky's, Hazel had liked Mr. Schröder. Now she hated him.

"Jack is friends with both of my kids," Mom said. "I've known him all my life. Blaming him, just because he's the only one of the Folk most of us have ever met, is wrong. He's been raised here. He's a citizen of Fairfold, just like the rest of us."

Hazel felt a profound sense of relief that her mother had spoken, but she could tell the others weren't convinced. They'd already decided.

"The Folk were good to us in Fairfold," put in old Ms. Kirtling, standing underneath two Spanish-American War sabers, looking particularly indomitable. She'd been mayor many years ago and had, as much as anyone could recall, been decent at it. "We had an understanding. Something scuppered that."

"They haven't always been *good to us*," Jack's mother said in a quelling tone. "Don't you try to rewrite history just to make what you're asking easier. No, it's no coincidence they got worse around when Jack came to us—if you'll recall, they didn't used to take our children the way they took Carter."

"Well, maybe *good*'s too strong a word," Ms. Kirtling said. "But you can't deny that living in this town is different from other places. And you can't deny that you like it here, because you dragged that man of yours back from that Ivy League school instead of going off with him. If normal was what you wanted, then you'd be living in Chicago. And there would never have been a Jack anyway."

Beside Hazel, Jack tensed.

"Now, you got your son back from They Themselves and you even got to raise one of theirs for a good long while, despite having no claim on him except the poor judgment of his mother. But you can't have thought you'd keep him forever."

Hazel had seen the college brochures on the Gordon sideboard. His mother had absolutely been planning on forever. Looking around the room, Hazel identified teachers from school, shopkeepers, the parents of people she'd known her whole life, even a few kids. Most of them nodding, acting as if handing over Jack to the faeries was more than just the means of assuaging their fears.

After all, in Fairfold, the Folk hurt only tourists, so if you got hurt, you must be acting like a tourist, right? You must have done something wrong. Someone must have done something wrong. So long as there was someone else to blame, no one ever had to admit how powerless they were.

"It's like when you find one of those adorable little buzzard babies," said Lexie Carver, Franklin's sister and one of the youngest women there. Her family was infamous in town for eating roadkill and—if rumor was to be believed—had a bit of troll in their distant bloodline. "You want to take it home and take care of it and feed it little bits of steak, but if you do, you'll drive the hunting instinct right out. It won't be able to survive on its own later, when it needs to. He doesn't belong here, Nia. It's not good for him. It's not right."

"Well, don't you think it's a little too late for that metaphor?" Carter said, unfolding himself from where he'd apparently been hiding on the stairs. "The damage is done. She already fed him the little bits of steak or whatever. What you're really saying is that Jack won't be able to survive if we send him back."

"*Carter*," Jack's mother said, her tone indicating that he wasn't supposed to have spoken.

"Sorry," he mumbled, about to swing back to his spot on the stairs, but then he startled, noticing Jack and Hazel standing in the hallway opposite him.

"We'll take all you've said under advisement, but I hope you understand that this is a decision for the family and—" Jack's mom began, but when she followed Carter's gaze, her whole body went rigid. All around the room, the buzz of conversation flared up and then went silent as townsfolk slowly realized that the person they'd been discussing was standing there, listening to every word.

"I'll go," Jack spoke into the silence.

There was only the squeak of fingers on Styrofoam cups and the nervous swallows of tea. No one seemed to know what to say.

"Yeah," Hazel said, maybe a little bit too loudly, grabbing for his arm, pretending a misunderstanding. "You're right. Let's *go*. As in let's get out of here. Now."

"No," he said, shaking his head. "I mean, I'll go. I'll go back to them. If that's what you all want, I'll go."

His mother shook her head. "You're staying." Her voice was steely, challenging, but around the room Hazel could see people nodding to one another. They'd already accepted his offer. Those few words, in a town like this, made a compact that might not be able to be undone.

At least, if he didn't say something right then.

"You can't," Hazel said, but Jack just shook his head.

"Tell them," she pleaded. "Tell them about the Alderking and Sorrow. Tell them the truth. I can vouch for you."

"They won't believe me," he told her. "And they'll find some reason not to believe you, either."

"Nia, be reasonable. Maybe he doesn't want to stay with us. We're not his people." One of the women was speaking. Hazel didn't notice which, because the rush of blood to her head made the beating of her heart seem to drum out all other thoughts. Her chest felt too tight, and all the colors of the room seemed to smear together.

"Don't worry, Mom," Carter said. "He's not going anywhere."

Jack whirled toward his brother, clearly frustrated. "You don't get to make my decisions for me."

"How about I go? Maybe they're mad *I* got stolen back from them? Did anyone ever think of that?" Carter looked around the room defiantly, as though daring them to tell him he wasn't a prize. "Maybe they'd like to have me and not him at all."

"That's very noble," Ms. Kirtling said. "But I don't think—"

"Jack, listen to me." His mother crossed the room toward him. "You don't want anyone to get hurt when you could prevent it, even if that means putting yourself in danger. You're a good boy, a boy who puts himself before other people, and so you have, volunteering where these cowards thought they'd have to force you or trick you." She looked around the room, daring anyone to contradict her. "They believe your father and I will insist you not go at first, but in the end, we'd put the welfare of the town before your welfare. They think that when push comes to shove, we'd give you up. And I bet your other family thinks so, too."

Around the room there were whispered comments.

Jack looked stunned. His face had gone blank in what might have been surprise but was also certainly fear of what she might say next.

His mother looked over at her husband. He was standing against one wall, arms folded across his chest. "Your mom and I had a long talk about this last night," he said. "As far as we're concerned, the whole town can burn; what we care about is you."

At that, Jack laughed in clear surprise and maybe delight and maybe even a little embarrassment. It was an odd reaction, however, and Hazel could see that register on the faces of the townspeople.

Faeries laughed at funerals and wept at weddings; they didn't have human feelings for human things.

"This is turning into a real show," Ms. Holt said, pursing coral-lipsticked lips and putting a hand to her eyes. Her fingers came away wet. She let out a soft sob and looked around in confusion.

Then the sheriff began to weep. Around the room it spread. Tears sprang to eyes. Hazel's mother gave a broken wail and began to pull at her hair.

Hazel looked toward Jack. His lips were pressed into a thin line. He shook his head, as though what was happening could be denied. Sorrow was here. Hazel heard her in her head. It was like being caught in the current of a river. Like a diver who had lost any sense of direction, thrashing around, not sure which way is up…

Hazel blinked. Jack was finishing tying a knot in her hair. He whispered against her neck, "You will not weep until I give you leave."

He'd enchanted her against Sorrow's spell. She realized her cheeks were wet. She had no idea how long she'd been lost to it, but around the room people wept and wailed still.

The front door slammed open and Ben ran into the room.

"We've got to get out of here!" Ben's voice had the effect of a glass crashing to the floor and shattering. Everyone stared. "The monster at the heart in the forest. She's coming."

Standing behind him was Severin. For a moment Hazel saw him as everyone in the room must. Tall and inhumanly beautiful, horns rising from his brown curls, moss-green eyes watching them. It didn't matter that he was wearing ordinary clothes; he wasn't ordinary. He was their vision of what faeries ought to be; he was the dream that brought them to Fairfold, that caused them to want to stay, despite all the dangers.

And in that moment, Hazel knew what they must feel, the mingled hope and terror. She felt it, too. He was her prince. She was supposed to save him and he was supposed to save her right back.

"Find cover," Severin said, walking to the wall where the two sabers rested and pulling them from their sheaths in one smooth move that set the metal ringing. For a moment he held a sword in each hand, moving them as if to test their balance. Then, looking across the room, he grinned at Hazel and tossed her a blade.

She caught it before she knew that she could. It felt right in her hand, like an extension of her arm, like a missing limb restored to her. The weight of the saber was decent; it was obviously an actual sword and not some pot-metal reproduction. She wondered if it was expensive, because she was pretty sure she was going to ruin it on that monster's hide.

Her blood began to race, thrilling through her veins.

"Normal blades can't cut her," Hazel said, moving toward the horned boy.

"We just need to drive her back," he said, heading for the door. "Tire her out. She doesn't really want to hurt anyone."

Jack snorted. "Yeah, right."

Outside, wind shook the trees like rattles.

Across the room, a weeping Carter stood in front of their mother.

Jack was stooped over his father, whispering in his ear, fingers fumbling in his gray hair.

Hazel braced herself. All her doubts rose at once. Her night self might have been trained by the Alderking, but her day self didn't know how to fight any better than she had at twelve. And she didn't have a magical sword anymore. She was going to make a hash of this.

She took a deep breath, closing her eyes.

You're a knight, she told herself. *You're a knight. A real knight.*

When she opened her eyes, the monster was in the doorway. All around her, those not already weeping began to scream. Some ran for another room or the stairs, some blockaded themselves behind furniture, and a few more stood, as though turned to statues by their terror.

Hazel held her ground. When she'd seen Sorrow in the glass, she'd imagined her as hideous, something foul and twisted, but her appearance was that of a living tree, one covered in moss and dried, decaying vine. She had branches instead of bone, and roots spreading from her feet like the train of a dress. From her head rose a wild thicket of tiny branches, sticking up along one side, matted with thick clumps of dirt and leaves. Black eyes peered out of knotholes in the wood. Sticky reddish sap wetted her face, running from the knotholes of her eyes, mimicking the paths of tears. She was as beautiful as she was terrifying.

She towered over them, at least a foot higher than anyone in the room.

"Sorrel," Severin said, taking a hesitant half step toward her. Even he seemed awed, as though whatever she was when he'd been shut away from the world had grown more terrible as he slept. "Sister, please."

She didn't even seem to see him. A voice, thick with tears, spoke from throats around the room, a chorus of her grief. "I loved him and he's dead and gone and bones. I loved him and they took him away from me. Where is he? Where is he? Dead and gone and bones. Dead and gone and bones. Where is he?"

More people fell prey to the weeping. Sobs racked bodies.

Sorrow took a step toward her brother, knocking a side table to the ground. When she spoke, she sounded more like the wind blowing through trees than any human voice. "I loved him and I loved him and he's dead and gone and bones. I loved him and they took him away from me. Where is he? Where is he? Dead and gone and bones. Dead and gone and bones. My father took him. My brother killed him. Where is he? Dead and gone and bones. Dead and gone and bones."

"You would not wish this," Severin said. "You would not do this. Sister, please. Please. Do not make me try to stop you."

Deeper into the room Sorrow went, Hazel and Severin moving to either side of her. People shrieked. Ms. Kirtling, in a panic, ran across the room, right into the monster's path. A long arm with willow-twig fingers reached out and brushed Ms. Kirtling aside as one might brush a spiderweb away. But that small gesture sent Ms. Kirtling hurtling into the wall. Plaster cracked, and with a moan, she slid to the floor.

In the new-formed crack, moss and mold began to spill into the room, like water into the hull of a leaking boat.

On the other side of the room, a woman began to cough up dirt.

Without any idea of what else to do, Hazel slammed her saber into the monster's side.

All her life, she'd heard about the monster in the heart of the forest. She'd imagined that if only the monster was slain, then faeries would go back to being only tricksy and magical. She'd imagined it enough times that even though she knew better, some part of her believed that when her blade hit the monster's flank, it would cut deeply.

It left no mark at all, but it did make Sorrow turn toward her, long fingers reaching. Hazel ducked, feeling the brush of dry leaves and smelling fresh-turned earth. She wasn't quite fast enough to keep Sorrow from catching a clump of her hair. A few strands ripped out and drifted through the air like sparks. The monster used the rest of it like a rope, to hurl Hazel, toppling her into a sofa, saber flying from Hazel's hand to clang against the floor.

Bruised, she pushed herself up. Her head hurt and her bones felt jangly, as if they no longer fit together. She made herself cross to where her saber was, made herself lift it and turn toward the monster.

Severin had leaped onto her back, holding on to the branches and vines, but she shook him off, then thundered toward where he fell. He rolled and rose to his feet, moving with a swiftness and sureness she had never seen equaled. His blade whirled through the air. He was a magnificent swordsman. And still his blade glanced off her. And still she knocked him back.

It was just then that Jack's dad came running down the stairs, a hunting rifle gripped in his hands. He set the butt against his shoulder pocket and gazed down the sight, aiming for Sorrow.

"Please, no," Severin called from the floor, but Hazel wasn't sure Mr. Gordon even heard him. He pulled the trigger.

The gun was loud in the room, like thunder, rocking Hazel back onto her heels. But the bullets struck the monster's bark and slid off as though they were mere pebbles hurled by a child. Sorrow went for Mr. Gordon.

Carter intercepted, swinging a candlestick at her, but the creature wrapped its long fingers around him, pulling him to her. Hazel raced toward them, slamming her saber into Sorrow's back. The monster didn't even seem to notice.

"Hey!" Jack yelled, and then something spattered the monster. The stinging smell of alcohol filled the air. He'd thrown brandy at her, brandy from his parents' now-open liquor cabinet.

"I'll set you on fire," he said, holding up a book of matches in trembling fingers. "Get away from them. Get out of here."

The monster seemed to regard him for a long moment, letting Carter slump to the ground. He was unconscious, a green stain spreading across his lips.

It had happened so fast.

Hazel heard her mother scream from the other side of the room.

She glanced to one side and saw that Ben was dragging her behind the old upright piano.

Jack struck a match.

The monster rushed at him, fast enough that the flame flickered out in his hand. Hazel threw herself between them, raising her saber, going for the creature's eyes. The blow grazed Sorrow's cheek, but no more sap ran.

Jack fumbled to light another match, but as he did, the room became full of rushing wind. Somewhere in the distance, crows called to one another.

With a howl, Severin launched himself onto her back again. Holding on to her branches, he pressed the saber to her throat, clearly hoping to still her, clearly hoping she might be afraid. But she shook herself, trying to throw him off. Hazel tried to slash at her, tried to cut her arms, her sides, even her impossibly long twig fingers. No blow made a single mark. Hazel was batted against a wall, thrown into a small knot of people who screamed as she fell against them.

She was sore all over. Standing took a great effort. Her head rang, and dizziness threatened to overwhelm her. She blinked blood and sweat out of her eyes. She was bleeding from a dozen cuts she didn't recall getting. She had no idea how many more times she could do this.

Severin crashed against the floor, rolling into a stand. He was still moving, but Hazel could see that some part of him had given up.

Then she heard the sound of the piano.

She turned, and Sorrow knocked her off her feet again. Hazel hit the wood floor of the house hard, slamming down onto it, the breath knocked out of her. She turned on her side and saw her brother sitting on the bench, his broken fingers splayed across the keys. Playing music.

The notes swelled around them. It was as though Ben was playing the sound of weeping. Sorrow howled into the air.

Then he seemed to slip. The music faltered. He couldn't do it. His broken fingers, the ones he'd never let set right, the ones he'd never let heal, weren't nimble enough for the piano. She shouldn't have been staring in astonishment; she should have been using that frozen moment he'd given her. Hazel pushed herself to her feet, hoping it wasn't too late.

She ran for Sorrow, but the monster was ready for her. It snatched her up and threw her down onto the sofa so hard that the legs cracked. It rolled backward, taking Hazel with it. Dazed, she looked up at the creature leaning over her. Branches and moss and shining eyes.

"Dead and gone and bones. Dead and gone and bones," Sorrow said softly. A long arm shot out toward Hazel.

Then Ben started to sing. Formless notes, like the ones he might have played had his fingers worked, rose from his throat. It sounded almost like weeping, like her wails. It was grief, terrible and immobilizing. Despite the knot in her hair and Jack's spell, Hazel felt tears in the back of her throat, felt them burn the backs of her eyes.

A keening, terrible sound came from Sorrow. She thrashed back and forth, knocking down chairs. The sharp broken ends of branches ripped the upholstery of the couch. She howled with grief.

"Ben," Hazel yelled. "You're making it worse."

But Ben didn't stop. He sang on. People wailed in despair, in rage. Tears wet their clothes, soaked their hair. They collapsed in heaps. They slammed fists against the walls. Sorrow thundered toward the piano, knocking it to one side. It fell with a terrible crash. Her branching fingers covered her face. The monster's shoulders shook with weeping.

And then Hazel understood. Ben was taking her through the storm of grief. He was singing her through the rage and despair. He was singing her through the terrible loneliness, because there was no way to shut off grief, no way to cast it aside or fight against it. The only way to end grief was to go through it.

As she realized that, his song began to change. It grew softer, sweeter, like the morning after a long cry, when your head still hurt but your heart was no longer broken. Like flowers blooming on a grave. One by one, around the room, the weeping stopped.

The monster grew still.

Ben ceased his singing. He slumped down onto the piano bench, exhausted. Reaching up, his mother twined her fingers with his. Mom was still crying.

For a moment there was only silence. Sorrow looked around her with her strange knothole black eyes, as though waking from a long dream. Severin pushed himself to his feet and walked to her.

She stared down at him, reached out with her long twig fingers.

This time she seemed conscious, aware. Her expression was unreadable. Hazel had no idea whether she would strike at him or not.

He reached up a hand and touched her mossy cheek. For a moment the monster leaned into his touch, almost nuzzling. Then, pulling away, she clomped out through the doorway, past the smashed furniture and stunned townsfolk, and was gone.

CHAPTER 19

H azel dropped the saber. It made an echoing clang. Her knuckles felt bruised. *Everything* felt bruised, but at least her bones
were intact. The sitting room of the Gordons' house was a mess of
broken frames, ottomans ripped open, leaves and dirt strewn across
the scratched wood floor.

A woman was moaning from one of the corners. Someone else
was weeping, sobs that no longer sounded forced from her throat.
She was crying all on her own.

"We need the monster's blood," Jack said to her from the floor,
where he was cradling an unconscious Carter. Hazel turned toward
him, startled, because he wasn't normally so vicious. Seeing her
expression, he shook his head. "That's what you said would wake
these people up, what's going to fix Carter. *We need her blood.*"

Hazel nodded. Of course. That was what the Alderking had told her. It was a puzzle, the math kind you got in school: To get the blood of a monster, you need a magical sword; to get a magical sword, you need to know whom your secret night self is in league with; to know whom your secret night self is in league with, you need to know who'd want to free Severin; to know who'd want to free Severin, you needed...

"Come," said Ben. His voice sounded low and rough, as though he'd hurt it singing as he had. He reached out a hand toward Jack, gripping his shoulder. "Let's get out of here. We're all looking for the same thing now, and we don't have much time to find it."

"Heartsworn," Severin said. He nodded toward Hazel, a dip of his head, an acknowledgment. "You fought well."

Instinct had propelled her into moving in a way she hadn't known she could. So long as she didn't think too much. The moment she considered why she was holding the blade at a certain angle or what she was going to do next, she'd faltered, all the momentum gone out of her. Fear had done a pretty good job of keeping her attention on the present, but now that she wasn't scared, she couldn't make her body do any more tricks.

Jack stood up reluctantly. All around them the people of the town were standing, too, coming down from the second floor or out from where they'd hidden, fleeing across the lawn, to their cars, to their homes, away away away. "Ben's right. We should get out of here."

At the door, Hazel looked back. Across the room, Mom was

standing, hand on a wall sconce, using it to keep herself upright. She stared at her children as though she'd never seen them before. Hazel turned to Jack. He was watching his own parents kneeling over Carter, his mother trying to lift her son's body. Hazel could see the anguish on Jack's face. His father had said the town could burn for all he cared, but she was sure he'd never meant Carter.

"It's not your fault," Hazel told him.

Jack nodded, and they walked out, past the deep, muddy tracks Sorrow had left in the grass, so different from the trample of footprints. Looking back at the house, at the sagging, broken boards of the porch, Hazel wondered how the town would explain this. Would the residents of Fairfold have to confront the bargain they made living there? Face that not all faeries were content to sup milk from chipped bowls, that some wanted blood?

"You okay to ride in a car again?" Ben asked the horned boy as they got closer to his Volkswagen.

"*Your* car?" Severin asked, following Ben's gaze. The wariness on Severin's face nearly made Hazel laugh, despite everything. Finally, he inclined his head. "If that is to be my fate, then I accept it."

The horned boy got in on the passenger side, and Hazel and Jack slid into the back. She took Jack's hand and squeezed it.

He squeezed back once, then let her fingers fall from his.

They drove back to the house quietly. The more time passed, the more Hazel's head throbbed, the more her arms felt bruised from where she'd hit the couch. One of her ankles was swollen and a little unsteady. Her body hurt, and at nightfall, if she slept, she would become someone else. Someone with different memories and maybe different allegiances.

She couldn't help thinking of the dream she'd had, of herself as one of the Alderking's company, just as cruel as the rest. Hazel wasn't sure she would like the person she became at night.

Once they got through the door of her house, Hazel went to the sink and took a long drink of water out of the faucet. Then she pulled herself up onto the counter.

Ben put the kettle on the stove and got down honey from the cabinet, then went to the bathroom for peroxide and bandages.

"What you did back there," Hazel told him softly. "That was amazing."

He shrugged. "I'm surprised it worked."

"That makes it even more amazing." She wiped her hands on her jeans.

Severin went to the table and straddled a chair backward, sitting on it as one might sit astride a faerie horse. A bruise was blooming along his jaw. Jack stood in the middle of the room, looking lost.

"So, Heartsworn," Severin said finally. "But there's more you're not telling us, isn't there, Hazel? I said you fought well and you did. I gave you the other sword because I saw from your stance that you could fight. Better it to be in the hands of someone with a little train- ing than none. But the *way* you fought, I recognize it. It's no mortal way of fighting."

Hazel reached up into one of the cabinets and took out a bowl. She poured peroxide into it and wet a kitchen towel to rub over her cuts. This was the moment she'd dreaded, the moment when everything came tumbling out. She didn't look at any of them as she started to speak. "At the revel, I discovered I've been in the service of the Alderking for the past five years. As soon as I go to sleep at night, I wake up and I'm someone else. And that person, I don't know what she's done, but she's been trained to fight, and I guess my body remembers that, even when the rest of me doesn't."

At least Jack already knew. At least Jack wasn't staring at her the way Ben was, as though she'd become a stranger.

"You have to understand," Hazel said, forcing herself to go on. "I made a bargain a long time ago, but I know—"

"You made a bargain with the Alderking?" Ben shouted, surprising her into flinching. "You grew up in this town. You know better."

Hazel watched the towel turn pink with blood as she drew it over her arm. "I was a kid. I was stupid. What do you want me to say?"

"Why did you do it?" Ben asked. "What did you bargain for?"

On the stove, the kettle began to howl.

After a few long moments, Hazel hopped down from the counter and turned off the stove. "Back when we were hunting faeries and having adventures," she said, turning to her brother. "I didn't want to stop. You know I didn't want to stop."

She expected him to look angry as he realized how stupid she'd been. She didn't expect him to look afraid. *"Hazel, what did you do?"*

"I made a bargain so that we wouldn't have to stop. You said that if you were better at music, we could keep going." There was a child's pleading in her voice and she hated it.

"You did this for me?" Ben asked, horror plain on his face.

Hazel shook her head ferociously. He'd got it all wrong. "No, I did it for *me*. I didn't want to stop. I was selfish."

"You got me that scholarship. That was you." His voice had dropped low. He almost sounded as though he was saying the words to himself.

"Ben..."

"What was the exact nature of this bargain?" Severin asked, his cool indifference a relief.

"I promised that I would give up seven years of my life. I thought it meant I would just die sooner. Like years of life were something they would shave off the end and bottle up somehow."

Severin nodded, his expression grim.

Ben didn't look as if he thought dying seven years too soon made for a better bargain. He looked like he wanted to shake her. Hazel wished she could just stop talking. She wished she could make all her mistakes go away.

"That's why you wouldn't tell me any of this," he said.

"That's why I wouldn't tell you any of this. It doesn't matter why I did it. And anyway, I obviously ruined everything that was supposed to happen in Philadelphia anyway. I ruined it and it doesn't matter what I intended, because I ruined it."

"What are you talking about?" He was staring at her as though he really had no idea.

"You know what I did." She hated having to explain. She hated that Jack was looking at her, all concern, and how differently he'd see her once he realized what she'd done. He'd said that anyone who offered up their heart on a silver platter deserved what they got, but he was wrong.

"Hazel, what you *did*? You mean when Kerem kissed you?"

"Obviously that's what I mean," Hazel bit out.

Ben threw up his hands, exasperated. "That's not what *you* did—that's what *he* did, because he was a jerk and he was thirteen and totally confused about everything. He was freaking out. Look, I've talked to him on Facebook and he's fine now. He's got a boyfriend, he's out, his parents came around. But back then he was freaking out and his parents were freaking out and he wanted to prove he didn't like me. You were there. That's all."

"I know what happened because of that kiss," Hazel said, keeping her gaze on the kettle, fixing cups of tea.

Ben's voice had gone soft. "That wasn't because...you can't blame yourself because I lost control. I kept losing control. I wanted to go to music school because I was already afraid of how much I was losing control. When I saw Kerem with you, the first thing I thought was that maybe I'd enchanted him to like me. Because I'd liked him *so much*. After what happened, after my teacher—look what I did with my hand. That was a good thing. What happened in Philadelphia was my fault and no one else's."

It was on Hazel's lips to say that no, it was all *her* fault, and then she realized how ridiculous that would sound. They had been hiding secrets from each other, resenting each other, and it had all been for nothing. Ben had never blamed her. For so long, her determination to hide this from Ben had been the center of so many of her choices. She felt almost impossibly light without the burden of it. "Smashing your fingers wasn't a good thing, Ben. What you can do is incredible."

"You sold seven fucking years of your life for my scholarship and you never even told me." Ben still sounded angry, but not with her. "You should have told me. Maybe we could have figured something out."

"Well, we *have* to figure something out," Jack said, interrupting them. "Tell them the rest."

And Hazel did. She told them about the messages, about waking up with mud on her feet, afraid that her debt had come due; she told them about the revel and the Alderking's words. In turn, Severin told them his story, with Ben nodding along.

"Why now?" Ben asked. "That's the question, right? What changed? What is the Alderking up to?"

"He found some way to control Sorrow," Hazel said. "Isn't that it?"

Jack shook his head. "We shouldn't be thinking about what changed recently. We should be looking back. Something set him off, made him lose his leash on the wild fey like the townspeople said at the meeting. Eight years ago, the Court in the East was taken over. Could that have pissed him off enough?"

"Too recent," Ben said.

"Who rules there now?" Severin asked, but Jack held up his hands helplessly.

"I don't pay attention to names," he said. "None of it means anything to me."

Severin nodded thoughtfully. "I still have some contacts in my father's court. No one with any real power, but some of the wild fey who knew my mother spoke with me. They told me that a little more than a sesquidecade back, the Alderking took another one of the wild fey as a lover. She tarried with a mortal, though, and bore him child. That's around when other mortals began dying in greater numbers, yes? And that's when he began in earnest to find a way to control my sister, turning her dead husband's bones into an enchanted ring."

"A sesqui-what?" Hazel asked, a shiver of horror going through her. She'd seen a bone ring on the Alderking's finger, but never would have supposed it was carved from a corpse.

"Sesquidecade. Fifteen years," Jack said, mouth moving like he tasted something bad. "It's an SAT word. And the woman you're talking about is my mother."

Ben's eyebrows went up. Even Severin looked surprised.

"Your mother?" Hazel asked. She remembered the elf woman in the faerie court, clutching at Jack's sleeve. There had been real fear in her face.

Jack nodded. "That's why she hid me. She was the Alderking's lover, but he wasn't very nice, so she took up with a human and wound up with me. That's why she wanted to leave me with humans, to keep me out of his path. At least until he forgot the slight."

Hazel wondered if he'd ever told anyone this story before.

Considering the way he was looking at his cup, not meeting any of their eyes, she suspected he hadn't.

Severin's expression was all regret. "If your mother broke faith with him, if she spurned him for a mortal, his vengeance would have been terrible. Not just on the town, not just on that mortal man, but on your mother as well. He would have hurt her."

Jack looked sick. "No. She would have told me."

"That seems like a good reason to want him dead," Ben said. "Could she be the one with the sword?"

Hazel hesitated, then spoke. "She did say an odd thing to me. When I told her I was there looking for Ainsel at the revel, she seemed to know something, but kept implying I should shut up."

Jack rubbed a frustrated hand over his mouth. "She made that odd remark about my being there to save you. Does this mean that people at that town meeting were right? This is all my fault?"

"No," Hazel said. "Never. This is never your fault."

"But Jack's mother—what's her name?" Severin asked.

"Eolanthe," Jack said.

"I knew her, once." Severin gave Jack a strange look, one that made Hazel think he knew her better than a little. "She's very beautiful, very clever, but no swordswoman. If she managed to take Heartsworn from Hazel, whether by trickery or force or out of the generosity of her night heart, she would still need someone to wield it."

"So, okay, play this through," Ben said. "Jack tells his elf mother offhandedly about this girl he knows, maybe says she found a sword. So Eolanthe decides to, what? Persuade Hazel to break the curse on Severin? Free a sleeping prince of Faerie—but then not give him the one thing that would let him face his father and defeat Heartseeker?"

Jack nodded. He'd started pacing the floor, not looking at any of them, caught up in his own thoughts. "I might have said something about Hazel and her sword, when I was younger. And Hazel probably wouldn't need a lot of convincing to break Severin's curse."

Hazel laughed. "Ben would need even less."

Her brother made a face at her.

"Your mother doesn't seem like the sort of person who'd ally with anyone," Hazel said. "Least of all me. She didn't like me much."

"What about just taking the sword?" Ben asked. "Maybe she stole it and then left a bunch of cryptic crap to confuse us. Made us chase our own tails while she put her plan in motion."

"So what about Severin's curse, then?" Hazel asked. "Why bother breaking it?"

"It could be a distraction for the Alderking," Jack said, looking over at Ben with a frown, as though they were making a particularly devious plan rather than guessing at one. "Plus it's the proof that Hazel had Heartsworn. Only Heartsworn could smash the casket and break the curse. So no point in stealing a sword until you're sure."

Severin raised his delicate brows. "Then we are back to her needing a swordsman."

Ben shrugged. "You said she was pretty and clever. Maybe she found someone who was good with a weapon and wanted to stop the Alderking. There have to be a few bravos at court, right?"

"Well, there's at least one," Hazel said with a snort that had nothing to do with humor. "I want to stop him."

"There's a way to send my mother a message," Jack said, going to the cutlery drawer and pulling out a slender steak knife. "Blood summons blood." He went out the kitchen door to the backyard. "If she has the sword, I'll promise her anything for its return. If she wants me, I will be hers. Whatever must be sworn, I will swear it."

"Jack," Hazel said. "You don't have to do this."

"It might not be her," said Ben. "It could be someone none of us has ever met—it could be someone that none of us *recall* meeting."

"Or it could be the person who hid her son from the Alderking and has good reason to hate him. Which is more likely?" Jack's face was haunted. "If we don't get that sword, Carter is as good as dead."

"Jack," Hazel said again, but Jack didn't turn, didn't flinch. He thrust the point of the knife into his index finger, lifted up a leaf, and wrote on it with blood, the way anyone else might scrawl on paper with a pen. Then he whispered something over it and sent it swirling up into the air.

But Hazel had seen his offer: *Mother, if you have Heartsworn, bring it to the house at the end of River Road and whatever you ask of me will be yours.*

⌒

After the message was sent, they waited.

Ben thought he remembered the name Ainsel from somewhere and, taking his mug of honeyed tea, went to look through some of the books in the den to see if he could find the word in one of their indexes. Severin went out to the shed to collect Ben's ax and see what other weaponry he could sharpen into usefulness.

Without her secrets, Hazel felt a horrible, anxious vulnerability. Shadows waited to flood in. To keep busy, she went to find all the iron and scissors in the house, all the salt and grave dirt, all the oatmeal and berries and charms. After Severin brought the weapons back inside, she spread some on every lintel and across each doorway.

When that was done, she sat down on one of the chairs and dozed. Whatever magic allowed her to serve the Alderking without sleeping seemed to be wearing off. Exhaustion overtook her.

She woke to find the sun going down in a blaze of molten gold. She heard Severin's voice upstairs, a low warm mumble, and then a bark of laughter from her brother.

"Hey," Jack said softly, coming over to where she was. His jeans were hanging low on his hip bones, exposing a slice of warm brown skin where his T-shirt rode up. She imagined resting her hand there and curled her fingers to keep from touching him. "I just came to wake you before you...changed."

Hazel flinched. She'd nearly forgotten.

"None of this is your fault," he said. "Just so we're clear."

"I lost the sword. I freed Severin. I made a stupid bargain. It's at least somewhat my fault." She began to finger-comb her hair and then braid it out of her face. "But I'm not letting her take you back if you don't want to go."

He gave her a smile that wasn't really a smile at all. "Eh, it wouldn't be so bad. I wouldn't have to study for the SATs or get a summer job or figure out my major. I can drink Elderflower wine all day, dance all through the night, and sleep on a bower of roses."

Hazel made a face. "I'm pretty sure there are some colleges where you can do that. I bet there are some colleges where you can *major* in that."

"Maybe," he said, then shook his head. "It's always been an elaborate game of pretend here in Fairfold, you know? Pretend you're human. Pretend no one thinks it's weird when Mom calls the relatives and tries to explain how she actually had twins, but one was really sick and that's why she didn't tell anyone about him. Pretend everyone believes her. Pretend that Dad doesn't think it's strange that I exist at all. Pretend no one in town stares. Pretend that I haven't been sneaking off to the woods for all these years. Pretend I'm never tempted to leave. Pretend I can't do magic. My life has always been a powder keg waiting for a match."

"Well, hello, match," Hazel said, pointing to herself with both thumbs, but she smiled as she did it, hoping to take the sting out of the words.

"Hello, match." Somehow his snagged-silk voice gave them an entirely different meaning. She thought about waking in the forest, about the smell of the pine needles in the air and the feeling of his mouth on hers with the uneven ground rough against her back, and squirmed.

But they were far from the heady, pine-soaked woods.

And she still hadn't told him the thing.

"I like you," Hazel blurted abruptly, the words coming out all wrong, like an accusation.

Jack raised his eyebrows. "Really?"

"Why else would I say it?" Now he knew and now they could go back to talking about colleges or killing things or strategy or something—*anything*—else. Now they could go back to worrying about his being taken away to Faerie. At least he knew. At least she'd said it.

"If you like me, why do you sound so mad about it?"

"I'm not *angry*," she said. She sounded angry, though. She sounded furious.

He sighed. "You don't have to tell me that you like me. Just because I am having a bad day or because I told you—you're not obligated."

"I know that." She did. She did know that. She'd loved Jack for ages, loved him for so long that her love was an ache that never left her body. Jack, who kissed her like nothing else mattered. Jack, who knew her too well. She'd loved him and had believed he couldn't ever like her, had believed it so firmly that even with the memory of his saying he did, she still felt as though he was going to snatch it back, declare that he'd made a mistake.

He probably should take it back. She was a mess. She couldn't even tell a boy she liked him the way she was supposed to.

"You don't owe this to me," Jack said. "And if this is because you don't think it matters, since I won't be here to find out you lied—"

She realized abruptly that he really didn't believe her. Her declaration was going even worse than she'd thought. "No. No, I'm not lying."

"Hazel," he started, voice flat.

"Look," she told him, interrupting, hoping she'd get it right this time. "After I made that bargain, I thought I was going to be taken away by the Folk. And I could have been! I didn't want to get close to anyone, okay? I'm not good at getting close to people. I don't have boyfriends. I don't date. I hook up with boys at parties, and I definitely don't tell them that I like them. I'm not good at it, okay? That doesn't mean it's not true."

"Okay," Jack said. "But I've known you all my life, Hazel. Your brother is my best friend. I hear the stuff you say to each other, and I hear a lot of the stuff you don't say, too. I know you don't want to get close to anyone, but it's not just because of the faeries."

"What do you mean?"

He shook his head. "We shouldn't talk about this."

"No," she said, although she felt cold all over. "Say what it is you're thinking."

He sighed. "I mean, you're the one who showed me how to forage for food in the woods. We were, what, nine or ten when you showed me how to find stuff to eat? Do you remember why you'd learned that—why you were such an expert? Or how about the time that you stayed for dinner at my house and hid food in your napkin to eat later because you weren't sure your parents would remember to feed you, but we all were supposed to pretend things were fine? The parties your parents used to throw were legendary, but I've heard the stories about you and your brother eating food out of the dog's bowl. Heard you tell the story, too, like it was a joke. You talk about your childhood like it was just wild, bohemian fun, but I remember how much it wasn't fun for you."

Hazel blinked at him. She'd been so good at shutting out memories she didn't like, so good at locking them away. None of what he said should have surprised her; they were only facts about her life, after all. But she found herself surprised anyway. All that stuff was so long ago that she'd felt like it didn't matter anymore. "My parents are fine now. They grew up. They got better at stuff."

He nodded. "I know. I just also know you always think it's down to you to fix things, but it doesn't have to be. Some people are trustworthy."

"I was going to save Fairfold."

"You can't save a place. Sometimes you can't even save a person."

"Can you save yourself?" Hazel asked. It felt important, as though his answer would be *the* answer, as though somehow he might really know.

He shrugged. "We've all got to try, right?"

"So do you believe me? That I like you?" she asked. But he didn't get to answer.

Ben strode into the room triumphantly, holding a book up in the air. "I found it. I found it! I am a genius! A memory genius. I am like one of those people who count cards in Vegas!"

Hazel stood up. "Ainsel?"

He nodded. "And by the way, Hazel, this was *in your room*."

She recognized it with alarm. The spine read, FOLKLORE OF ENGLAND. It was the book she'd found in the trunk underneath her bed. Had she not understood its significance?

Her brother flipped it open. "There's this story from Northumberland about a little kid who won't go to bed. His mother tells him that if he stays up, the faeries are going to come and take him away. He doesn't believe her, so he keeps on playing anyway as the hearth fire burns down. In time, a faerie does show up, a pretty little faerie kid who wants to play with him. The boy asks the faerie's name, and she says, "Ainsel." Then she asks the boy's name and he says "*my* ainsel" with a wicked grin.

"So they play a little more, and the boy tries to get the fire going. He stokes it, but one of the dying embers rolls out and burns the faerie child's toe. She howls like crazy, and the huge, scary faerie mother barrels down the chimney. The boy hops into bed, but he can still hear the faerie mother demanding her child name the one who burned her. 'My ainsel! My ainsel!' the faerie girl howls. Apparently, 'my ainsel' is what 'my own self' sounds like when said with a Northumbrian accent, so hearing that, the faerie mother becomes very stern. 'Well, then,' she says, grabbing the faerie child by the ear and dragging her up into the chimney, 'you've got no one but yourself to

blame.' And that's the whole story. Ainsel. My ainsel. My own self."
Ben bowed exaggeratedly.

"But what does that mean?" Jack asked.

Myself. My own self.

"Give me a pen," Hazel said, in a voice that trembled only slightly.
She opened the book to a blank page in the back.

Ben got a Sharpie out of the kitchen junk drawer and handed it
over. "What's wrong?"

Taking the marker in her right hand, she wrote *seven years to
pay your debts*. Then, switching hands, she wrote the words with
her left.

It was the same handwriting she'd seen on the walnut messages,
the same handwriting that had marked AINSEL on her wall. For a
long moment, Hazel just stared at the page in front of her. The word
scratched in mud on her wall wasn't the name of a conspirator or
enemy. It was a signature. Her own.

There was no one else. No shadowy figure pulling the strings, leaving clues, guiding her hand. Just herself, discovering the way to open
the casket, figuring out the value of the sword she had. Just herself,
realizing what the Alderking intended to do to Fairfold and trying to
stop it.

My Ainsel. My own self.

A coded message, because the Alderking had forbidden her from
revealing the nature of their bargain to her daylight self, so all she'd
been able to do was leave a few desperate riddles and hints.

She recalled what Severin had said about being woken. He'd

heard her voice, but *by the time I came awake—truly awake—the sky was bright and you were gone.* Of course she'd been gone; she'd had to rush to her bed and become day Hazel. She must have barely made it there—not with enough time to even clean the mud off her feet. Panicking, writing on the wall, dumping a book into the newly empty trunk. She'd smashed the case with some plan in mind, some idea of bargaining with Severin or returning his sword to him. Whatever she'd intended, when he hadn't woken, she must have realized that her ownership of Heartsworn would be discovered.

So she'd hidden it somewhere no one would think to look, someplace where the Alderking couldn't find it, even if he found her.

And then—well, Hazel had stayed up through the whole next night, following Ben into the woods and being menaced by Severin. She'd slept for only a few moments, near dawn. Only long enough for her night self to write the note that Hazel had found in her book bag: *Full moon overhead; better go straight to bed.*

But Hazel hadn't obeyed. She'd stayed awake throughout a whole other evening, giving night Hazel no time to retrieve the sword, no time for an alternate plan, no time for anything.

The first note—the one in the walnut, the one she found at Lucky's—might have been her night self's test, to see if she could send a message to her day self without being caught by the Alderking. And the next one would have been at the height of her panic, when she wasn't sure whether she was about to be discovered and wouldn't want to leave anything incriminating in case one of the Folk saw it.

She wouldn't want to give her day self so many clues that she'd put herself in danger without knowing all of the story, either.

What a mess she'd made of things.

Severin came down the stairs, holding a spear-like thing he'd made from saw blades and a wooden shaft of a rake. "Someone's outside," he said.

Hazel went to the window and saw them circling the house. Knights on faerie steeds, Jack's mother behind one of them in a green-and-gold gown that swirled through the air. Eolanthe swung down from the horse, striding toward the house.

"Mom," Jack said, and went to the door, throwing it open.

"Wait," called Hazel. "She doesn't have it."

But Ben had already scattered the salt and berries with his foot so that the faerie woman could step inside. Her eyes were silver and her hair was the green of new grass. She looked toward Severin and her smile turned frosty.

"I thought I might find you here," she said.

He made a small, courtly bow. "My lady Eolanthe. To what do we owe this pleasure? Those are the king's guards with you and I do not hold favor with the king."

"You must understand," she said, turning toward Jack, who was standing, frozen, his hand still on the doorknob. "When I told him where his son was, he promised to spare mine. He has guaranteed your safety. Jack, you don't know what this means."

Hazel already suspected they'd been wrong, grievously wrong, about Eolanthe having Heartsworn. Now she realized they'd also been wrong about her loyalties. They'd been wrong about everything.

"How could you do this?" Jack spat out the words. He was shaking all over, as though he was going to shake apart. "How could you call yourself my mother and bargain away my friends' lives?"

She took a step back, unnerved by the force of his anger. "For your safety! I have but a few moments to bring you from this place. Come. Whatever you think of me, you will be able to do more for your friends if you're not clapped in chains with them."

"No," Jack said. "I'm not going with you. No."

"Heed her," said Severin. "There is no shame in living. Without Heartsworn, we cannot win."

But Jack only shook his head.

Hazel had to do something, but she could think of only one possible move. She remembered the story Leonie had told her, the one where Jack commanded Matt to punch himself in the face and Matt had done it. She remembered the way Jack had knotted her hair and commanded her not to cry.

"Jack," Hazel said, grabbing hold of his arm so he had to look at her. "Can you make me sleep?"

His eyes were full of anguish. He didn't seem to understand what she was saying.

His mother frowned. "Jack, you must come away with me."

"*Can you make me sleep?*" she asked again, raising her voice to a near shout. "Like a spell—like the way you made it so I couldn't cry.

It's still night, so if I sleep and then wake up again, I won't be myself. I'll be her. The other Hazel. She'll tell you everything."

They all stared at her with blank incomprehension, but she couldn't say more with Eolanthe standing right in front of her, ready to tattle to the Alderking.

"What if night Hazel isn't entirely on our side?" Severin asked, raising a single arched brow. "At least our Hazel will fight for us."

She smiled at that—their prince calling her *our Hazel*. Just as in one of their stories.

"Hazel's always on our side," said Jack. He touched her brow gently. She thought he would give her the command then, but instead he leaned in and kissed her. She felt the soft pressure of his mouth against hers, felt the smile stretching his lips. Then he pulled back a little ways and spoke. "Sleep," he said. "Sleep."

She felt the magic rolling over her, a vast wave, and at the last second, even though she'd asked him to do it, she fought the enchantment. Trying to keep her eyes open, she surged up off the cushion. Then she staggered forward and fell. The last thing she remembered was Ben's shout and Jack's hand catching her moments before she slammed her head against the floor.

CHAPTER 20

Between one blink and the next, Hazel woke.

She was marching, along with several of the Alderking's knights, through a cave-like opening. Overhead, milky light filtered through the leaves and the wind made the branches dance. Day had come. Then they moved into the darkness of the hollow hill, full of worming roots above them, like pale waving arms, and thorned vines blooming with strange white flowers crawling up the walls. Blue-footed mushrooms lined their path.

And creaking along behind her, guarded by ten knights on each side, was a cage—black metal twisted in the form of bent branches set on large, ornate wheels. It held Severin and her brother. Ben sat on the floor of the cage, looking terrified but unhurt. Severin paced it like a beast in a zoo, his rage seeming to radiate out. His cheek was slashed, and there was a dark stain in his midsection that even at this distance she knew was probably blood.

Her step faltered. Why was she free when they'd been captured, when they'd fought? What had she done?

Why hadn't she fought with them? Why wasn't she in that cage?

"Sir Hazel?" an unfamiliar voice asked. She realized she was standing among the Alderking's knights, dressed like one of them— dressed in the stiff doublet she'd found where her sword used to be, the one that had been beside the book. Looking at the knight who had spoken, she realized she wore the mirror of his garb, although he had plates of shining golden armor down one of his arms, an exaggeratedly large piece at his elbow, and a golden plate along his lower jaw. It was strange, menacing, and beautiful.

Marcan, Jack had called him. He'd been at the full-moon revel.

No, she wasn't just standing near the Alderking's knights, wasn't just dressed like them. She *was* one of them. That was why Marcan was saying her name in concerned tones. He knew her—knew nighttime Hazel, knight Hazel, the Hazel who had served the Alderking and served him still, the one who must have been standing in her place just moments before. She remembered Marcan's words from the revel: *Hazel doesn't mind coming with me. We've crossed swords before.*

"I'm fine," she said. She reached for her belt automatically, but there was no sword at her hip. Of course not; her blade was gone. She'd hidden it.

"You're in a lot of trouble," Marcan said under his breath. "Be careful."

The procession halted in front of the throne of the Alderking, where he waited with his courtiers. Beside him was a casket of black metal and crystal, this one even more intricately wrought than the one that had rested in the woods. Beside it, standing with a proprietary hand on one glassy pane, stood a small wizened creature with a cloud of silver hair and a scarlet doublet. He wore intricate jeweled bracers at his wrists and a pin attached to the cloth of his shirt with wings that moved in the wind, as though a gold-and-pearl moth with gemstone eyes could be alive. *Grimsen*, she recalled, from Severin's story. The blacksmith whose powers were so great that the Alderking stole him away from the old court.

Grimsen, who, with his brothers, had made Heartseeker and Heartsworn. Who could coax metals into any shape. She must have stared at him too fixedly, because he turned toward her and gave her a mendacious smile. His black eyes gleamed.

Frantically, she searched the crowd of grim courtiers for Jack— and spotted him, riding before his elf mother on a dappled faerie steed. He wore an expression that was no expression at all, a curious unreadable blankness. Her gaze rested on him, until he finally noticed. His eyes widened and he opened his palms and mimed looking down at them.

Confused, she did the same.

Her heart sped all over again. On her right, in black ink, like that of a Sharpie, were the words *carrots* and *iron rods* in the same scratchy handwriting of all the other messages. And on her left were the words *Remember to kneel* in a familiar hand—her own.

The first two clues were a reference to that story about the farmer and the boggart, the one she thought hadn't made any sense. Those were the same words that had been circled in mud, but she no more understood the clue now than she had then.

And the third clue—a reminder about etiquette?

Scanning the crowd, she looked for Jack again, her eyes sweeping over a bent-backed woman holding a gnarled cane, a long-nosed green man with a shock of black hair, a golden creature with long grasshopper-like legs.

No one met her eyes. Jack wasn't there.

"Sir Hazel," the Alderking said. "The sun is risen and so you are no longer my little marionette."

Several of the courtiers, some in tattered lace finery, some in nothing at all, began tittering behind hands and fans. One phooka laughed so hard that he brayed like a pony.

She closed her hands into fists, trying to fight down panic.

"Your face!" the phooka shouted, strange golden goat eyes rolling up in his head with mirth. "You should see your face!"

Hazel glanced back at Ben, in the cage. He was standing, hands curled around the bars. When he saw her turn his way, he gave her a somewhat unsteady smile, like he was trying to put on a brave face—a smile that she couldn't possibly deserve.

"But you are still mine," the Alderking continued. "You would do well not to forget it, Hazel. Come forward and kneel before me."

She knelt, feeling the cold of the stone seep up into the strange, almost metallic cloth of the pants she wore.

Remember to kneel.

"Look at me," the Alderking said.

She did, seeing the poison green of his eyes and the long raven-feather cape draped over his shoulders, each feather the glimmering blue-black of an oil slick. He was ruinously beautiful in the way that knives and scalpels can be beautiful. She'd tried to avoid thinking about that, since he was Severin's father and it wasn't right that he should be equal in beauty to his son, but staring at him made it impossible to ignore. He was a fairy-tale king, radiant and terrible. Part of her *wanted* to serve him, and the more he gazed down at her, the stronger that feeling became.

She forced herself to look away from his eyes, forced herself to study his lips instead.

"Imagine my surprise to find Severin hiding in your house. Not only have you failed at your task, but you have squandered my goodwill."

She stayed silent, biting the inside of her cheek, and bowed her head.

The Alderking had clearly expected nothing less. "Will you deny it, little sneak? Will you pretend that you intended to betray him? Will you claim that you're still my loyal servant?"

"No," she said, trying not to show panic on her face. "I will not."

For the first time since she'd been brought before him, he looked wary. "Come here, Eolanthe. Tell the court what you know."

Jack's elf mother stepped forward, a leaf in one of her hands. Hazel knew what it was immediately. She read out the words written in her son's blood, and when she named Heartsworn, the buzz of conversation among the courtiers was silenced, as though the name of the blade itself was a spell.

Eolanthe was shaking a little. The Alderking watched her with blazing, possessive eyes. He looked at her as though he'd remembered that he was angry with her and that the memory of his own anger excited him. Hazel could see why Eolanthe hadn't wanted Jack to draw the Alderking's attention.

A moment later, the full force of that stare was turned back on Hazel. "Tell me, why would you believe one of my courtiers had Heartsworn?"

Hazel swallowed. "Someone has to have it. That's the only way that the casket could have been broken, the only way that Severin could have been freed."

He leaned forward eagerly. "And who shared that bit of the curse with you?"

Hazel shook her head. This part was easy. "Severin told me."

The Alderking signaled and the cage was wheeled closer to him. He studied his son with an odd possessiveness, gazing at him the way one might look at a particularly valuable painting put away in storage because it had acquired a scratch. A painting you no longer wished to hang where others could see, but neither were you willing to part with.

Severin stared back, eyes hungry. Ben had stepped into shadow, so that it was hard to see his face. Hazel wondered what he was thinking.

"Who freed you?" the Alderking asked his son. "Tell me where the sword is and I will forgive you. You may sit at my side, my own heir restored. What do you think of that? I have the means to take my revenge on the Court in the East. With your sister under my control and the twin swords back in my possession, nothing stands in my way.

"Let us destroy Fairfold, destroy all those who gawked at you these long years as you slept. I will show you the might of your sister brought to harness. You will see how easily we will take back the Eastern Court, wrest the throne from the upstart knight who rules it."

Hazel sucked in her breath. He spoke about destroying Fairfold as though it were nothing, a smudge to polish away.

In the cage, Ben whispered something to Severin, but the horned boy shook his head. When he turned back to his father, his eyes were hot and bright. "Let the mortals go and I will sit beside you, Father. Let me out of the cage and I will take my place by your side."

A thin smile appeared on the Alderking's mouth. "Where is Heartsworn?"

Severin shook his head. "You first. I'm the one in the cage."

For a frozen moment Hazel wondered if the Alderking would let Severin out, if Severin would betray them. But then the Alderking laughed and called over a creature in red armor, with a tail that whipped around behind him and ears like that of a fox. "Take the mortal out instead and bring me the Bone Maiden and all her knives."

Ben shouted as a dozen knights gathered around the cage,

shoving their swords between the metal branches to keep Severin back as they unlocked the door and dragged Hazel's brother through it. Severin grabbed one of the knights, twisting his arm hard, nearly pulling him between the bars. The faerie screamed and she heard a sharp sound, like bone cracking.

Hazel started toward them.

"Halt, Sir Hazel," said the Alderking. "You will stay just as you are or I will cut young Benjamin's throat."

Hazel stopped moving. Three knights pressed their blades to Severin's skin. He was breathing hard, but no longer struggled. Two knights seized Ben and dragged him across the stone floor to thrust him in front of a hag with a face as blue as woad in a tattered black gown who had appeared at the Alderking's summons. She pressed long fingers that tapered to bare white bone against Ben's forehead, inspecting his birthmark.

"Now, you or my son will tell me what has happened to Heartsworn. If you don't, the boy will suffer." The Alderking's smile was horrible.

"Blessed and cursed, cursed and blessed," the blue woman said, then took one of his fingers and twisted it hard.

He screamed, artlessly and uncontrollably.

"Stop," Hazel shouted. If she'd known where the sword was, she might have told him, but it was impossible to think, impossible to puzzle anything through with Ben screaming. She was glad for the knot Jack had put in her hair. Without it, she would have wept. "Stop. Stop or I will stop you."

At that, the Alderking laughed. "Ah, yes, there's that true nature of yours coming out. You play at obedience, but it isn't obedience if you only answer the orders you like. Much as my son does."

Ben screamed again. A second finger.

The Alderking had Heartseeker on his right, sheathed in the furred skin of some creature. Could Hazel get herself another weapon and slit his throat before he drew on her? Hazel thought it was unlikely, but she eyed the courtiers, noticing a goat-footed girl with a knife strapped to her belt, and wondered. She pictured herself grabbing the blade. She counted how many steps to the throne there were and calculated how fast she could take them at a run. Her fingers twitched.

She had to do something.

"One cannot heal a musician's fingers without breaking them," said the Alderking. "Your brother is in pain, but his suffering may be a boon to him. If you both continue being obstinate, I will do far worse. There are some torments so terrible they change a person forever. There are some torments so terrible that minds refuse to withstand them. You had best tell me what you know and you better tell me now."

"Leave Benjamin alone," Severin said. "Your grievance is with me, Father. Leave him!"

Hazel had to do something. She had to stop Ben from being hurt.

"Me," Hazel said. "I freed Severin. Me. So leave Ben alone. I did it and I did it by myself."

"You?" The Alderking stood, eyes blazing. "You who came to

our sacred hawthorn tree and asked for our help? Was it not you who gave up seven years of your life voluntarily, gladly, even? I could have taken those seven years any way I wished, but I wasn't cruel. Instead, I gave you not just what you asked for, but all the things you never dared ask. When you came to me, you were a child, eleven years old, and we stole you from your bed to fly through the skies on rushes and ragwort. We trained you to swing a blade and to take a blow. We taught you to ride on our swift-footed steeds, like you were Tam Lin himself. Some part of you recalls it, recalls the wind whipping your hair and the howl of the night sky before you. Recalls the lessons in courtly manners. Recalls laughing when you rode down a girl from Fairfold out by the highway, the footfalls of the other knights behind you, your horse outpacing theirs—"

"No. You're wrong. I didn't do that," Hazel said, trying to keep her voice from shaking. But they didn't lie—*couldn't* lie, so some part of it was true. She thought of the dream she'd had, the one where she'd tormented a family and laughed when they were cursed to stone. How much had she been changed in his service? How much could she trust her other self?

"I made your wishes come true." The Alderking spread his hands wide in a gesture of acceptance, smiling. "And if our gifts have barbs, you know enough of our nature to expect that. And so, tell me, who told you how to free my son? The real answer now. Who gave you Heartsworn? And where is my sword?"

"I don't know," Hazel said, panicked, because she *didn't* know where the sword was, yet he had no reason in the world to believe her.

He beckoned to the Bone Maiden, who advanced toward the throne, drawing a thin and jagged blade. It looked as though there was dried rust or blood marring the metal. "Mortals are born liars," said the Alderking. "It's the only thing your kind has any exceptional talent in."

Hazel swallowed and prepared herself. She let herself be afraid, let herself get lost in the moment, tried not to think too much. She needed her instinct. She hoped she seemed stunned enough that the Bone Maiden expected her to be passive, to allow herself to be tortured, to scream and weep and never fight back. And when the creature got close enough for Hazel to smell the crushed-pine-needle scent of her, to see the strange gleam of her ruby eyes, then Hazel went for the rusty knife.

It scraped the skin of her arm as she moved, hand closing on the blade. It cut her palm, but she jerked it out of the hag's hand and slammed it into the creature's throat. Black blood gouted out. The hag's long fingers scrabbled at her neck, but her eyes were already dulling, the shine going out of them.

A knight grabbed hold of Ben, jerking his hands behind his back, careless of his fingers. Ben howled with pain.

Three of the knights circled Hazel, wary of the thin, rusty knife. She slipped into a crouch, watching them.

"No," commanded the Alderking. "Let her keep it. You see, Sir Hazel, so long as I have your brother, it's my hand that holds the knife."

"It looks like your hand slipped," she said as the hag's body gave a final twitch and was still. Hazel was flushed with victory and violence. She felt like her most dangerous self, the self who had once walked through the woods of Fairfold and believed herself to be their defender. Around her, the crowd of courtiers had gone silent. She had brought death to this place, to these deathless and ancient people, and they watched her with wide, puzzled eyes.

"Observe," he said, speaking as though he were giving a lesson to a very small child. "Now, Hazel, I want you to recite the rhyme to summon the monster at the heart of the forest, my sweet daughter. You know it, don't you? Say the words or he'll gut your brother."

Hazel hesitated for a moment, realizing how trapped they all were. "Fine," she said, taking a deep breath. The singsong tone of it brought back memories of skipping rope, of the feeling of bare feet hitting hot pavement on a summer day, and of the ever-present temptation of saying that final word. "There's a monster in our wood. She'll get you if you're not good. Drag you under leaves and sticks. Punish you for all your tricks. A nest of hair and gnawed bone. You are never, ever coming...home."

Hazel felt the ripples of magic, felt the breeze that blew through the hollow hill, felt the touch of cold that accompanied it. Sorrow was coming, and if he could really control her, they were all doomed.

The Alderking nodded. "Very good. Now, let's see what else you can do. Slash your own arm or my knight will slice open your brother's face. See how you hasten to obey? Go ahead, hasten."

Hazel pushed up the sleeve of her shirt with trembling fingers. She raised the Bone Maiden's crooked little blade, pressing the tip to her skin. Then she pressed down until sharp, bright pain bloomed across her arm, until a thin trickle of blood ran all the way to her palm, spattering onto the stone.

The smile that cut across the Alderking's face was awful.

"Hazel, stop," Ben yelled. "Don't worry about me—"

"Enough, Father," Severin shouted, his voice commanding. "She doesn't have Heartsworn."

"She's a liar," said the Alderking. "They lie! All mortals lie."

"It's me that Hazel is protecting," Jack said, stepping away from the other courtiers, eyes flashing silver, head held high. Eolanthe reached for him, but he shrugged off her touch. All around him, courtiers went quiet. He walked before the Alderking's throne and made an elaborate bow, one that Hazel had no idea he even knew how to make. "I conspired to betray you. Let her go. Let her go and punish me instead."

"No!" his mother said. "You swore! You swore not to harm him."

"Jack?" Hazel said, frowning. She felt light-headed, maybe from the blood running down her arm. For a single moment, she wondered if there was some truth to it, if there was another secret yet to be revealed. Then she saw the flash of panic on his face, heard the catch in his voice.

He was buying her time. Time for her to puzzle through the clues she'd left herself.

Carrots. Iron rods.

Remember to kneel.

What did it mean? The human farmer had tricked the boggart

by planting carrots underground. And the iron rods were buried as well.

Maybe she *buried* the sword.

"You? The boy who plays at being mortal?" The Alderking studied Jack through narrowed eyes and then moved to his throne, sweeping back his cape and sitting. "What possible reason could you have to stand against me? Your birth was proof of your mother's betrayal and yet here you are, alive and unharmed."

Remember to kneel.

"What does it matter why?" Jack said, and there was something in his expression—as though he was daring the Alderking to press him further.

"You presume much, changeling child." The Alderking's brows rose. "I may have promised your mother that I would order no hand raised against you, but Sorrow will welcome your pain—your death—because all she knows is pain and death and grief. Put him into the cage with my son."

Jack took a deep breath and then half smiled, allowing himself to be forced back from Hazel, toward the cage. Despair flooded her. They were all going to die. She wanted nothing more than to sink down onto the cold stone and beg, offer up anything, everything. But she had nothing to offer.

Carrots. Iron rods.

Remember to kneel.

Then she realized what the answer must be. She knew where she'd hidden the sword.

Heartsworn, a blade that could cut through anything, a blade so sharp that it could be sheathed in stone itself. And that's where she must have hidden it, just as she first found it, buried blade deep in the dirt and sand beside Wight Lake. The Alderking would no more look for it paving the ground of his throne room than he would look for it among the clouds.

Remember to kneel.

Her gaze dropped to the floor, looking for any shine in the dirt between the massive stone tiles. She spotted what she thought might be a shimmer, but it could have been a trick of the light. She had one chance to find it.

Three knights in gleaming gold marched Jack to the cage and gingerly opened the door. As it swung wide, though, Severin ducked down, rolling under the swords knights pushed through the bars to hold him back. He'd clearly been anticipating them, and he moved fast. Fast enough that by the time they'd pulled their swords out to face him, he was through and straightening up.

Wounded from whatever fight had taken place earlier, he wore the ripped and bloodstained remains of a shirt wrapped around his waist—Jack's undershirt, she realized.

The knights who had been standing near Hazel ran toward Severin, swords flashing. Hazel had her chance. She crossed quickly to where she thought she'd seen a glimmer of the hilt.

Then, despite herself, she looked back toward the cage.

The knights had surrounded Severin, none of them bold enough to come at him, despite the fact that he was unarmed. Severin spoke.

"Give me your sword," he said to Marcan. He looked like the prince of Hazel's childhood, the one who was going to wake up and make everything right. "Give me your sword and let me die with a blade in my hands. I don't want to fight any of you and my father has Heartseeker. You can hardly fear for him. Surely, he will fight me. I cannot win."

The courtiers looked from one to another, a nervous energy taking hold of them.

The Alderking stood, drawing Heartseeker from his sheath with a terrible scrape of metal on metal. He looked at the assembled throng. They were watching with eagerness and something else— something she thought might be hatred. The Alderking could not lose with the enchanted blade in his hand, but no one would delight in his winning.

"Take mine," Marcan said, and placed his sword in Severin's hand.

"I didn't give you leave to arm him," the Alderking snapped.

"No prince should die for want of a sword," said Marcan, a muscle moving in his jaw. It was no safe thing to lecture a king.

The Alderking sneered. "And yet so many do."

But even with a faerie-wrought blade, Severin would die. Even were he the best swordsman in the world, he would die. No skill could guard against a blade that never missed. If Hazel couldn't get him Heartsworn, he was doomed.

She found what she thought might be the shine of the bottom of a pommel and dropped to her knees. Fingers sliding over it, she tried to get a grip, tried to pull it up. It slipped from her fingers. No one had noticed her yet, crouched there, but they would, surely. She had to work quickly.

On the other side of the floor, Severin and his father circled each other. Heartseeker darted out toward Severin's shoulder. The horned boy tried to block the blow, but the other sword was too fast. It sank into his arm, making him cry out. His grip on his own sword wavered. Metal rang against metal in a flurry of furious blows. Severin couldn't block swiftly enough. Again and again, Heartseeker sliced into his flesh. Already wounded, he quickly became a mess of small cuts, bleeding freely.

And yet, Hazel could tell the Alderking was frustrated. Severin was clearly the better swordsman. The Alderking was constantly thrown off his balance by his own sword; it jerked him into the position it needed to strike. He dealt sloppy blows, blows that went wide and then corrected themselves. And Severin continued on, relentlessly parrying, ferociously striking, even when there was no hope of winning out, even when his defeat was assured. The Alderking might be able to kill him, but he could not break him.

"As amusing as this is," said the Alderking, out of breath, "it cannot continue. Subside. Your sister is coming. She will rip you limb from limb if I don't cut your throat first. Either way, this time when you lie in the glass coffin, you will truly be dead, dead and on display for all the rest of the forest."

Severin slashed his blade at his father's side and hit, slicing through fabric to show a thin line of welling blood. The Alderking looked at his son as though seeing him for the first time.

"Heartseeker means *you* never miss, Father," Severin said, circling again. "It doesn't mean I always miss you."

The Alderking roared forward, heedless of form. Abruptly, brutally, he thrust Heartseeker into Severin's gut. The horned boy howled and fell to his knees, hand pressed to his stomach. The Alderking had stabbed him where he was already wounded.

But as the Alderking stepped back, his hand went to his own arm. It was bleeding freely, the red wash of blood covering his hand like a glove. He'd struck his son, but Severin had dealt him another blow.

"Enough," the Alderking shouted, breathing hard, pointing to his knights. "Finish him."

They stood rigidly, as though they hadn't heard the command. Because they might be cruel and capricious, might care nothing for mortals, but they were still knights, like the kind in books she'd read when she was little. Knights, like in Ben's stories. What the Alderking was asking was against their code of honor. They did not swarm a wounded man, certainly not one who'd been so clearly beaten in no kind of fair fight.

After a moment, Marcan stepped forward. One of the others pressed a blade into his hand. They seemed to have come to the decision that though they were bound to follow the Alderking's orders, they would do so facing Severin one-on-one, as honor demanded.

Hazel finally caught hold of the edge of the sword. She pushed her fingers deeper into the ground, as far as they would go, hooking her nail beneath the metal and insinuating her fingers until she could grip it. Carefully, she pulled the sword up, up from the stone where she'd buried it, up through the deep slice in the rock. Up until it was in her hand.

Her sword, the golden blade gleaming, black paint long chipped off. The one she'd borne on her back. The one that had made her a knight. Heartsworn.

Hardly believing what she'd done, she took several steps toward Severin, realizing in that moment that she was too late. He was bleeding too freely from too many wounds. As Marcan circled him, Severin stumbled. He was barely on his feet. He couldn't wield the blade and win against his father, no less his fearsome sister.

She had failed. She was too late.

"Ben," Severin called as he slumped to the ground. "Benjamin Evans, you're wrong, but you're not stupid."

"What?" Ben called back from where he stood, at the edge of the cage, the broken fingers of his hands curling around the bars. His gaze flickered between Severin and Hazel, as though he wasn't sure whom he feared for more.

"I love you," Severin said, looking up, looking at nothing at all, his face exultant. "I love you like in the storybooks. I love you like in the ballads. I love you like a lightning bolt. I've loved you since the third month you came and spoke with me. I loved that you made me want to laugh. I loved the way you were kind and the way you would pause when you spoke, as though you were waiting for me to answer you. I love you and I am mocking no one when I kiss you, no one at all."

Ben tried to move toward him, clawing at the bars of the cage, but a gleaming knight held him back. "You're insane," Ben shouted, and Severin started to laugh.

Hazel crossed the floor in front of the throne. She wasn't sure if the other knights recognized what she held or if they just weren't paying enough attention to her.

The Alderking whirled, eyes widening in surprise. Then he decided on amusement. "What are you thinking, little knight? Do you even remember how to hold a sword? Do you think you're being honorable? He won't be able to save you."

"No," Hazel said. "I'm the one who's supposed to save him."

He swung at her, but she'd had time to think about this. She didn't bother aiming to block him. She aimed Heartsworn not at him, but at his sword, and swung with all her might.

Heartsworn cut the blade of Heartseeker in half with a terrible crack, like that of shattering glass. The Alderking looked at her, as though he couldn't believe what she had done. Then his gaze went to something she couldn't see, and he managed a smile. His expression froze Hazel in place, filling her with fresh dread.

Sorrow had come.

Courtiers had their hands pressed against their mouths, smothering small shrieks. Behind her, Hazel heard the heavy, thudding tread of the monster, heard the shiver of her branches. Hazel shuddered, taking a deep breath.

She pressed the edge of Heartsworn against the Alderking's throat. It nicked his skin, blood beading like a single garnet where the point touched him.

"She's coming closer, ever closer," the Alderking said, swallowing, holding out the broken blade in one hand, as though in surrender, as though he meant to drop it. Hazel was fairly sure he wouldn't, though. "Remember that I have the bone ring. Remember that with it, I can influence her."

Hazel swallowed, coming to a decision.

"If you turn, you'll have a chance," he said. "All you have to do is turn. You have the sword. But if you don't strike now, you'll be hers. She'll make you cough up dirt and vine, make you sleep in a bed of your own tears."

There was a rush of air, like something moving very fast. Maybe the monster was pulling back to strike. Hazel knew what it was like to lose, knew it so well that it had washed the taste of winning from her mouth, so that she wasn't sure she even remembered the savor of it.

She might be about to lose again.

Hazel thought of the creature she'd seen in the school, of the creature she'd seen the day before in Jack's house. She thought of the strange, shambling beauty of her treelike shape, the impossibility of her. She thought of the way Ben had sung and the way the monster had let Severin touch her face.

Was Sorrow still under the Alderking's influence? Or was she awake, conscious, no longer able to be fooled by a bit of bone?

"Go ahead," said the Alderking. "Quick now, trust me or trust a monster?"

"Don't—" Jack yelled, but Hazel couldn't wait until he finished what he was going to say.

Quickly, she moved, slicing down fast, so that the very tip of Heartsworn sliced the grim bone ring in two. "I swore I would defeat the monster at the heart of the forest—and I have. It was never her. It was always you."

It was then that the monster's twig fingers grasped the Alderking. Astonished, his eyes went wide and he howled, calling for his knights, screaming curses. She held him and kept on holding him until his body went slack, broken sword sliding from his grasp.

Then she dropped him onto the stone floor.

Hazel bent down to take what was left of Heartseeker away. As her hand closed on the hilt, the Alderking's eyes opened suddenly and he reached for her. The pad of his finger ran down her cheek and rasped out words from a mouth painted with blood: "Remember, Sir Hazel. Remember, my disloyal knight. I curse you to remember. I curse you to remember everything."

"No!" Hazel cried out, shaking her head back and forth, stumbling back from him. "I don't want to. I won't!"

The Alderking's eyes closed, his face smoothing out into sleep.

But Hazel kept on screaming.

CHAPTER 21

Once, there was a girl who found a sword in the woods.

Once, there was a girl who made a bargain with the Folk.

Once, there was a girl who'd been a knight in the service of a monster.

Once, there was a girl who vowed she would save everyone in the world, but forgot herself.

Once, there was a girl...

Hazel remembered everything at once, all the locks come undone, all the memories rising up from the deep, murky place where she'd buried them, all of herself crashing into herself. Not just the memories that the Alderking had taken from her. Faerie curses were more powerful than that. She got back every memory she ever tried to lock away.

—

The night after Hazel had slain the hag, her parents hosted a party. It went on until late, growing more and more boisterous as the evening wore on. A loud argument about the artistic value of illustration versus fine art turned into a fight about someone cheating on somebody else.

Ben and Hazel sat outside beside their dog's fresh-dug grave and listened to the distant sound of a bottle smashing.

"I'm tired and hungry," Ben said. "And it's cold."

He didn't say *and we can't go back in there*, but Hazel understood that part anyway.

"Let's do something," she said.

Ben looked up at the stars. The night was bright and cold. They'd both had an exhausting and terrifying day, and he looked wary of any more excitement. "Like what?"

"In your book, there's a ceremony you have to go through to be ready for knighthood. A vigil. We should do that. To prove ourselves."

The book was on the porch where they'd left it. Her sword was hidden in the shed where the machete used to be. She went and got them both.

"What does it say we're supposed to do?" Ben asked, his breaths clouding in the air and rising like specters.

According to the book, first they had to fast. Since they hadn't had dinner, Hazel thought that counted. Then they were supposed to bathe to purify themselves, dress in robes, and stay up all night praying on their knees in a chapel. Then they'd be ready to be knighted.

"We don't have a chapel," Ben said. "But we could make an altar."

And so they did, using a big rock. They found a couple of old citronella candles and lit them, giving the yard an eerie glow. Then they undressed and washed in the ice-cold water from the garden hose. Shivering, they wrapped themselves in tablecloths swiped out of the laundry area.

"Okay," Ben said. "So now we pray?"

They weren't a particularly religious family. Hazel couldn't even remember being to church, although there were pictures of her being baptized, so she must have been. She didn't know exactly what praying entailed, but she knew what it looked like. She tugged Ben down to his knees next to her.

The ground was icy, but the sword slid into the earth easily. Hazel gripped the hilt and tried to concentrate on knightly thoughts. Thoughts about bravery and honor and trueness and rightness. She rocked back and forth on her knees, murmuring under her breath, and after a moment Ben copied her movements. Hazel felt as though she was falling into a dream. Soon she could almost ignore how cold she was, could almost not feel the heavy weight of her hair clumping as it froze, could almost control her shivering.

At some point, she was conscious of Ben getting up, of telling her it was too cold and urging her to come inside. She'd just shaken her head.

At some point, people had left the house. She'd heard cars starting, tense words exchanged, and the sound of someone noisily puking in the bushes. But no one noticed her kneeling in the back garden.

At some point, the sun rose, turning the grass to gold.

Hazel's parents found her kneeling on the lawn later that morning when they stumbled out of the house, hung over and panicked at discovering her not in her bed. Mom was still in her dress from the night before, makeup smeared across her cheek. Dad was in a T-shirt and underwear, walking barefoot on the frost-covered grass.

"What are you doing out here?" Dad said, clasping Hazel's shoulder. "Have you been out all night? Jesus, Hazel, what were you thinking?"

She tried to stand, but her legs were too stiff. She couldn't feel her fingers. As her father lifted her up into his arms, she wanted to explain, but her teeth were chattering too loudly for her to get any words out.

———

And she remembered another night, too, slinking home through the woods after being in the Alderking's service, a shudder never quite leaving her shoulders.

She had ridden with the Folk and pretended to laugh as they tormented mortals, aped their cruelty along with all else they taught her.

Let us curse them to be rocks until some mortal recognizes their true nature.

She knew she was the best hope of breaking the curse. Lying alone in her bed in the moments before dawn, waiting for her memories to wash out like a tide, she went over the conundrum. All she had to do was go out to the grove where they were and their true nature would be recognized. She would recognize them.

But only if she remained her night self. Her day self wouldn't know.

Briefly, she imagined leaving a note for Ben. Maybe if she worded it right, he could break the spell. But no matter how she worded it, he would probably say just the wrong thing to her day self—a self she wasn't sure she trusted.

Day Hazel was her, but with all the sharp edges blunted. Day Hazel didn't know what it was to ride beside the Folk on sleek faerie horses, hair streaming behind her. She didn't recall swinging a silvery sword with such force that the air itself seemed to sing. She didn't know what it was to outwit them and to be outwitted. She hadn't seen the wild and grotesque things night Hazel had seen. She hadn't told the many, many lies.

Day Hazel needed to be preserved, protected. There would be no help there.

And so she concocted a plan. The terms of her service were simple. *Every night, from the moment you fall into slumber until your head touches your pillow again near dawn, you're mine,* the Alderking had said.

The way she thwarted him was simple, too. She put her head down on her pillow but didn't allow herself to sleep. Instead, she got back up again—and stayed night Hazel until dawn broke on the horizon and her memories fled with the dark.

Some nights, she was able to steal almost an hour. Other nights, mere moments. But it allowed her to break curses, to undo damage.

And, in time, it let her concoct a plan.

She knew what the Alderking intended to do with Sorrow. He flaunted Fairfold's looming destruction before her, boasted about his plans for conquest and revenge on the Court in the East. Just as he let slip details he hadn't thought mattered, about his lost sword and the means of releasing the horned boy. Slowly, Hazel had realized the value of the blade she had found all those years ago. Slowly, she had come to see that she was the only one with the means to stop him.

I may be stuck in his service, Hazel had thought, *but if I free the prince, he could defeat his father. He's not bound by any promises. He's got enough vengeance in him for both of us.*

That was when everything went wrong. Hazel remembered the panic that rose in her when the casket shattered, but the prince didn't wake. She remembered the terror of trying to hide the sword, of leaving herself hasty, cryptic hints and then rushing to her bed before the first rays of light touched her.

She'd thought she'd have more time, but she had stolen only minutes when she woke next, until finally she'd awakened in her own house, with her brother and Jack and Severin standing over her and half the Alderking's court outside.

"Where is it?" Ben asked her.

That was when the first of the faeries burst through the front door. Hazel scrabbled for the Sharpie and ran up the stairs to don her armor.

⌒

Hazel remembered all those things, slumped on the ground, as Ben told her they'd won, as Severin ordered his father's body moved to the casket, where he could sleep away all the rest of his days, as the court crowded around the monster, as Jack said Hazel's name over and over, until the words bled together.

She closed her eyes and let the darkness take her.

CHAPTER 22

Hazel woke up in an unfamiliar place, the air redolent with honeysuckle and carrying the distant playing of a harp. She was lying in a large, elaborate, carved bed with a silvery gray blanket over her that felt lighter than silk, but was warmer than goose down. She wanted to burrow back down in the coverlets and go on sleeping, although she knew there was some reason why she shouldn't.

She turned over and saw Jack, sitting so that he was in profile. He was in a tipped-back chair, balancing it with a single booted foot against the wall. He had a book open on his lap, but he didn't seem to be turning the pages. There was something in the way the soft light of the candles resting beside him defined the planes of his face, something in the heavy lash of his eye and the softness of his mouth that was both familiar and endlessly strange in its beauty.

Hazel realized that as many times as she'd seen Jack before, she'd never really got to look at him with night Hazel's eyes.

Who was she? Hazel wondered. *Knowing what she did, having done what she had done? Was she enough of the Hazel Evans he'd liked? Was she even a Hazel Evans she herself could like?*

Once her service to the Alderking was complete, if he hadn't tricked her into becoming his eternal servant or killed her outright, she'd assumed he'd take back all her memories of her time in his court. She'd thought of her night self as expendable, thought of what she'd endured as being scars that would simply, one day, vanish.

Now she knew they wouldn't. But the Alderking had left her with talents, too. And knowledge.

She'd heard the story of how Jack came be a changeling so many times as her daylight self, but as she watched him, she realized she'd heard it in the faerie court, too. She'd heard his elf mother tell it, explaining how she'd chosen Carter because he was such a beautiful child, warm and sweet and laughing in her arms. Telling of the horror of the hot iron scorching Jack's skin, the smell of burning flesh and the howl he'd given up, so anguished that a banshee would despair to hear it. How the mortals were indifferent to his pain and kept him for spite, for a curiosity to show off to their friends, how she feared they would make him the servant of their own son. Hazel had heard stories of the way the hobs would peer in the windows, making sure he was safe, how they would pile up acorns and chestnuts outside in case he got hungry at night, how they would play with him in the garden when his human mother's back was turned and pinch Carter until he cried.

Thinking of that, Hazel took a breath and got ready to turn over and speak, when she heard someone come into the room.

"I have sent you a dozen messages," Eolanthe said. "You have deigned to reply to none."

"I've been here." Jack closed the book and set it down beside the candles. "You knew I was here. You could have come to speak with me anytime—as you have."

Hazel slitted her eyes to see the faerie woman, standing near the earthen wall.

"I understand your anger over my bargain with the Alderking, but you don't see why it was necessary—"

"What makes you think that?" Jack asked. There was a warning in his voice.

Hazel knew that it was a bad thing to listen as she was, to pretend she was asleep and let them talk in front of her. But it seemed awful to sit up and admit she was awake, as though she was accusing them of saying something they wanted kept secret, when they were just talking.

Indecision kept her quiet too long, because once Hazel heard that tone in Jack's voice, she knew they were going to discuss secrets.

"I wondered when you hesitated during your little speech before the Alderking—as though there was something you thought you might say, but then thought better of it," Eolanthe told him.

"When I wondered if you had Heartsworn, it got me thinking about all the things that didn't add up."

"Yes, you thought I was the architect of all this. You were wrong, but you were right to guess I had a plan. Once I found out that

Heartsworn was discovered, I thought that you and I might bide our time and wait for them to kill one another." There was a soft sound of fabric, as though she was moving around the room. "If Severin and the Alderking were both dead, then there would be only one person poised to inherit. If you just hadn't spoken when you had, if he had fought his son for a few more minutes, things might be very different. Don't you want to ask me what I mean?"

"I do not," he said.

"Are you afraid I would tell you who your—"

"I said I wasn't asking you," Jack interrupted her. "And I'm not. If you do tell me, I'll pretend you didn't."

"Then I don't need to tell you," she said. "You already know."

For a long moment, he didn't speak.

"It is your gift," she said, "to guess what is in another's heart. Severin would need someone with your gift, someone by his side who knows the mortal world as you do. You need not hide any longer."

"Nothing has changed," he said. "I'm going home now—to my human home, to be with my human family. I don't care who my father was."

Hazel heard the rustle of fabric. "They will never really love you. They will always fear you."

"It doesn't matter. Let me have this time being human," he said. "Over and over you tell me that I will never be mortal, that the span of one human life is so short as to mean nothing. Fine, then let me have my human life. Let all the mortals I love die and blow away to dust. Let me have Nia for a mother and Charles for a father and Carter for my brother. Let me be Jack Gordon, and when I am done, when all is dust and ashes, I will return to you and learn how to be your son."

She was quiet.

"Let me have this, Mother, because once they are dead, I can never have it again." In his voice, Hazel heard the eerie agelessness she'd associated with Severin and the Alderking. He was one of them, eternal and inhuman. But he was going to stay in her world a little longer.

"Go," she said finally. "Be Jack Gordon. But mortality is a bitter draught."

"And yet I would have the full measure," he told her.

Hazel kept her eyes closed, trying to control her breathing, sure one of them would discover her deception. But after a few minutes of steady inhaling and exhaling, she was asleep again.

The next time she woke, it was Ben who was beside her, sitting on the other side of the bed, propped up by more of the soft pillows she'd been snuggling with. One of his hands was bandaged too heavily to use, but he was texting with the other.

She forced herself to shift into a sitting position and groaned.

"Is this Faerieland?" Hazel asked him muzzily.

"Maybe," Ben said. "If there is such a place. I mean, if we all occupy the same dimensional space, then, technically, we're always in Faerieland. But the jury's still out on that."

She ignored the second part of his statement to focus on the first. "So you're texting in Faerieland. *Who* are you texting? What network are you even on?"

He made a face at her. "Mom and Dad. Mom freaked out, like

everyone else at the Gordons', and it sounds like half the town went to the big old church on Main Street with all the protections carved into the foundation. They locked themselves in with charms and canned food and whatnot. Mom thought we'd go there, too, but obviously we didn't, because we are badasses. Dad drove down to look for us. I told her that you'd be home tonight, if you're feeling up to it. You think you're going to feel up to it?"

"Me?" Hazel stretched. "Where's Jack?"

"He had to go take some more of Sorrel's blood to the hospital. He had a hell of a time convincing them it was the antidote, but once he did and it started working, they wanted more. Sorrel let Severin cut her with Heartsworn and bled into a vial."

"Is she still...?"

"A giant, creepy tree monster?" He mimed branches with his fingers, reaching for Hazel. "Oh yeah. Her blood was a bright green, too. But she spoke to us and she sounded—I don't know—*nice*. The way Severin described her."

Hazel yawned. For the first time, she really took in the room. The rug on the floor had an intricate pattern that seemed to shift the more she looked at it, green lines coiling like vipers and making her dizzy. She blinked and turned her attention to a sideboard carved with oak leaves and topped with a copper bowl. Beside it rested three glass decanters with different liquids in them and a goblet.

There was a large bench covered in thick green velvet with glimmering gold tacks along the edge of the upholstery set near a fireplace, where a cheery fire was burning. Atop it were folded clothes.

"So, without you saying anything about dimensions, where are we?" Hazel asked.

"In the palace of the Alderking." Ben put down his phone and slid out of bed. He was wearing new clothes—black jeans and a rusty orange sweater the color of his hair, with a black unicorn rearing up across the front. Hazel recognized it as a purchase he'd been particularly proud of, but one she was pretty sure he hadn't had with him the day before. There hadn't been any reason to pack overnight bags.

He followed her gaze, looking down at his sweater. "Severin commanded a hob to go to our house and get some stuff. It picked up some clothes for you and . . . more stuff for me."

Ben waited, as though expecting her to react.

Hazel didn't like where this was going. "Does this have something to do with your telling Mom and Dad that I'd be coming home tonight, but not saying anything about yourself?"

He nodded. "I'm staying with the faeries."

Hazel scrambled out from under the covers. Whatever had to be done, whoever had to be fought, she'd do it. She might not have Heartsworn, but she'd faced worse odds. "What did they promise you? What did you bargain for?"

Ben shook his head. "It's not like that."

"What is it like? Is this because of Severin?"

Ben winced. "It's not about him. Or at least mostly it's not about him." His whole face blushed a deep, ridiculous red.

"He looooooves you," Hazel crowed, dizzy with relief at being alive. "He told you he loooooooved you in front of everyone."

"*Hazel*," he moaned. It was fun to torture her brother. It made her feel like she was still herself.

She grabbed him by the shoulders, shaking him, and they fell back together on the bed, laughing.

"You better have kissed him! You better have kissed him so hard that he just about choked on your tongue. And if not, you better go kiss him like that *right now*."

"Shut up." Ben tried to pretend he wasn't holding back a smile. "Oh my god. That's so disgusting."

Hazel shoved him deeper into the mattress. "But none of this explains why you're not coming home."

Ben sighed. "I can't just go around with this ability to play music inside me like some unexploded bomb. I need to learn what it is and how to control it. And I'm not going to be able to learn that in the human world. I have to learn it here."

"But—" she began.

"I need to stop fantasizing about running away to some other life and start figuring out the one I have."

"You could come home first," Hazel said. "Explain things to Mom and Dad. Say good-bye to people at school."

"Maybe." Ben nodded, as if she was making sense, but he still wasn't going to agree. "But in all the stories, you have a single chance; and if you miss it, then it's gone. The door isn't there when you go back to look. There is no second invitation to the ball. This is my chance."

Hazel wanted to protest, but this wasn't about her. Maybe the music could live again for him. Maybe he could love it the way he'd never let himself before, because it was too terrifying to love something he couldn't control, because it was too awful to hurt people and love what hurt them.

"I'm going to miss you like crazy," he said, looking down at her, his hand pushing hair out of her face. "I'm sorry we weren't honest enough before."

"Don't talk like that," she said. "We might not be sharing the same bathroom, but I'll still see you, won't I? I mean, I spent half of the last five years of my life in Faerie, so it's not like I don't know my way around, and your boyfriend is more or less in charge now, so that's got to count for something."

"More or less," Ben said. "Yeah, of course we'll see each other. I didn't mean we wouldn't. But things will be...different. Just promise me you'll try to be happy."

Maybe, Hazel decided, maybe they could both learn how. Not just making-up-stories-in-which-you're-happy happiness, but the real thing. She leaned across the bed and hugged him with all the strength in her limbs, hugged him until her bones ached. But no matter how hard she hugged him, she knew it would never be enough.

"I promise," she whispered. "I'll try."

⁓

Ben left her in the room to get dressed. She stripped off the doublet, revealing a map of bruises and slashes across her torso. She splashed water into the metal basin and cleaned off most of the blood and dirt. She washed her mouth with an elixir that tasted of pine resin and combed her hair with a golden comb that magically turned her tangles into soft ginger ringlets.

The hob had chosen leggings, a black T-shirt with a steaming mug of tea on the front, an oversize gray button-up sweater, and a pair of bright green Chucks. Hazel put the clothes on, glad to be in familiar things. She left the tattered remains of her knight's uniform on the bed. Even if it could be repaired, she couldn't imagine ever wearing it again.

Without anywhere else to go, she started for home.

She stepped out of the room, into long, branching passageways with strangely sized doors, some massive, some tiny, some slender, and others wide. Knobs and knockers were shaped into silver goblin faces with sinister smiles and pointed ears or golden branches dripping berries. Sometimes she heard music or laughter; sometimes it seemed as though there were voices muttering in the distance.

Soon she came to steps that spiraled up into the hollow of a massive tree, and she found her way out through a long, narrow opening in it, like the mouth of a cave. Overhead, the sky was bright and the air sharp. Hazel pulled her sweater more tightly around her shoulders, wishing that the hob had thought to bring her a coat.

She trudged through piles of fallen leaves, through brush and bracken, until she came to her house. The front door hung from a single hinge. There was a splintered crack where a faerie knight's boot had hit it.

When she stepped through into the kitchen, her father and mother both stood up from the worn wood table, coming toward her.

"Oh, kiddo," her father said, putting his arms around Hazel's shoulders. "Kiddo, we're so glad that you're home."

"Ben's gone," Hazel blurted out, because it seemed cruel to let them be relieved when they weren't going to get to stay that way. "He's not coming back. He's going to stay with them."

"Come sit down," Dad said. "We know about your brother. He called and told us himself. Said to imagine Faerieland like an exclusive boarding school in Switzerland. I told him it was more like an exclusive boarding school in hell."

"You're okay with that?" Hazel asked, but she let herself sit. He'd probably told them it was for the good of his music. They would have accepted that, even if they didn't like it.

"No, we're not okay with it," Dad said. "But other than telling him we're not thrilled with his decision, there's not much we can do."

Mom frowned, pressing her finger to a burn mark in the wood table. "We have some questions for *you*, though. You fought alongside the horned boy from the casket in the woods, whom you and your brother appeared to know? Hazel, how did you know to fight like that? How did you get involved in this?"

"It happened a long time ago," Hazel said. Her parents had changed so much since the day she'd found the dead boy and the sword in the woods. They'd become the sort of parents who could never have spawned a child like Hazel.

Maybe that was why it was so hard to tell them just what kind of child she was.

Mom shook her head. "We're just relieved you're both okay. We were so worried."

"You don't have to worry about me—not now. There's no point. It's too late to worry." Her parents might have been able to transform themselves, but they couldn't transform her. She'd been too busy transforming herself.

"It's never too late to worry," Mom said, reaching across the table and taking Hazel's hand.

When she squeezed it, Hazel squeezed back.

———

School reopened a few days later. The administration sent home slips reporting that the recent crisis used up all available snow days for the academic year and if there was another closure, students would be attending Fairfold High through the end of June. There were still some cracks in the walls and the roof was still greenish with moss, and occasionally, a stray spiral of wind would blow a single black feather or a clump of dried fern down a hallway, but most of the rest of the vines and leaves had been removed.

Carter and Amanda were back in classes. Amanda was making much of her newfound celebrity, giving scandalous details of things she'd overheard while in her magical sleep. She and Carter were no longer dating.

Everything seemed as if it was normal again.

Everything seemed as if it was normal again, except that people called out to Hazel in the halls. People, even Robbie, wanted to ask her what the horned boy had really been like, how she'd found him, whether she'd been the one to free him from the casket. Tom Mullins wanted to see her fighting moves, using a borrowed mop from the janitor's closet. Three separate times over lunch, Leonie forced Hazel to tell the story of Ben and Severin getting together, and Molly wanted endless reassurance that Sorrow wasn't coming back to get her.

Everyone had something to say to Hazel, and no one had much to say to Jack. She saw people turn away from him in the halls, as though their fear and guilt had combined to make him invisible. But Carter was still beside him, shoving his shoulder and laughing and making their friends laugh, too, making sure he was seen. Talking about colleges and the next football game and where they were going that Saturday night.

Everyone would get over their fear of him soon enough. They would forget that he had magic in his blood.

But not Hazel. When she caught his eye, his gaze had a fathomless intensity that made her feel as if she were drowning. His mouth tilted crookedly, and she felt it like a blow.

He liked her. He liked her—or he *had* liked her daytime self. He liked her and she loved him. She loved him so much that it already hurt. It already felt like he'd broken her heart.

Anyone who offers up their heart on a silver platter deserves what they get.

Jack Gordon was a good boy, going to a good school far away from here. Going to have his normal, human life before he started his other, grander, immortal one.

"Hazel," he said, jogging up to her after last period. They hadn't spoken for three days, and she didn't want him to know how glad she was to hear his voice. He looked different from the way he had before the defeat of the Alderking—his ears a bit more pointy, his face a bit thinner, his hair full of greenish shadows—but his smile was that same old smile, the one that twisted up her insides, the one that had never belonged to Carter, the one that was Jack's and Jack's alone. "Hey, wait up. I want to talk to you. I was wondering if you might like—"

Just talking made her want to smile. A jolt of happiness washed over her so intense that it was almost pain.

"I don't think I can do this," Hazel blurted out.

"Do what?" He looked puzzled.

She kept on going, not sure what to say next, but determined. "I'm not okay. As a person. I guess I am just starting to realize how not okay I am, you know? I keep remembering things I've done—and stuff that happened to me—and it all adds up to the fact that I am not someone that any normal person should have a relationship with."

"Good thing I'm not exactly normal," Jack said.

"I'm going to mess this up," she told him. "I've never had a boyfriend before. I don't usually do dates, no less second dates. I'm kind of a coward about love," she continued. "I said I wished boys would show me some secret side of themselves, but you did and now all I want to do is run away."

He reached out a hand and she took it, threading her fingers through his. She sucked in a breath, looking down at their twined fingers.

Down a path worn into the woods, past a stream and a hollowed-out log full of pill bugs and termites, is a glass coffin. It rests right on the ground, and in it sleeps an elf with a golden circlet on his head and ears as pointed as knives.

The townsfolk know there was once a different boy resting there. One with horns and brown curls, one whom they adored and whom they have begun to forget. What matters is that they have a new faerie, one who won't wake up during the long summers when girls and boys stretch out the full length of the coffin, staring down through the panes and fogging them up with their breath. Who won't wake when tourists come and gape or debunkers insist he isn't real, but want to take photographs with him anyway. Who won't open his poison-green eyes on autumn weekends while girls dance right on top of him, lifting bottles high over their heads, as if they're saluting the whole haunted forest.

And elsewhere in the woods, there is another party, one taking place inside a hollow hill, full of night-blooming flowers. There, a pale boy plays a fiddle with newly mended fingers while his sister dances with his best friend. There, a monster whirls about, branches waving in time with the music. There, a prince of the Folk takes up the mantle of king, embracing a changeling like a brother, and, with a human boy at his side, names a girl his champion.

ACKNOWLEDGMENTS

I started this book thinking that it was going to be about revisiting the faerie folklore I loved, but it turned out to be about a lot of other things, too. It was a tricksy book to write, constantly transforming itself and trying to slip through my fingers. I believe it was Gene Wolfe who said, "You never learn to write a novel, you just learn to write the novel that you're writing." Never was that more true for me than with this book.

I am indebted to the folklorists who've compiled the materials that have informed my understanding of faeries. In particular, for this book, I am indebted to W. Y. Evans-Wentz's *The Fairy-Faith in Celtic Countries*; the chapter that concerns changeling stories in *Yoruba-Speaking Peoples of the Slave Coast of West Africa*, by A. B. Ellis; Johann Wolfgang von Goethe's poem "Der Erlkönig"; *Notes on the Folk-Lore of the North-East of Scotland*, by Walter Gregor; "Kate Crackernuts," from *English Fairy Tales*, by Joseph Jacobs; "The Farmer and the Boggart," from *County Folk-Lore Vol. V*, collected by Mrs. Gutch and Mabel Peacock; and many bits of *Folklore in the English and Scottish Ballads*, by Lowry Charles Wimberly.

I also need to thank the many people who held my hand, provided suggestions and support, and suffered with me—especially those of you who suffered through multiple drafts.

Thank you to all those who were in Arizona on the writing retreat where I started the book, to everyone in San Miguel de Allende who helped me plot out an early and possibly unrecognizable draft, and to those who were with me in Cornwall to help me figure out what to do once I'd doubled back and changed a ton.

In particular, thank you to Delia Sherman, Gwenda Bond, and Christopher Rowe for your wise advice. Thank you to Steve Berman for guiding me toward a better understanding of Benjamin's storyline. Thank you to Paolo Bacigalupi for checking in on me and commiserating on deadlines. Thank you to Cassandra Clare for continually reassuring me that the book would eventually be done and that despair was part of the process. Thank you to Sarah Rees Brennan for all your structural advice and for reading the book so many times. Thank you to Kelly Link for also reading the book so many times and thank you for telling me where to put the kissing. Thank you to Libba Bray for taking the bullet by turning in your draft, so I got another week of work on my own. Thank you to Robin Wasserman for sitting with me and a newborn baby in a Starbucks, listening to me cry about my plot while he cried for his bottle, and thank you for that brutal and necessary Christmas Eve edit. Thank you to Joshua Lewis for helping to figure out the endgame. Thank you to Leigh Bardugo for fighting to make my plot and conflict and pacing better—I appreciate it more than I can say and probably a lot more than it seemed. Thank you to Cindy Pon for talking through the story with me over delicious Russian food and spicy ginger beer. Thank you to Kami Garcia, who let me lounge around in her hotel room and eat all her gummy bears while we were both finishing drafts. Thank you to Ally Carter for talking me through the reveals and off the ledge.

I owe a special, huge, heartfelt thanks to everyone at Little, Brown Books for Young Readers, especially my fabulous editor, Alvina Ling, who believed in this manuscript even when it was very late and very messy. Thank you to Bethany Strout for being an amazing, generous reader, and to Amber Caraveo at Orion Books in the UK, for knowing what wasn't working. Thank you to Lisa Moraleda, publicist extraordinaire, who always knows what we're going to eat, and thank you to Nina Douglas, my publicist in the UK, who made travel fun. And, of course, thanks to Victoria Stapleton, for awesomeness and also booze.

Thank you to my agent, Barry Goldblatt, for support, advice, chasing down that epigraph, and believing I would actually ever finish this book.

Really, thank you, anyone who believed I would finish, because I wasn't so sure I would.

Most of all, to my husband, Theo, and our son, Sebastian, who put up with all my absences and my long hours in front of the computer, and who listened as I read this whole book out loud to them (okay, Sebastian mostly slept through that part). Your vast patience and love is deeply appreciated.